ACCLAIM FOR
DAVID ROSENFELT'S
NOVELS

DOG TAGS

"Compelling...laugh-out-loud funny...I couldn't put the book down...a first-place winner."
—Examiner.com

"A novel that you just can't put down till you finish reading the whole book...will keep you guessing till the end."
—*American Dog Magazine*

"Well-plotted and paced...Rosenfelt knows how to entertain, delivering thrills, laughs, heart, and likable characters...Nerd verdict: Clever DOG."
—PopCultureNerd.com

"Rosenfelt's wisecracking humor, likable good guys, and evil baddies are all part of a writing style that makes his books immensely enjoyable...If you love a good mystery, read DOG TAGS. Then go back to the first in the series, *Open and Shut,* and enjoy.
—BookReporter.com

"Nice writing, great plot...I love David Rosenfelt's dog-infused mysteries...Rosenfelt's melodic and paced writing only creates more friction...What's not to like?"
—TheReviewBroads.com

NEW TRICKS

"Packed with shootings, explosions, murder, and gritty courtroom drama...*New Tricks* is a treat for dog lovers, but it's also a great way for mystery lovers to spend time with a terrific storyteller. And you'll never guess the ending."
—USA Today

"Lollops at a golden retriever's vigorous pace...fun to read and...if there's a better mystery to take on a plane or train, I can't imagine it."
—Washington Times

"A funny, warm-hearted mystery, *Tricks* moves quickly."
—People

"Excellent...Rosenfelt injects this clever installment with courtroom twists, a peek into some scary DNA research, and a romantic surprise."
—Publishers Weekly (starred review)

"A winner...In the same vein as Harlan Coben's Myron Bolitar or Robert Crais's Elvis Cole, Rosenfelt's Andy has some great one-liners that complete his rich-lawyer, dog-loving persona. This hard-to-put-down read will please not just mystery fans (especially those who enjoy canine mysteries like Spencer Quinn's *Dog On It*) but others seeking the perfect summer escape. Put on the list of good reads."
—Library Journal (starred review)

"A fetching tale...If you're unfamiliar with this enjoyable series, it's a safe bet that this one will have you hunting down the previous six Andy Carpenter novels in your library or bookstore."

—Newark Star-Ledger

"Just when you think the story's about to end, there's a big surprise waiting in the final pages."

—Tampa Tribune

"Fans of the series will be pleased to reconnect with familiar characters, and new readers will be happy to discover something genuinely different in the world of pet mysteries."

—Booklist

PLAY DEAD

"Riveting...No shaggy dog story, this puppy's alive with reliable Rosenfelt wit and heart."

—Publishers Weekly (starred review)

"There is no way you can read this novel without becoming completely caught up in the story. As always, Andy's offbeat, outspoken personality shines on every page, and the balance of humor and mystery is dead-on."

—Booklist (starred review)

"Enjoyable...Carpenter continues to amuse and engage."

—Library Journal

"A terrific tale…Fans of the series will enjoy *Dead Center*."

—*Midwest Book Review*

"Witty…cleverly plotted…very enjoyable."
—*About Books*

SUDDEN DEATH

"The author handles the material deftly, mixing humor and whodunit but never letting the comedy overwhelm the mystery."

—*Booklist*

"Another touchdown!"
—*Publishers Weekly*

BURY THE LEAD

A *TODAY SHOW* BOOK CLUB PICK

"Absolute fun…Anyone who likes the Plum books will love this book."

—Janet Evanovich

"A clever plot and breezy style…absorbing."
—*Boston Globe*

"Exudes charm and offbeat humor, sophistication, and personable characters."
—*Dallas Morning News*

FIRST DEGREE

"Entertaining...fast-paced...sophisticated."
  —Marilyn Stasio, *New York Times Book Review*

"Suspense just where you want it and humor just where you need it."
            —*Entertainment Weekly*

"Entertaining."
            —*Cleveland Plain Dealer*

OPEN AND SHUT

"Very assured...packed with cleverly sarcastic wit."
            —*New York Times*

"Splendid...intricate plotting."
            —*Cleveland Plain Dealer*

"A great book...one part gripping legal thriller, one part smart-mouth wise-guy detective story, and all-around terrific."
  —Harlan Coben, author of *No Second Chance*

"Engaging and likable...The action is brisk."
            —*San Francisco Chronicle*

DOG
TAGS

Also by David Rosenfelt

DOG TAGS

DAVID ROSENFELT

GRAND CENTRAL
PUBLISHING

NEW YORK   BOSTON

Copyright © 2010 by David Rosenfelt

All rights reserved. In accordance with the U.S. Copyright Act of 1976, the scanning, uploading, and electronic sharing of any part of this book without the permission of the publisher is unlawful piracy and theft of the author's intellectual property. If you would like to use material from the book (other than for review purposes), prior written permission must be obtained by contacting the publisher at permissions@hbgusa.com. Thank you for your support of the author's rights.

Grand Central Publishing
Hachette Book Group
1290 Avenue of the Americas
New York, NY 10104
Visit our website at www.HachetteBookGroup.com

Grand Central Publishing is a division of Hachette Book Group, Inc. The Grand Central Publishing name and logo is a trademark of Hachette Book Group, Inc.

The Hachette Speakers Bureau provides a wide range of authors for speaking events. To find out more, go to www.hachettespeakersbureau.com or call (866) 376-6591.

The publisher is not responsible for websites (or their content) that are not owned by the publisher.

Printed in the United States of America

Originally published in hardcover by Hachette Book Group
First mass market edition, June 2010

10 9 8 7 6

OPM

To Lillian Churilla, wonderful friend to Debbie, mother to Tina, grandmother to Madeline, lover of books, and all-around great lady

DOG
TAGS

• • • • •

IT FELT SO much like being a cop. The fact that the two occupations were so similar was an irony that was never lost on Billy Zimmerman, who was certainly in a unique position to know. Until three years ago, he was a cop. Now he was a thief.

And at times like this, he was damned if he could tell the difference.

Much of the similarity was in the waiting. Back then he might be assigned to follow someone, to simply watch and see where they were going, and to move in if they did something illegal. If things got hairy, there was an unlimited supply of backup to call upon.

In his new occupation, there was just as much downtime, but now it was spent waiting for a potential victim to make a mistake, to reveal a vulnerability. Of course, being a thief came with more built-in pressure. If you failed a mission as a cop, the captain got pissed off. Fail as a thief, and it's a warden you're dealing with.

And calling in backup was not a viable option.

Standing outside Skybar on River Road in Edgewater, New Jersey, Billy was hopeful that something good was about to happen. It was Friday evening, and his target had been standing outside the building for twenty minutes, frequently checking his watch, and obviously waiting for someone.

Billy noticed the man held his right arm tight in against his ribs, as if pressing something against himself. He seemed to exert a constant pressure, which could be extremely tiring. This was no anonymous target; Billy knew him very well, and he had no doubt that there was something valuable inside his jacket, something he wanted to completely control.

Which made it something that Billy wanted.

Billy looked toward his partner, Milo, a classic, powerful German shepherd. Milo stood to the left of the club, near the curb, thirty feet away. A casual observer might have observed that Milo was wearing a leash around his neck, with the other end tied to a signpost. A more keen observer might have noticed that there was no knot on the leash; it was simply wound loosely around the post.

Milo could free himself whenever he so chose, and he was planning to do so as soon as Billy gave him the sign.

Milo, more than anything else, made Billy feel like he was back on the force. They were partners then, before Iraq, before the sixteen-year-old girl who calmly blew herself up and took Billy's left leg with her.

Getting Milo back was the best thing that had happened since, and not just because of his particular, immense talent. Billy loved Milo, and Milo loved him right back. They were a team, and they were friends.

And for now they both waited for the moment they knew was coming.

• • • • •

"You're Andy Carpenter, right?"
The man speaking is four inches shorter than me and at least forty pounds heavier. That makes him short and fat. He is standing in front of large platters of shrimp and crab. I've been eyeing them for a while, until he came and blocked my view.

I nod confirmation. "That's me."

I reach out my left hand to shake his, which is the only hand I have available. My right hand is securely in my right pocket, which is where it has been for three hours, ever since I got dressed.

That hand isn't just hanging out in that pocket. It is holding on to the ring that Kevin Randall, the junior partner in our two-lawyer firm, will be slipping onto Kelly Topfer's finger in about twenty minutes. I'm a little paranoid about stuff like this, and as the best man I want to make sure that when the minister says Kevin's ready for me to provide the ring, I don't come up with air or pocket lint.

Kelly and Kevin met only five months ago, and for Kevin it's a match made in heaven. He is the world's biggest hypochondriac, and Kelly is an internist. If it were left to Kevin, the couple would have registered for gifts at an online medical supply store.

The wedding is being held at the Claremont Hotel in Closter, New Jersey, thirty-five minutes from my house in Paterson. The pre-ceremony cocktail party has been an hors-d'oeuvrian challenge for me. If you don't believe me, try to take the tail shell off a shrimp with one hand while standing. And even if it were possible, how do you dip it in cocktail sauce? And what do you do with your drink?

"Eddie Lynch. People call me Hike" is how he introduces himself.

The name *Eddie Lynch* rings a bell somewhere in the recesses of my mind, but since there are already two bloody Marys sloshing around in there, I'm not thinking too clearly.

"You a friend of Kevin's?"

He shrugs. "We were roommates in law school."

The name clicks into place. Kevin has told me about him a few times, describing him as the smartest lawyer he knows. Since I'm also a lawyer whom Kevin knows, I half pretended to take offense, but Kevin wouldn't back off his assessment.

"You're the best man, right?" he asks.

"Yes," I say in a solemn voice. "I am. By far."

He shakes his head. "I'm glad he didn't pick me. I'd probably lose the damn ring."

The conversation, not exactly scintillating up to this point, takes a turn for the worse, as we both just stand there with nothing to say. It's getting uncomfortable, so I pipe up with, "They make a great couple, don't they?"

He shrugs again. Shrugging seems to be his movement of choice. "If it works out. But when was the last time one of these worked out?"

I'm a life-half-empty kind of guy, but "Hike" is making me look like Mr. Sunshine.

"Let me guess," I say. "You're not married."

"No way," he says. "Not me. I'd beat them off with a stick if I had to."

"Have you had to?"

He takes a step back and holds out his hands, palms up, as if inviting me to look at him. "Not in this lifetime," he says, then laughs a surprisingly pleasant laugh and walks away.

A few moments later Laurie Collins, better known as the love of my life, walks over. She has a small plate of food in her hand, and watches Hike as he walks away.

"Who was that?" she asks.

"The Prince of Darkness."

She decides that isn't worth a follow-up, so she asks, "Have you eaten anything? The shrimp are wonderful."

"I haven't been able to figure out how to get the tails off with one hand. And then there's the dipping-them-in-cocktail-sauce problem."

"Why can't you use two hands?" she asks.

"Because I'm holding on to the ring in my pocket."

"Isn't the pocket supposed to hold it? Isn't that why pockets exist?"

"You're talking philosophy and I'm talking reality," I say. "I'm afraid if I take my hand out I'll drop the ring."

"Why would you do that?" she asks.

"It wouldn't be on purpose. It might slip out and fall on the floor, and then what the hell would I do?"

"You could pick it up."

"It might fall down a drain."

"A drain in the carpet? You've got serious mental problems, you know?"

Just then the lights flash on and off, signaling that it's time to head into the other room for the ceremony. "It's showtime, Mr. Best Man. Get the ring ready."

I squeeze it a little tighter in my pocket. "It's under control," I say.

We start to leave the room, and I cast a glance back at the shrimp. "You think they'll still be here later?" I ask, but Laurie just frowns a look of disgust.

I take that as a no.

• • • • •

THE MAN WAS proving tough to wait out.

He stood near the front of the bar for over an hour, all the while under the watchful eye of Billy and Milo, though Billy was across the street, and out of the man's line of sight.

Milo looked over at Billy as if to say, *Let's get this show on the road.* Occasionally, passersby would approach Milo, often clucking about how terrible it was for someone to have left their dog tied up like that. Milo would give a low growl, not menacing enough for them to call animal control, but powerful enough to make them walk away.

But Billy was not changing targets. He instinctively knew the man would do something that would put what he was protecting in a place where they could get to it.

And with what he knew about this man, it could be very valuable.

So Billy and Milo waited until past midnight, which qualified as the wee hours of the morning by New Jersey standards. There weren't many cars going by, but Billy noticed that the man watched each one as it approached. He was meeting someone arriving by car.

If Billy's instincts were right, the upcoming meeting was to pass whatever was in the man's inside jacket pocket to the person he was meeting. If that was the case, Milo would have first dibs on it. If not, then Milo would probably just take the man's watch and be done with it. Either way, it would be a profitable night, and revenge would be sweet.

At twelve twenty, a Mercedes came down the street from the north, driving more slowly than normal. Billy tensed as it pulled over to the curb about thirty yards past the bar. The man Billy had been watching looked toward the car, nodded almost imperceptibly, and started walking in that direction.

The man walked past Milo, who did not look at him but was instead looking toward Billy, waiting for a signal. Billy just held one hand in the air, palm facing Milo, the signal to wait.

The driver of the car pulled his car to the corner and got out, leaving the door open. He walked a short distance toward the bar and then stood on the sidewalk, waiting for the man to reach him. Billy could see that the driver was tall, maybe six foot five. Billy moved closer to them, almost to where Milo was, about thirty feet from the driver of the car.

If the men greeted each other, it was inaudible to

Billy, and they didn't shake hands. They stood together for two or three minutes, though Billy could not hear them talking.

The man from the bar started to reach into his jacket to take out whatever he had been protecting all this time. Billy moved closer, straining to see. Even in the darkness, he could clearly make out a thick envelope. The man started to hand it to the driver.

Billy gave Milo the signal to spring into action, and the dog reacted instantly. He raced toward the men just as the driver was himself taking something out of his own pocket. The glint off it sent a jolt of panic through Billy; it was a gun.

Billy never carried a gun himself; to do so would be to inflate any possible burglary charge to armed robbery. Instead he ran toward the men, though his prosthetic leg hampered the speed at which he could move.

"Erskine!"

Milo was by this time launching himself into the air, intent on grabbing the envelope now held by the driver. Just before he arrived, the man from the bar took a brief, frightened step back, and then a gunshot rang out. He was blown farther backward by the force of the bullet.

Milo's perfectly timed jump allowed him to grab the envelope from the driver's hand and take off down the street. The driver was clearly stunned, and it took a few moments for him to gather himself and point the gun toward the fleeing Milo.

As the man started to pull the trigger, Billy reached him and grabbed for the gun. It fired as they were both holding it, and the bullet went off target. The driver wrestled with Billy for the gun, but Billy carried the day with a well-placed knee to the groin.

The man grunted in pain and staggered toward his car. Billy considered chasing him, but opted instead to quickly glance at the license plate, memorizing the number, and then went over to try to help the man who had been shot.

He put the gun on the ground and felt the man's neck for a pulse, but there was none. Three men appeared from nowhere and fanned out into the area. Billy had been the first to arrive at a lot of crime scenes, and he knew with certainty that these were not city or state cops. But he had no idea who they were.

By this point, a crowd of people was starting to gather, and Billy yelled, "Somebody call nine-one-one! Hurry! Get an ambulance here!" He said this even though his substantial experience with gunshot victims made it clear to him that they hadn't invented the ambulance or doctors that could help this guy.

Within a few minutes local police cars and ambulances arrived, and the men who had gotten there first seemed to melt away. This gave Billy time to look around for Milo, but he was nowhere to be found.

When homicide detective Roger Naylor showed up, he took command of the crime scene. Naylor heard what the officers who were already there had to say, and then walked over to Billy. They had known each other for years.

"Hey, Billy. They tell me you're a witness?"

"Unfortunately."

Naylor nodded. "You know the drill. Hang out until we can question you, and you'll need to make a statement."

Naylor didn't wait for a response; he just walked

over to the area where the forensics people were doing their work. Billy noticed that detectives were questioning other witnesses, probably patrons from the bar.

It was almost an hour before Naylor came back to Billy, along with another detective and two patrolmen. It wasn't the waiting that bothered Billy; it was not knowing where Milo was. The sound of the gunshot at that close a range had undoubtedly spooked him, of that he was certain.

"Can we get this over with?" asked Billy.

"I'm afraid it's a little more complicated than that," Naylor said. "We're going to have to do this down at the station."

"Why is that?"

"Because you're under arrest," Naylor said as he and the patrolmen took out their weapons. "Stand and place your hands against the wall."

• • • • •

"DO YOU HAVE the ring?" The minister's question takes me by surprise, because I was waiting for the part where he asks if anybody knows any reason why the marriage shouldn't take place. Could it be that only movie ministers use that line?

I rise smoothly to the occasion and take the ring out of my pocket, and then hand it to Kevin. In doing so I am graceful but deliberate, focused but with the apparent calm assurance of someone who has been taking things out of his pocket for years. It is a standout performance.

After the ceremony we head into the main ballroom for dinner. There is a DJ who plays music way too loud and spends most of his time begging people to go out on the dance floor.

Dancing, other than slow dancing, makes absolutely no sense to me. I don't understand the enjoyment anyone could get from standing in one place and wildly gyrating. If it's such a blast, do these people turn on the radio when they're alone at home and start doing contortions? I don't think so.

So if they only do it in public, it must be because they're being watched by other people. They clearly think they look good doing it. They don't. If rooms like this were ringed with mirrors, 95 percent of all dancing would be eliminated.

This kind of dancing also violates my space-alien principle. I judge things by the measure of whether aliens, landing on earth for the first time, would observe something and deem it stupid. And unless the aliens were from the Planet Bozo, dancing would land squarely in the "stupid" category.

But Laurie likes to dance, so I cave in about once every four songs. I do this because I'm a terrific guy, and because I think on some level that it will increase my chances of having sex when we get home. Sex would also look stupid to aliens, but who cares what they think? They're aliens; are we going to let them run our lives?

Sitting at our table are Vince Sanders, Willie and Sondra Miller, Pete Stanton and his wife, Donna, and Edna Silver. Vince, Pete, and Willie are my three best friends in the world, with the notable exceptions of Laurie and Tara, my golden retriever.

Pete is a lieutenant on the Paterson, New Jersey, police force, which is where I grew up and where Laurie and I live. Willie is a former client and my partner in the Tara Foundation, a dog-rescue operation that we run.

Edna is what I used to call my secretary, but she now refers to herself as my administrative assistant. She's in her sixties, though she'd never admit it, and has occasionally talked of retirement. Since she doesn't do any actual work, I've got a hunch that her retirement isn't imminent.

"You going to write this up for tomorrow?" I ask Vince, the editor of the local newspaper. I'm sure Kevin would like it, but he'd never ask Vince, who can be rather disagreeable approximately 100 percent of the time.

"This wedding? Only if somebody gets murdered on the dance floor."

As the evening is nearing an end, Kevin comes over and says, "I just want to thank you again for being my best man."

"It was an honor. And I thought I handled the whole ring thing flawlessly."

He smiles. "Yes, you did."

"So, are you guys going to stay in your house, or move?" Kevin has a small house in Fair Lawn, where they have been living.

"That's what I wanted to talk to you about," he says. "We're going to move to Bangladesh."

I do a double take. "Bangladesh? Is there a Bangladesh, New Jersey?"

"No, I'm talking about the real Bangladesh. Andy, I should have told you this earlier, but Kelly and I are leaving the country. She's going to practice medicine where people really need her, and I'm going to offer whatever services I can."

I'm having trouble getting this to compute. "Bangladesh?"

He nods. "Bangladesh."

"You know how hot it is there? You can throw a Wiffle ball and hit the sun. The cement sweats."

"I know."

It's an amazingly selfless thing that they're doing, and since it doesn't seem like I can talk him out of it, I might as well try being gracious. "That's incredible, Kevin. Really remarkable."

"Thanks for understanding," he says.

"Really, I totally admire it, but aren't there other, closer Deshes that you could go to? Maybe a Desh with plumbing?"

"We've researched it pretty well," he says. "And since we haven't taken on a client in six months…"

"We'll be okay." I smile. "Edna will just pick up the slack."

"If you need help, you should bring Eddie Lynch in. I think he's left already, or I would introduce you."

"I met him. He's a real room brightener. When are you leaving?"

"A week from Wednesday."

"So this is the last time I'm going to see you?"

He nods. "You want to hug good-bye?"

I smile, because Kevin knows I'm not a big fan of guy-hugs. "No, but Laurie will want to."

"Good," he says. "She was my first choice anyway."

On the way home I tell Laurie about Kevin's decision. "I know," she says. "I think it's wonderful."

"He told you tonight?" I ask.

She shakes her head. "No…maybe two months ago. He asked me not to tell you."

"I can't believe he told you before me," I say.

"He told pretty much everybody before you," she says. "I think he was afraid you'd be disappointed in him."

This is annoying me no end. "For devoting his life to helping people? I'd be disappointed with that?"

"I'm not sure I'd put it that way," she says.

"How would you put it?"

She thinks for a few moments, then smiles. "I guess I would put it that way."

As we get near the George Washington Bridge, I get off the Palisades Interstate Parkway and take city streets to Route 4. Like everybody else who lives in northern New Jersey, I wear my knowledge of back streets and shortcuts in the area near the bridge as a badge of honor.

Suckers take highways.

We're on Lemoyne Avenue in Fort Lee when we see flashing lights from at least five police cars down a side street.

"I wonder what that's about," says Laurie. As an ex-cop, I think she'd like to help out in whatever is going down. As a non-ex-cop, I want to get home and go to bed.

My point of view changes when I see that there are three animal control trucks intermingled with the police cars. As a certified animal lunatic, I want to know what could provoke such a massive government response.

"Let's check this out," I say.

Having seen the animal control trucks, Laurie knows exactly why I'm interested. "Why, you think a bunch of Chihuahuas might have broken into a PetSmart?"

The incident must have just begun, because the police have not yet set up a perimeter. Laurie and I get out of the car and walk right into the middle of it. She recognizes one of the cops and asks what's going on.

He shrugs. "Beats me. A dog got loose, and the alert

went out for all cars in the area. You'd think it was Osama bin Laden."

At least fifteen people, mostly cops and the rest animal control officers, have cornered a German shepherd whose back is literally against the wall of a building. He is an absolutely beautiful dog, well built and powerful, with two of the coolest ears I've ever seen.

Two of the officers are pointing guns at him. They are strange-looking weapons, and I assume they're some kind of stun guns. Even in his cornered position, the dog does not seem afraid, or even hostile. In fact, he almost looks bored.

I certainly don't want to see this dog hurt, so I yell, "Relax, everyone! Calm down! No reason to hurt that dog!"

One of the officers says, "Who the hell is that? Get him out of here."

I take out my cell phone and point it in the general direction of the dog and the officers surrounding him. "I'm videotaping this," I say. "Anything happens to that dog, it's going viral."

Of course, I barely know how to use the cell phone, and I can't imagine it has video capabilities, but it's dark out, and the officers would have no way of knowing that.

This time the officer is more insistent. "Get him out of here."

Two officers move toward me, including the one Laurie knows. "That dog is not going to hurt anyone," Laurie says. Then she yells out to the others, "Just put a damn leash on him. Give one to me and I'll do it."

As I'm being led away, one of the animal control officers approaches the dog with a leash, and the dog calmly lets him slip it around his neck. The officer then leads the docile dog away toward an animal control van.

When I get to the car, I look back and see Laurie talking to some of the officers. Having been in the Paterson Police Department for a number of years, she pretty much knows everybody.

When she finally joins me at the car, I ask, "What was that about?"

She shrugs. "Nobody seems to know, but it was made very clear that the dog was not to get away."

We get in the car. "I don't see how Kevin could leave this kind of excitement. You don't see drama like this in Bangladesh."

● ● ● ● ●

JERRY HARRIS HAD always taken pride in his work. Since that work usually consisted of theft and murder, he understood that most people would have trouble understanding the gratification he felt when a job was accomplished smoothly.

But Jerry realized that sometimes events beyond his control got in the way, and that's what had just happened. First there was that dog, and then that other lunatic who attacked him. It seemed like they had been waiting to make their move, though he had no idea who they were or why they were there.

So when it was time to report back to his employer exactly what had transpired, he felt some regret that he couldn't claim total success. It wasn't a complete failure; the target was effectively eliminated. But the point of the operation, securing the envelope, simply did not happen.

Jerry sat in his car at three in the morning behind a strip mall in Hackensack, the meeting place that had been designated last week, when he had been hired. At that time he had been given one hundred thousand dollars, in cash, with the promise of another hundred to follow the successful completion of the job.

The second hundred, Jerry understood, would now be the subject of a negotiation.

A Lexus pulled up alongside him, and his employer got out. It irked Jerry that he did not even know the man's name, or what his interest was in all of this.

Jerry had mentally nicknamed him Smooth, since he conveyed a calm, unruffled demeanor. He wore expensive clothes and jewelry, with a watch that probably cost more than Jerry's car. "Smooth" was obviously used to getting what he wanted, but that wasn't going to happen this time.

It might be unpleasant, but Jerry would handle it. He'd handled a lot tougher situations before.

Smooth entered the car and sat in the passenger seat without saying a word. His real name was Marvin Emerson, called M by the few people who knew him well. Not even Marvin himself really remembered if that started because it was his first initial, or the sound at the beginning of "Em-erson." In any event, he had never given his name or nickname to Jerry, and saw no reason to do so now.

"Hey, how ya doin'?" said Jerry.

"Please report on the evening's events."

"Well, we had a bit of a problem. It's going to sound nuts, but right after the guy gave me the envelope, I put a bullet in him, but then this dog comes out of nowhere and grabs the envelope and runs off with it."

"A dog...," M said. It was a way to prompt Jerry to finish the story, although M already knew everything that happened. He'd had a person in place, hidden across the street, who saw the entire thing.

"Yeah, and then some guy comes charging at me as I was trying to shoot the dog. He grabbed the gun, and I got the hell out of there." Jerry decided to leave out the part about getting kneed in the groin; it was humiliating and would cast him in a bad light.

"That's quite a story," M said. "Did you know this man?"

Jerry shakes his head. "Never saw him before. But the guy who gave me the envelope won't ever bother you again."

"The envelope is what was important. I thought I conveyed that to you."

"Hey come on, I did the best I could. How could I know that dog would do that? For all I know, you set it up."

"You'll get the remainder of the money when I get the envelope," M said.

Jerry was now annoyed. "That's bullshit. How the hell am I going to get the envelope now? I don't know where the damn dog went. You tell me where it is, and I'll go get it."

By now M was convinced that Jerry was telling the truth—that he really had no more knowledge of the dog or the other man than he said.

So he reached into his pocket, and in one remarkably swift motion took out a gun and shot Jerry in the right temple.

It didn't give him pleasure, or make him feel better.

Jerry was a loose end that had to be removed, no more, no less. But killing him did not solve M's problem; only finding the envelope would do that.

M got out of the car and signaled across the street to two men who would come over and do the cleanup, getting rid of the body and car so that they would never be found.

M then got into his own car and drove away, already focusing on the next step, which had to be getting his hands on that dog, and the guy who owned it.

• • • • •

FOR THE LAST three weeks, I have been living a nightmare.

Charlie's, the greatest sports bar in the history of the civilized world, has been undergoing renovations. They chose to do it now because it's July, and except for baseball there isn't much going on in the sports world. Apparently they ignored the fact that in the heat of summer there is plenty going on in the beer world.

Vince, Pete, and I generally spend at least three evenings a week at Charlie's. It used to be five, until Laurie moved back here from Wisconsin, where she briefly lived for a miserable year. It's not that she objects to my being out with my friends; it's just that I'd rather spend time with her than them. Of course, I would never tell them that.

Sports, lubricated by beer, is the glue that holds

us together. But I sometimes wonder if they would be my friends, if I would have any male friends, without sports. It represents at least 70 percent of what we talk about.

My attitude toward sports has evolved as I've grown older. For years I wanted to play professionally, though down deep I knew that was never going to be a realistic possibility. Then I got to the point where I lived vicariously through modern athletes, and that was reasonably satisfying.

Now, approaching forty and fading fast, I think I'm embarking on a new phase. I'm going to start living vicariously through someone who is already living vicariously through an athlete. It should be far less exhausting. All I have to do is find someone to fill the role; I think this is why men have sons.

The renovation is scheduled to last for six weeks, although I have no idea why they would be doing it at all. Charlie's is perfect, and in my experience perfection is generally a tough thing to improve upon.

So we have been spending our time at The Sports Shack, an upscale restaurant-bar located on Route 4 in Teaneck. It has a ski-lodge-impersonation motif, and it operates under the assumption that if you have enough TVs, and a gimmicky enough decor, everything else will take care of itself. Nothing could be further from the truth.

The hamburgers aren't thick enough, the french fries aren't crisp enough, and unless you tell them otherwise every single time, they serve the beer in a glass. Clusters of TVs sometimes all show the same baseball game, when there are plenty of others to choose from, and the other night one of the TVs was tuned to a *Best of the X Games* retrospective.

Best of the X Games? Now, there's a show that should run all of ten seconds. In any event, what is it doing in a sports bar? What is happening to the country I love?

But here we sit, drinking our beer, eating our food, and watching our games, thereby trying to restore a sense of order out of this chaos.

Tonight Pete is late in arriving, and Vince is in a bad mood because the Mets are losing. He would also be in a bad mood if the Mets were winning, or if they were not playing, or if there were no such thing as the Mets.

He stares in the direction of the bar. "Do you see that?" he asks, then shakes his head. "Unbelievable."

I look over there but don't see anything that would be considered difficult to believe. "What are you talking about?"

"That guy is in a three-piece suit. With a tie."

"So?"

"So?" he sneers. "So it's supposed to be a sports bar. What's next, flowers on the tables? That smelly stuff in a pot?"

"You mean potpourri?"

He looks at me like a bug he found in his soup. "Yes, Mr. Foo-Foo. That's exactly what I mean."

Pete arrives, and not a moment too soon. Vince is harder to handle one-on-one than LeBron James. Pete doesn't say hello; for some reason greetings have never been a part of the relationship among the three of us. We don't say good-bye, either. Or *How was your day?*

"I need a favor" is the first thing Pete says to me.

"Dream on," I say, though we both know that I will do whatever he asks. Since I am a criminal defense attorney,

Pete's job as a police lieutenant makes him a valuable source of information for me, and I call upon him all the time. He grumbles, but he always comes through.

Even if that weren't the case, I would do whatever Pete needs. Doing favors fits squarely within our definition of friendship, and to refuse one would be highly unusual. But pretending to resist is a necessary part of the process.

"Actually, I'm doing you a favor," he says. "I've got you a client."

"Just what I need," I say. I am independently wealthy, a result of inheritance and a few major victorious cases. Since hard work in general, and hard legal work in particular, is not my idea of a good time, I rarely take on new clients.

"You read about the murder in Edgewater last night?" Pete asks.

"Was it on the sports page?"

Vince chimes in with "You're an asshole." I can't decide if he says that because it was on the front page of his newspaper and he's annoyed that I didn't see it, or because he just thinks I'm an asshole and thought this was a good time to remind me. Probably both.

"I read about it," I say.

"The guy they arrested for it is Billy Zimmerman. We graduated from the academy together, and we were even partners for a while."

"An ex-cop?" I ask, and immediately regret the question.

"Wow, you figured that out all by yourself?" Pete asks. "Just from what I said about him going to the academy and being my partner? You are really sharp."

"Get to the favor part," I say.

"All in good time. Anyway, Billy was also in the National Guard, and he volunteered to go to Iraq. He was there less than a year and got his leg blown off. So he comes back and gets screwed by everybody. Medical care is bad; it was like they were doing him a favor by treating him. And all he could do on the force was get a desk job, which is not for Billy. So he told them to shove it."

"What did he want?"

"He wanted his old job back, working the streets."

"With one leg?"

"He has a prosthetic; it works fine," Pete says. "He could outrun you."

"So can my grandmother," Vince says.

"Both your grandmothers are dead," I say.

He nods. "Either one of them could still spot you ten yards in the hundred and wipe the track with you."

I'm not going to get anywhere by talking to Vince, so I turn my attention back to Pete. "So he wants me to represent him?" I ask, cringing.

"Maybe. We didn't talk about it," Pete says. "But that's down the road."

The answer surprises me. "What's up the road?"

"His dog."

"He wants me to take his dog?" I ask, my relief probably showing through. Willie and I have already placed hundreds of dogs through our foundation, and adding one is no hardship at all.

"No. He wants you to defend his dog."

"From what?"

"The government."

• • • • •

"HE'S LIKE A celebrity here, Andy."

Fred Brandenberger is talking about Milo, who has been placed in the Passaic County Animal Shelter. Fred is the shelter director, a thankless job in a world in which there are far more dogs and cats than available homes.

I am following through on Pete's request for me to try to help his friend by helping his friend's dog. The first step in that process is to visit with my new "client," whom Fred tells me is occupying a special dog run in the back of the shelter.

"What do you mean by 'celebrity'?" I ask.

"Well, for one thing, four cops came with animal control when they brought him in. Then they told me I couldn't take him out, not even for a walk."

It hits me that it's probably the dog I saw under police siege the other night. "Is it a German shepherd?" I ask.

"How did you know?"

"I was there when the arrest went down. But you can do whatever you want with him," I say. "This is your show here."

"I don't think so," he says. "You'll see what I mean in a second."

Fred brings me into a back room that I've never been in before, and which I didn't realize existed. The room is completely empty except for a large dog run against the back wall. In that run is the same German shepherd, pacing in his five-by-eight space, as if frustrated and not completely understanding or tolerating the fact that he is a prisoner. When they say that someone is acting like a caged animal, this is literally what they're talking about.

I've got a thing about dogs; I am totally and completely crazy about them. I thumb through *Dog Fancy* the way most guys look at the *Sports Illustrated* swimsuit issue. And this dog is even more spectacular than he looked in the dark the other night; there is immediately no doubt that he does not belong in these circumstances, and I am going to change them.

He is getting out.

Sitting on a chair in front of the run, and complicating matters considerably, is a uniformed police officer. He stands when he sees us, and lets his hand rest on his holstered gun.

"What's going on?" he asks.

"What are you doing?" I ask. "Guarding the dog?"

"Who are you?"

We seem to be asking a lot of questions, but none of

them are getting answered. I decide to break that streak. "I'm the dog's lawyer."

"What the hell are you talking about?"

"Which part didn't you understand? I'm Milo's lawyer, and I'm here to discuss the case with my client. If you'll excuse us..."

"Forget it," he says. "Nobody gets near that dog."

"Except for me," Fred offers. "I get to feed him and clean up after him."

"Why are you guarding my client?"

"Because they assigned me here," the officer says. "You think I decided to do this on my own?"

This isn't turning into a very productive conversation. "Why did they assign you here?"

He shrugs. "Beats the shit out of me. But nobody's going near that dog." He nods toward Fred. "Except this guy."

I'm not going to get anywhere with him, and I sort of have nowhere to get anyway. It's not like I was going to have a meaningful client conference with Milo; I just wanted to get another look at him. He's a spectacular, powerful dog who certainly doesn't look like he needs an armed guard to protect him. It annoys me to see him locked up like this.

"Okay," I say, and then look past him so I can talk directly to Milo. "Milo, don't talk to anybody about anything. Anybody asks you something, refer them to your lawyer. If you need anything, cigarettes, reading material, whatever, just tell the guard."

The officer looks like he's going to shoot me, so Fred and I go back into the main area. "You have no idea what this is about?" I ask.

"Nope. They came in like they were dealing with Al Capone and wouldn't tell me anything. But there's a guard there twenty-four hours; maybe they think somebody is going to try to steal him. Stealing dogs is not usually a problem here."

Fred is referring to the fact that he frequently has the very unpleasant task of having to put down some of the dogs here. It's why Willie and I have our foundation.

I call Pete from my car and tell him what happened, and I'm surprised when he doesn't sound surprised at all. "Yeah, I was going to call you," he says. "I just heard about the guard."

"What's this all about?"

"I don't know, but the situation is locked down. And the word is that the FBI is involved."

"FBI? Who did your friend kill?"

"What happened to innocent until proven guilty?" he asks.

"All of a sudden you're an ACLU member? Who is your friend alleged to have killed?"

"I don't know."

"So I suppose you don't know where the dog fits in?"

"Not a clue."

"Thanks. Your involving me in this situation has really affected my life in a positive way."

"You bailing out?" he asks.

"No."

"Because you got a look at the dog, right? You saw him in a cage and you want to get him out."

I'm annoyed that he's right, and I can't think of a quick comeback, so I don't say anything.

He laughs, knowing full well that he's scored a point. "You actually prefer dogs to humans."

"Maybe I need to start hanging out with a better class of humans."

Click.

• • • • •

I NEED TO speak to Billy Zimmerman's lawyer. That way I can have him get the court to allow me to represent Milo. I have to admit that my semi-involvement in all of this doesn't feel quite so much like a chore anymore. Not only do I want to get that dog out of his undeserved imprisonment, but I'm more than curious to find out why it is considered necessary to post a twenty-four-hour armed guard outside his cage.

I call Rita Gordon, the court clerk, to find out who is representing Zimmerman. I had a forty-five-minute affair with Rita a few years ago, when Laurie had left for Wisconsin and we were broken up. Rita's sexual prowess and energy level are such that if the affair had lasted for fifty-five minutes, they would have had to get me out of bed with a soup ladle.

"Hiya, big boy," she says when she hears that it's me.

She's taken to calling me big boy lately, and I don't know what to make of it. I stifle the desire to ask her what she means or if she's kidding, because I'm afraid to hear the answer.

We banter a bit, since that is the price I have to pay for information. Then I ask, "Who is Billy Zimmerman's lawyer?"

"Does the name Nobody ring a bell?"

"What does that mean?"

"It means he refuses to have a lawyer," she says. "The PD handled it for the arraignment, but after that Zimmerman said he didn't need one."

"So he's going to represent himself?" I ask.

"As far as I know he hasn't said that, but eventually he's going to have to make a decision."

This is becoming more complicated by the minute. "I need to see him."

"We all have our needs."

"Can you get a message to him? Tell him it's about Milo."

"Who's Milo?" she asks.

"His dog."

"Again with the dogs? Don't you think you might be overdoing this dog thing?"

"Come on, Rita. Tell him I need to talk to him about Milo. Tell him it's life or death."

"Is it?"

"No."

She considers that for a few moments, and then shrugs. "Okay. I'll get word to him."

"Thanks."

With nothing else to do, I head back to the office. It's

not like I have anything to do there; I just feel that if I spend afternoons at home, I'm one step from watching soap operas and eating bonbons. It's a dignity thing.

Edna isn't in, which does not exactly qualify as a news event, so I take the time to ponder what I should do about Kevin's announced departure from the firm. His leaving means that we lose 50 percent of the firm's lawyers, while retaining the 50 percent, me, that doesn't like to do any of the work.

This would leave something of a gap, if we had any clients. The fact that we don't makes the problem somewhat less urgent, but that is subject to change. Despite my best efforts, clients and murder cases seem to show up out of nowhere.

Kevin is a brilliant attorney, and the perfect complement to me. He takes great pleasure and pride in writing detailed legal briefs and obsessing over the minutiae that can be so critical in the course of a trial. I see myself as more of a big-picture strategist, which means I'm lazy and I bore easily.

There's a good chance I can deal with this minor Milo issue on my own, but in the future I'm going to need somebody, at least on a part-time basis. Kevin's friend Eddie Lynch is a possibility, though based on my one conversation with him, he could probably talk me onto a window ledge.

Having resolved nothing, not even in my mind, I turn my attention to the Internet to read what I can about the murder that Billy Zimmerman stands accused of. The name of the victim is still being withheld, which is very unusual for this situation.

The victim was standing in front of a relatively expensive club, and is not being described as homeless or a vagrant. It would seem far-fetched that he cannot be identified, and the police are not even claiming that is the case. They simply are not yet releasing his name.

The incident has not been treated by the press as a major story, so I would imagine there is little pressure on the police to be more forthcoming. For now it is just strange, though not nearly as strange as an armed guard around Milo.

Just as I'm preparing to go home, having exhausted myself from thinking nonstop for forty-five minutes, Rita Gordon calls. She has contacted Billy Zimmerman, who had previously been not at all responsive to any contacts from representatives of the justice system.

"Milo was the magic word," she says. "He says he'll see you at ten o'clock tomorrow morning."

I'm a little irritated by a prisoner, no less one I'm doing a favor for, dictating the time of our meeting. "Gee," I say, "that barely gives me time to find something to wear."

"Shall I set it up?" she asks, choosing to ignore my sarcasm.

My inclination is to tell her to tell him to shove it, but I can't get the image of Milo in a cage out of my mind.

"Okay. I'll be there."

• • • • •

BILLY ZIMMERMAN ISN'T just any county jail inmate. He gets special accommodations, separate from the others awaiting their turn at the justice system. That's because Billy is a former cop, and that's a group that generally doesn't do well in this type of environment. For instance, they get stabbed a lot.

Beyond the separation from the other inmates, the treatment former cops get from the guards can be hit or miss. Some guards feel a kinship with the prisoner, a carryover bond from his former career. Others view the ex-cop as a traitor, a turncoat, and someone even more despicable than the average crook.

When Billy is first brought out to see me in a private room set up for the occasion, my guess is that he's one of the lucky ones. He seems relaxed, surprisingly so, for a man facing a murder charge. Billy has to know how difficult this is going to be, and he must be aware that he may literally never spend another day enjoying freedom. Yet if he's panicked or tormented, he's hiding it well.

"Hey, Andy Carpenter, right?" He extends his hands to shake mine, an awkward movement since his hands are cuffed together. I extend both of mine in sort of a solidarity gesture, and we do a four-handed shake.

"Right."

"Thanks for coming. Pete said I could count on you."

"Pete's a good friend."

He nods vigorously. "Of mine, too. Stand-up guy."

Since I'm pissed off that Pete got me into this in the first place, I'm of a mind to cut short the Pete-praising portion of the conversation. "He said you wanted me to help your dog, which I am trying to do."

He nods. "Good. That's great."

"I tried to contact your lawyer about this, but you don't seem to have one."

Another nod. "Right. No problem. You can talk to me."

There's something weird going on here; his affect is one of being in charge of his situation, and it doesn't come close to fitting with the facts as I know them.

"Okay," I say. "I went to see Milo, who is currently at the county shelter."

"Is he all right?" Billy asks, the first concern I've seen so far.

"He's fine. He's being treated basically like you are, away from the other prisoners."

"Good. That's good."

"The unusual part is that there's an armed guard outside his cage."

Still another nod. "Good."

I'm obviously pleasing him, even though I don't have a clue as to what I'm talking about. "You have any idea why the guard is there?"

"So nobody can come in and steal him."

"Why would they want to do that?" I ask.

"I can't get into that right now. But I'm sure there are people who think he can help them."

"People think Milo can help them? How? Why?"

He holds his hands out, palms upward, and shrugs. "Sorry, I really can't go there."

I've had more than enough of this, so I stand up. "I've got to tell you, Pete is a good friend, but nobody is that good a friend. I like to help dogs, and I would have helped yours. But there's plenty of dogs in that shelter who don't have armed guards to protect them, so I'm going to focus my efforts on helping them."

For the first time, I see worry in his face. "Hey, come on, I'm not trying to be difficult. It's just that the things you're asking...I really can't go there."

"I understand," I say. "So I'm going to go there." I point to the door so he'll know what I'm talking about, and then start walking toward it. My hope is that he won't say anything until I'm safely out the other side.

"Wait. Please," he says, in a tone that no longer contains arrogance or confidence. It has just enough vulnerability to stop a sucker like me in my tracks. I stare at him and don't say anything; if this is going to get anywhere, he's going to have to do the talking.

"I need you to be my lawyer," he says.

That is something I have a singular lack of interest in. "We're talking about Milo," I say. "Besides, I thought you didn't want or need a lawyer?"

"I don't. But if I'm going to tell you anything, I have to be sure you're bound by confidentiality. The only way I can be sure of that is if I hire you as my attorney."

He's right about that, of course, so I nod. I tell him that I'll draw up an agreement in which he can hire me for a finite time for a fee of one dollar. For now the agreement can be verbal, and I will honor it.

He thinks for a few moments, and then seems to decide that this will be acceptable. Lucky me.

Once that's accomplished, he says, "Okay, here's what I can tell you. When I returned from Iraq, I tried to get my old job back on the force. There was no way."

"Why?"

"They told me that with the economy and all, there was a freeze on hiring, that they might be able to give me a part-time desk job. It was bullshit; they had no interest in a one-legged cop. They always viewed me as a pain in the ass anyway."

"Were you?"

"A pain in the ass?" He laughs. "Sure. A major one. Anyway, Milo used to be my partner on the job; he rode in the squad car with me. And I found out he was about to get dumped as well."

"For being a pain in the ass?" I ask.

"No, for being too old. He was about to turn seven. That's the limit for the department. So when I made the request, they were happy to give him to me."

"Why did you want him?"

He looks surprised by the question. "I love that dog; it sounds stupid, but he is my best friend in the entire world. Pete told me you're a dog nut, so you should get it."

"I get it," I say, because I do.

"Milo was trained to disarm perpetrators. He was amazing at it; the best in the department. Somebody would be holding a gun one second, and the next thing you know Milo is flying through the air and taking it right out of his hand."

"So?"

"So once I got him back, I enhanced that training a little bit. Now he can take anything he wants from anyone; he could take the fillings out of your teeth."

"He's a thief?" I ask.

Billy grins. "We both are. And we're as good as it gets. Milo and Clyde."

"Who do you steal from?"

"Well, the good news is that people worth stealing from are the ones who can afford it. You know, they're insured and all. So we're pretty selective, and we aren't out to get rich. Just get by."

"So that's what you were doing the night of the shooting?"

He nods. "Yes. Milo grabbed something from the victim just before he got shot."

I don't want to ask him who did the shooting, because I don't want to hear the answer. But implicit in his story is a denial of guilt; if they were out to steal something utilizing Milo's talents, the fact that he had just stolen it would have made the shooting unnecessary. There could have been additional circumstances, but for now, that's how I read what he is saying.

"I didn't shoot him," Billy says, reading my mind.

"Who did?"

"I don't know."

"Where is the item that Milo stole?"

He grins again. "That is the billion-dollar question."

● ● ● ● ●

A GOOD NUMBER of lawyers think they can instinctively tell when someone is lying. I am not among them. I have my instincts and hunches about the veracity of the things people tell me, but I am probably wrong as often as I am right. In this case, my hunch is that Billy is telling me the truth, but I don't have great confidence in it.

He tells me that he knew the victim, a man named Jack Erskine, and that he served with him in Iraq. He also stands by his claim not to know what was in the envelope that Milo took, but adds that a number of people will likely be desperate to get their hands on it.

I could push it and try to get more out of him, but it's not necessary for what I have to do. I also feel that the less involved I get with Billy and his story, the better.

"So that's why Milo is being guarded? Because the police are afraid that someone will take him in the hope he'll lead them to what he stole?"

Billy nods. "That's what they think, but he won't do it. At least not for them."

"But he'll do it for you?"

He smiles. "Could be. I told you; we're buddies. He trusts me."

Billy's strategy is becoming clear to me now, even if the facts of the case aren't. "So the reason you're not worried about yourself is that you think they'll come to you with a deal. You and Milo find the package, and they drop the charges."

"Pete said you were smart," Billy says. "He was right."

"I'm only smart compared with you," I say.

"What does that mean?"

"It means you're facing life in prison, and you're doing nothing to protect yourself. Instead you're sitting in your cell plotting a strategy that consists of hoping everything will fall neatly into place."

"It will."

"Maybe. Or maybe they'll find out what was in the envelope through other means, or maybe someone in power will decide they're better off not finding the envelope at all. Or maybe someone will get by the guard and take a shot at Milo, or figure out a way to poison his kibble. Any one of those maybes, or a hundred others, leaves you with an hour a day's exercise in the yard for the rest of your life."

I think I can see in his face a sign that I'm getting through to him, or maybe not. I'm not even sure that

I want to, because this is one human client I definitely don't need.

"Can you get Milo out?"

"I don't know," I say. "And what would I do with him if I did?"

"One step at a time," he says. "He doesn't belong in a cage."

Finally, a statement that I'm sure is true.

I promise Billy that I'll do my best, then I head home rather than to the office. I find I do my best thinking when I'm walking Tara, and some productive thinking is certainly going to be required here. A law enforcement system that considers it necessary to put an armed guard around a dog is not going to passively let that dog walk out the door.

Whatever the approach I decide on, it's going to take an ample dose of legal maneuvering. To that end I call Kevin. He and Kelly had decided not to take a honeymoon, since they were to be leaving for Bangladesh in less than two weeks.

"Kev, we've got a case."

"You've got a case" is his response. "I'm going to Bangladesh."

"What's your rush?"

"Poverty, hunger, illiteracy..."

"And you think if you don't hurry and get there all that stuff will be gone?" I'm admittedly sounding pathetic, but I really could use Kevin's help.

"Andy, I wish I could help you, but I can't."

"Okay," I say. "I understand. I guess my not losing the ring doesn't mean you owe me."

"Is the client at least a human this time?"

"Damn close. He's a German shepherd, but a really smart one." I tell Kevin the basics of the case, and I can tell he's intrigued by it, but he's firm that he and Kelly are off to save the world.

"Get Eddie Lynch," he says. "He writes legal briefs that make mine look like they were done with crayon."

"Kevin, he's Mr. Doom and Gloom."

"He thinks of himself as a realist. In any event, there are two reasons you should have him write the briefs."

"And they are?"

"He'll do a great job, and when he does, you won't have to."

The man has a point.

● ● ● ● ●

TARA IS NOT as young as she used to be, but you could never tell that by her attitude when we go for a walk.

Her tail is always wagging, her nose is always sniffing, and she's always alert to her surroundings. When she hears an unusual sound, her ears perk up and she looks around to see if a new adventure awaits her.

I admire her in terms of her attitude toward life, and I would like to emulate it. Unfortunately, I can't get my ears to perk.

In any event, while I don't think I have ever encountered a golden retriever who is less than extraordinary, Tara has somehow ascended to an even higher level.

Many people, when talking about their dogs, laughingly praise them by saying that the dog thinks it's human, as if being human is something a dog might aspire to. Maybe it's because I've spent a lot of time dealing with the criminal justice system, but the average dog I know is paws and shoulders above my species.

Dogs almost unanimously possess dignity, compassion, and innate intelligence. In these areas, humans tend to be a little more hit or miss. But Tara rises above them all.

In case you haven't noticed, I'm a bit of a dog lunatic.

The task at hand is to represent Milo against the system that has imprisoned him. In addition to having no idea what kind of tactic to use, I don't even know what I want the final result to be. If I get him out, where will he go, with his owner in prison? And if an armed guard is necessary to protect him in the shelter, who will protect him on the outside?

On the other hand, I am keenly aware that a dog's life is all too short. The average life expectancy for a German shepherd is twelve years, and every day spent in a cage is a day he'll never get back.

By the time I get back from my walk with Tara, I have reaffirmed my decision to get Milo out. I just have to figure out how.

Laurie is waiting for us at home when we arrive. She has taken something of a career turn since she moved back to New Jersey and in with me. Her previous résumé includes stints as a cop in Paterson, a private investigator working mostly for me, and a year as the police chief of Findlay, Wisconsin.

Last year, while visiting me in New Jersey, she was shot and badly wounded. Still suffering mild aftereffects of her injury, she decided to teach criminology at nearby William Paterson University. It's no surprise to me that she fully embraced this new line of work, or that she loves it.

I relate the situation to her over dinner, spending most of my time describing Billy's rather cavalier attitude about his predicament, and the fact that he knows more than he's willing to reveal.

She stops me midstory. "I'm sorry, Andy, but none of that is important, at least not now."

"What do you mean?"

"Your goal is to help the dog, right? So all you need to focus on is how to get him out of the shelter. The rest of the stuff doesn't matter."

"Except that whatever is behind this is the reason they're paying so much attention to him. Most dogs in the shelter don't have their own bodyguards."

She shakes her head. "It still doesn't matter. You're going to fight it out on legal grounds; they either have the right to keep Milo or they don't. And it doesn't sound like they would be willing to make everything public anyway."

She's right, of course, but it still leaves me without a concrete plan of action. "The legal grounds are the problem," I say. "At the moment I don't have any. I don't even know what their official reason is for keeping him."

"What could it be?"

"As far as I know, the only valid reason for keeping the dog would be if he was dangerous. If he had bitten someone."

"He didn't, right?"

"Not as far as I know. All he did was steal an envelope."

She smiles. "So he's a thief. You've represented a few of those before, haven't you?"

"Never. All my clients are innocent." I say this with a straight face, but Laurie clearly knows better.

"So then defend Milo like you defended them."

I think about it for a few moments, and the idea that is forming in my mind causes me to smile.

"You know something? I can do that."

• • • • •

"YOU'RE HERE TO talk about his dog?" Eli
Morrison is obviously surprised by my announcement,
and probably more than a little annoyed. As the county
attorney handling the Billy Zimmerman murder case, he
cleared his schedule to make time for me when I told him
Billy had hired me, and that an immediate meeting was
necessary.

Eli is considered an old-timer in the prosecutor's office: His tenure there began when my father was in
charge of the department. He's one of the few who never
attempted to use it as a stepping-stone to a more lucrative
career on the defense side, or for political gain.

We've had a pretty good relationship over the years,
and I can't say that about too many prosecutors.

In this case, chances are Eli figured I was going to

broach the possibility of a plea bargain for Billy, though I don't know if he would have been amenable to it or not.

"Yes," I say. "His name is Milo, and he's being unfairly detained."

"He's a dog, Andy," he explains, though I assume he knows that I'm already aware of that.

"He's a dog with rights."

"You've got to be kidding."

"Why are you holding him?" I ask.

"Well, for one thing, he's a thief. Witnesses saw him run off with an envelope that we believe belonged to the victim. We've also tied him to two other thefts that he and Zimmerman pulled off over the last few months."

"So why don't you charge him?"

"Charge who? The dog?"

"Yes. And his name is Milo; it's demeaning to keep calling him 'the dog.'"

Eli laughs, demonstrating an ability to move from incredulity to amusement. "You want me to charge the dog... Milo... with theft?"

"No, I want you to let him go."

"Where is he going to go?" he asks.

"That's not your problem."

"Andy, this thing you have with dogs may not be completely healthy. Maybe you should see a shrink." He laughs again. "Or a trainer."

"Look, Eli, I'm handling this as a favor for a friend. If you can't release the dog because he stole something, that's your call. But just so I can close the lid on this thing, can you write me a letter to that effect? I'd really appreciate it."

"Sure. No problem."

"Thanks. Let me know when it's ready and I'll have it picked up."

"Anytime tomorrow morning," he says. "Now, you're not representing Zimmerman for the murder?"

"Nope. Just Milo."

"This has been a pretty weird meeting."

"Really?" I ask, standing up. "For me it's just business as usual."

I leave Eli's office having accomplished everything I wanted. Once I get the letter from him accusing Milo of being a four-legged crook, I need to get another letter from Billy. After that I'll be able to make my legal move, which will be at best a long shot.

Unfortunately, there's actual work, detail-oriented work, that goes into the legal process. It's unfortunate because the actual work, especially the detail-oriented work, is the part I hate.

With Kevin unavailable, I definitely need someone to help me. My choices are to ask around and start interviewing prospective candidates, or hire Eddie Lynch, the incurable pessimist that Kevin recommended. The first approach would involve a substantial commitment of time and energy from me, while the second approach would consist of making one phone call.

Mmmm...many hours of work, or one phone call. What to do? What to do?

"Eddie?" I say when he picks up the phone. "Andy Carpenter. We met at Kevin's wedding."

"I remember," he says. "I hope you didn't eat the crab cakes. I had diarrhea every twenty minutes for two days."

"Well, I—"

"It left me with hemorrhoids the size of basketballs. I can't sit down without tipping over."

"Thanks for sharing that," I say. "I was calling to see if you were interested in doing some legal work with me on a case. Kevin recommended you."

I can almost see him shrug through the phone. "Might as well."

"Great, Eddie. That's the kind of enthusiasm we're going to need."

"Call me Hike," he reminds me. "What's the case?"

I tell him all about Milo, and my plan to get him out. "That's not bad," he says, grudgingly. "I like it. We'll probably get our clock cleaned, but I like it."

We talk about the legal brief he will write supporting our position, and I'm impressed by how quickly he grasps it. I shouldn't be surprised; Kevin told me what a brilliant lawyer Hike is, and I would pretty much take Kevin's word on something like that over anybody's.

We come to terms on an hourly rate that I will pay him; the fact that he agrees immediately means I could have gotten him for less. We plan to meet at my office the next morning. I ask him if he'll stop off at the jail and get the letter from Billy, and he's fine with that. He'll also stop at Eli's office and pick up the promised document about Milo.

My sense is that as long as Hike's getting paid by the hour, he'll shovel shit if that's what I want. That's okay with me; I think I'm going to like having a work slave again.

● ● ● ● ●

"MAN, I LOVE when you do this stuff," Willie Miller says. Because he's my partner in the Tara Foundation, our dog-rescue operation, I've come to the foundation building to talk to him about the situation with Milo, and what we might do with him should we get him out.

"What kind of stuff?" I ask.

"Lawyer stuff. Stuff like this thing with Milo. You know, with judges and witnesses and shit. Damn, I should have been a lawyer."

"Did you ever consider it?"

He shakes his head. "Nah. It would have meant finishing college, and high school, and eighth grade, and seventh grade..." He stops talking, no doubt exhausted by the amount of education he is contemplating.

"It's not all fun and games," I say.

"You have fun at my trial?" he asks. Willie was on

death row for seven years for a murder he did not commit; we got him off on a retrial.

"I was scared out of my mind at your trial. I thought we were going to lose, right up until the time the verdict came in."

"Not me," he says. "I knew it was in the bag all along. I'm lucky like that."

I refrain from asking him how come, if he's so lucky, he was wrongly imprisoned for seven years of his life. Instead I ask, "You want to sit at the defense table with me for this one? Kevin's gone, so you can be my assistant."

"No shit? Man, that'd be great." Then, "What does an assistant do?"

"You get me coffee, or soda, or M&M's, and every once in a while you tell me how great I'm doing."

"That's easy," he says. "I can do that."

"If we win, what are we gonna do with Milo?"

"You really think somebody's trying to kill him?" he asks.

"Either that or steal him. The cops seem to think he needs protection."

Willie thinks for a few moments. "Well, he can't stay here. Not unless we hire a guard ourselves."

We talk about it for a while but don't reach a final decision. We can worry about that later, if we win.

Having recruited a trusty assistant, I head back to the office, where Eddie Lynch is waiting for me with the brief he has written to file with the court. It's only six pages, minute by legal standards, but it is outstanding in every respect.

"This is absolutely great, Hike," I say.

He shrugs. "Yeah, right."

"I'm serious. It's exactly what I need."

"You're going to need a hell of a lot more than this," he says.

Buoyed by his optimism, I drive down to the courthouse to fire the opening salvo in the legal war over Milo. I tell Rita Gordon that I want to get a bail hearing on the court's calendar for my client.

"For Billy Zimmerman?" she asks. "Bail was already denied when the PD was handling his case."

I shake my head. "Different client. This is for Milo Zimmerman."

"The dog? You want a bail hearing for the dog?"

"Correct. On an expedited basis. He was entitled to it already. Which judge is assigned to the Zimmerman case?"

"Judge Catchings. I was just going in there now."

That's actually a break for me. Of all the judges in Passaic County, he's probably the one who hates me the least. He also has a terrific, dry sense of humor, which he's going to need. "Let me talk to him," I say.

"Sorry, Andy. That's not the way it works. You want to file a brief?"

"Okay, sure," I say, taking the envelope out of my pocket. "Here it is."

"That was convenient. Anything you want me to add to it when I talk to him?" she asks.

"You mean like I won't be going to the media with this unless he turns me down?"

Rita has seen how my previous cases with dogs have become national news, often making the authorities look bad, so she knows exactly what I'm saying.

"You don't think he'll take that as a threat?" she asks, smiling.

"Not if you smile like that when you say it. And maybe bat your eyes a little."

"How about if I take off my top?"

"Even better."

She laughs and stands up. "You want to hang out here until I get back?"

"Will he look at it right away?"

"Are you kidding? Absolutely."

"Okay. I'll wait. That way if I have to I can call Matt Lauer from here."

It takes Rita more than forty-five minutes to return to her office. Obviously they had more business to discuss than just *New Jersey v. Milo Zimmerman.* She finds me stretched out on her couch, hands clasped behind my head.

"Make yourself comfortable," she says.

"Without a pillow? I don't think so. Did we get the hearing? It took you long enough."

"Nine o'clock Wednesday morning. He cleared his calendar."

"Did he say anything?"

"I couldn't tell. He was laughing too hard."

• • • • •

COMPARED WITH BILLY Zimmerman, Milo's case is a slam dunk.

That's because the police finally revealed the identity of the guy that Billy is accused of murdering the other night. The victim was, as Billy said, one Jack Erskine. The problem is that his full name and title was Major Jack Erskine, recently returned from a four-year deployment in Iraq.

The negative implication for Billy in all this is that Erskine was in charge of security operations in and around the Baghdad area, which meant that Billy was under his command. The papers are already speculating that this was a revenge killing, that Billy somehow blamed Erskine for his terrible injury.

In any event, the Carpenterian theory holds that there are no such things as coincidences in murder cases, and there's no way that this has a chance of disproving it. Billy's connection to the victim, whatever the circumstances, is going to be a mountain for his lawyer to scale.

I spend the day with Eddie Lynch in the office, going over preparations for tomorrow's hearing. Eddie's starting to grow on me; I'm finding that if I absolutely tune out everything he says, he's not that annoying. And his mind is sharp as a tack. He might even be Kevin's equal as an attorney.

"By the way, why do people call you Hike?"

He shrugs. "My brother is four years older than me. When he was around ten, he wouldn't let me play football with him and his friends. So I used to cry to my mother about it, and she forced him to let me play."

"Let me guess," I say. "All they would do is let you hike the ball."

"You got it."

Having solved that mystery, I turn my attention back to the hearing tomorrow. Once I'm sure we are as prepared as we're going to be, I head home. Laurie and I take Tara for a walk through Eastside Park, and then drive over to The Bonfire for dinner. It's a restaurant that's been in the same location on Market Street forever; my parents told me they used to hang out there when they were in high school.

Laurie and I don't do small talk; we never have, and hopefully we never will. We have the ability to either talk about things that are of consequence to us, or stay silent without any discomfort at all.

As soon as we sit down, Laurie starts asking me questions about how I'm doing on Milo's case, which leads into more probing questions about Billy Zimmerman.

I can see that she's much more interested in it than I am. "You miss it, Laurie."

"Is it that obvious?"

I nod. Laurie has spent her entire life in law enforcement, either public or private, and I can tell that she misses the action. "It is. I thought you liked teaching?"

"I do. I really do. But teaching is something I enjoy. Being out on the street is something I am."

"You're not ready. You know that." It took a while for her to recover from the shooting; she bled so severely that her brain did not receive oxygen for a while, long enough to sustain some damage. She still has some weakness on her left side, and she tires easily. Her progress has been tremendous, amazing even her doctors, but she's not all the way back yet.

"My mind is ready."

"So?"

"So I want to help on the case."

"It'll be all over one way or the other tomorrow."

"I'm not talking about Milo. I'm talking about Billy Zimmerman."

"He doesn't want a lawyer," I say. "He thinks he's going to deal himself out of it."

"When he finds out he can't, he's going to come to you for help."

I shake my head. "Not me. I'm a one-Zimmerman attorney. Milo is my man. Billy can find somebody else."

"You know better than that, Andy. You'll come up with a reason to take him on as a client. Maybe you'll want Milo to have his father back, or maybe it'll be as a favor to Pete. Or maybe you'll think the guy's innocent. But you'll do it, and I'll help you."

"What about your teaching?"

"I'll do that as well. It's called multitasking. I can do a lot if I set my mind to it."

"And you'll still take care of my ravenous sexual appetite?"

"I'm not a miracle woman, Andy. I can't do everything."

"Laurie, I want to be up front about this. I'm not taking on Billy Zimmerman as a client to keep you busy, or to get you back in the action."

"Fair enough. But there will be other clients."

"Don't depress me," I say. "I'm having a nice dinner, and I want to focus on what I want for dessert."

"Really? I was looking forward to getting you into bed and showing you how I multitask."

"Check, please."

• • • • •

DONOVAN CHAMBERS LEARNED of his impending death in the newspaper. That was unusual in and of itself, but to find it buried on page seven of the *Nassau Advocate* was also a little demeaning. To read it sitting on a glorious beach while simultaneously soaking up sun and a piña colada... well, that was about as weird as it got.

Not that Donovan was mentioned by name in the story; he wasn't even referred to indirectly. But the message he received was as clear as if the headline had read, "Donovan Chambers About to Be Murdered."

The story was a two-paragraph item that identified the victim of a murder outside a New Jersey club the week before. Donovan couldn't remember reading about the murder previously, but he knew that it would not have interested him if it hadn't named the victim as Major Jack Erskine.

The identity of the victim meant that Donovan himself was going to die. And living in this exotic, out-of-the-way locale would not protect him at all. These were the kind of people that would find you no matter where you were hiding.

He never should have confided in Erskine.

Donovan had no way of knowing whether the story was itself dated. The *Nassau Advocate* would sometimes run pieces days after picking them up from mainland newspapers. If this was one of those cases, then those who'd be after him already had a head start.

Not that they would need it.

Donovan wasn't feeling fear, though he assumed that would come later. His dominant emotion was sadness. He was finally living the life he always wanted, but never thought possible. And now it was over.

Donovan wasn't going to give up; that wasn't his style. And he certainly wasn't going to go to the cops and tell them what he knew, or what he had done. That would simply guarantee a prison sentence, and that would be the easiest place of all for his killers to find him.

What he would do would be to run, and to hide, and he was good at both. It would make things easier that he had so much money; there would be no need to get a job and risk exposure in that way. He had concocted better plans for the money, but that was now in the past.

Donovan briefly considered whether to spend the rest of the afternoon on the beach, since it would be the last time he was there. He decided against it. Time was not something he had the luxury of wasting; it might be too late already.

He walked up the beach toward his house, a sprawling one-level place sitting on a small cliff overlooking the water. It was an absolutely spectacular setting. He was renting it with an option to buy, an option he had been about to exercise. Now he was glad he hadn't yet done so, since the process of selling it would no doubt provide clues to his whereabouts.

At this point, Donovan himself did not have any idea as to the location of those future whereabouts. It would have to be someplace unexciting, and modest, where he would be unlikely to attract attention. It would be boring, but he would be alive, until the moment that he wasn't alive anymore.

There would not be any flights off the island until the next morning, so he called and reserved a seat. He would pack right away, so that all he'd have to do in the morning would be to wake up and leave.

Donovan took his loaded gun out of the desk drawer and put it in his pocket. He hadn't carried it in a while; there wasn't any need, and it was illegal. Now it made him feel more comfortable, more secure, as it always had in the past.

But he knew that the feeling of comfort was illusory. When they came at him, it wouldn't be a gunfight at high noon in the center of town. He wouldn't see them coming until it was too late to do anything but die.

Donovan had finished packing and was carrying the suitcases out to the car when the first bullet penetrated his brain. He never felt it, nor the two that followed.

And he never saw his killer.

• • • • •

"ARE YOU OUT of your mind?" is the greeting that Eli Morrison gives me instead of hello. He's just arrived in court and come straight over to me at the defense table.

"Fine, how are you, Eli?"

"A bail hearing for a dog?"

"Justice works in strange and wonderful ways."

"I understand you have fun with this stuff, but some of us have important work to do," he says.

"Eli, let me ask you something. Are you aware that there is an armed guard stationed around Milo twenty-four hours a day?"

"What?" he asks, though he doesn't mean that he didn't hear what I said. It's clear by his face and tone that he had no idea about the armed guard, nor can he imagine why it would be done.

"If Milo is important enough to be guarded, he's damn sure important enough to have a bail hearing."

I can tell that Eli has more questions, none of which he has the time to ask, or I have the ability to answer. The bailiff signals the arrival of Judge Catchings, which forces a bewildered and irritated Eli back to the prosecution table.

Judge Horace Catchings takes his seat behind the bench, which he has been doing for thirty-two years. The first African-American judge in Passaic County, Judge Catchings stands six foot six, and his frame looms out over the courthouse. It seems as if he can reach out and touch the principals in the room. Baseball hitters might describe the experience of facing tall pitchers like Randy Johnson in much the same way. Judge Catchings can't throw the curveball, but he has a wicked contempt of court.

The judge has already agreed that I can call witnesses to support my case, but that my presentation is to take no more than two hours. I pretended that it would be difficult to stay within that time frame, though in reality I couldn't stretch it that long if I included a rendition of "MacArthur Park."

I have avoided notifying the press about today's hearing, mainly because I used them as a threat to get the judge to allow it in the first place. While they may be valuable to me later, bringing them in now would only risk pissing Catchings off, and since there is no jury, that wouldn't be wise.

Willie Miller is next to me, sitting in his seat and looking around as if he were at a Broadway theater. "This is really cool," he says. Kevin's courtroom comments, as I recall, were generally more helpful.

Eddie Lynch is not here. I didn't think it necessary

that he come, and he seemed to show no great desire to do so. But I will be relying on his brief to a considerable degree.

Judge Catchings welcomes us to his courtroom and admonishes us not to be long-winded. He also asks us if we have anything to say before we begin.

Eli stands and says, "Your Honor, while we have not had much time to prepare on this issue, and it is unique to say the least, I cannot find in any statute any right to bail for an animal."

"That may be true," the judge says. "The way I look at it is that we are here to decide if the continuing confinement of the dog known as Milo is warranted. As Mr. Carpenter's brief points out, there are any number of ways that his release could be handled legally. Bail is simply one of them."

That is already a small victory for me. Now I just have to show that Milo shouldn't be kept captive; I don't have to jump through quite as many legal hoops as I anticipated to manage it.

I nod my thanks to Judge Catchings and say, "Your Honor, the defense calls Thomas Basilio."

Thomas Basilio is the forty-one-year-old head of animal control in Passaic County. It is not a coveted position; dogcatchers are not exactly widely loved in most communities, and he is the king of the catchers. Because of the overwhelming number of unwanted dogs, it means that his department must euthanize a good number of them. It's not a position I'd want to be in.

I have spent some time socially with Basilio, and he's a decent guy with a disarming sense of humor. He's not going to get a chance to use it today.

"Mr. Basilio, you are aware that you have a German shepherd named Milo in your custody?"

"Yes."

"He's at the shelter in Paterson?"

"Yes."

"How did he come to be incarcerated there?"

"The police turned him over to us."

"Why? What did he do wrong?"

"I don't know that he did anything wrong. They didn't share that with me."

"Are you aware that they have stationed a guard outside his cage twenty-four hours a day?"

"Yes."

"Did they tell you why?"

He shakes his head. "No. I asked, but they said it had to do with a case and was confidential."

"Under what circumstances do you keep dogs in the shelters?" I ask.

"There can be a few reasons. Dogs can be found stray, and we hold them until perhaps their owner can find them. If not, we hope they will be adopted by a new owner. Or an owner might not want a dog anymore, and he brings it to our shelter."

"Is that it?"

"No. If a dog is a danger to the community, say if he has attacked or bitten someone, then we keep him confined. Often we have to put those dogs to sleep."

"That means kill them?"

"Yes."

"Which of those reasons speaks to why Milo is there?"

He thinks for a moment. "I'm not sure. His owner is,

as I understand it, unavailable to take care of him. As far as whether he's dangerous, I suppose the police would know better about that."

I introduce as evidence a letter from Billy Zimmerman giving me ownership of Milo. I had privately assured Billy that it was a temporary, though necessary, move.

"So if I am the owner of Milo, and I want to take him home and care for him, that would remove one of the reasons for his confinement?"

Basilio shrugs. "I suppose it would."

I turn the witness over to Eli, but he doesn't have any questions. I suspect that Eli will be reluctant to ask many questions throughout the hearing. Lawyers classically will not ask questions they don't know the answer to, and since Eli didn't even know about the guard, he'll be extra careful.

We're off to a good start.

• • • • •

DETECTIVE CARL OAKES looks like he would rather be anywhere else but on the stand. His body language and facial expressions seem to indicate that taking his time up on a matter as trivial as this is beneath his dignity. As his adversary, that gives me an advantage, because nothing is beneath my dignity.

"Detective Oakes, you personally gave the order for Milo to be incarcerated in the Passaic County Animal Shelter?"

"It wasn't an order. It was a request."

"Did he bite anyone?" I ask.

"Not that I know of," he says.

"Have you ever made a request like this before?"

"When we arrest someone who has an animal, and there is no one to care for it, it is turned over to the shelter."

"You personally do that?" I ask.

"Not usually."

"Ever?"

"I don't recall," he says, obviously annoyed.

"Why did you personally make the request in this case?"

"I told you. There was no one to care for the dog."

That doesn't come close to answering my question, but I let it go.

"So if I told you I was Milo's new owner, and that I would care for him, that would alleviate your concern and you would tell the shelter you no longer wanted him held there?"

"I didn't say that. The dog committed a theft."

I smile. "Milo is a crook?"

"He committed a theft."

"Okay, now we're getting somewhere." I introduce as evidence the letter I got from Eli, confirming that Milo was being held because of the robbery.

After I read it out loud, I ask Oakes if he agrees with it.

"I do," he says.

"So now the police and prosecutor are on record as saying that Milo is in jail because he committed a theft. Has he ever been arrested or charged before?"

Oakes can't conceal his disgust with my questions. "Come on...," he says.

"Is that a no? Has he ever been arrested or charged before?"

"Not that I know of."

"Not a member of organized crime? Not part of a canine Cosa Nostra?"

Oakes is not about to be humiliated, so he turns to Judge Catchings for help. "Judge..."

I turn to Judge Catchings as well. "Your Honor, we've established that this is Milo's first arrest. Bail for a first-time offender is certainly warranted. And he can be released on my recognizance; I will assume full responsibility for his future actions."

"I'll reserve judgment on that," he says. "Continue." Then he adds, sternly, "In a serious manner."

Before I can ask another question, Oakes says, "The dog is a danger to the community. He could keep stealing things; that's how he's been trained."

"Where was he trained?"

"At the police academy."

"He learned to be a thief at the police academy?" I ask, and the fifteen or so spectators in the gallery laugh.

Oakes doesn't seem inclined to answer that question, so I ask another one. "Detective, why is an armed guard stationed outside Milo's cage?"

"I can't say," he mumbles, obviously uncomfortable with the subject.

"You don't know, or you feel you shouldn't say?" I ask.

"I can't say." His emphasis is on "can't."

"Do you want to use a lifeline? Maybe phone a friend?"

Eli objects that I'm being disrespectful to the witness, which I never knew was an official objection, but the judge sustains it anyway, and asks me to rephrase.

"At taxpayers' expense, an officer is sitting in an animal shelter twenty-four hours a day, and you can't tell us why?"

"No."

I turn to Judge Catchings. "Your Honor..."

"Detective Oakes," he says, "you're going to have to do better than that."

Oakes thinks about it for a few moments and then says, "We received a request from the federal authorities."

Pete was right; the feds are somehow in on this. What is puzzling to me is why they would go to such lengths to guard Milo, but then take no action to intervene in this hearing.

Neither the judge nor Eli seems to know what to make of this, and I certainly can't shed any light on it. Catchings lets Oakes off the hook, accepting the cryptic reference to the feds as his final answer. I wish I could probe more, but he won't let me.

My final witness is Juliet Corsinita, a dog trainer whose home and office are in Teaneck, but who has developed a geographically wide clientele. She has a local TV show in which she dispenses training tips, and her dry sense of humor and easy way with dogs have earned her quite a following.

Juliet has a training camp of sorts on her property, and people bring their animals to her for six weeks of "boot camp" during which they learn pretty much all a dog can learn. I've watched her in action, and the training is done with love and care; there is no fear or punishment, and certainly no physical violence involved.

As soon as Juliet is called, Eli stands up to object. "Your Honor, I fail to see the relevance. It is my understanding that Ms. Corsinita, whatever her qualifications, has never worked with the dog in question, and has no direct knowledge of the incident itself."

Eli has obviously had his staff do quick homework on this; when he saw Juliet's name on the witness list, he must have had someone question her in advance of her appearance.

"Your Honor," I say, "Ms. Corsinita is being called to testify about my client's state of mind." This draws a roar from the gallery and a loud laugh and thigh slap from Willie, whom I will have to admonish about correct conduct at the defense table.

Eli has to stifle a smile himself, and he says, "Your Honor, this has moved from the ridiculous to the bizarre."

The judge turns to me and asks, "How can Ms. Corsinita possibly testify to this dog's state of mind? And why is that relevant?"

"Your Honor, Ms. Corsinita is an expert on dogs and how they think. She has studied Milo's history, and will be able to inform the court substantially as to the general way that a dog in his situation would react. If the court feels it is unhelpful, it can certainly disregard her point of view. There is no jury impact to worry about."

"It's a waste of the court's time," Eli says. "And it has the potential to further send this proceeding into chaos."

Judge Catchings stares daggers at Eli; apparently he doesn't like being accused of running a chaotic courtroom.

"Your Honor," I say, "I think everyone will agree that Milo is being held on a simple charge of theft. The prosecutor and arresting officer have admitted it. In such cases, when it is a first offense, there are two factors among those to consider as it relates to bail or an outright acquittal. First, is the accused a continuing threat to the community? And second, is he a flight risk?"

Now Judge Catchings turns his withering stare at me. "You do not need to educate the court."

"I know that, Your Honor. But there is another factor that I would also ask you to consider. In order to be ultimately convicted of this crime, the accused has to know the difference between right and wrong. Ms. Corsinita can help with that."

Eli jumps from his chair; this is too much. "Right and wrong? He's a dog!"

"I think Your Honor is already aware of the species we are talking about."

Judge Catchings shakes his head, probably unhappy with how far afield this has gotten. But the train has left the tracks, and there's no stopping it now. "I'll allow the witness," he says.

Juliet describes the type of training that Milo would have had at the police academy, and I get her to focus on the specific manner in which he was taught to grab weapons out of the hands of dangerous criminals.

"So his job was to take deadly weapons out of the hands of criminals who were using them to threaten people?"

"That's correct," she says.

"So he's a hero?" I ask, and before Eli can voice an objection, Juliet says, "In my mind he certainly is."

"So let's assume for the sake of argument that after he left the police force, he was trained to take other items from people who were holding them. Though this is strictly hypothetical, would that have been an easy thing to teach him?"

"Very. I could do it in a day."

"If he then used that training and took certain items, as directed, would he think he was doing something wrong?"

"Certainly not. That was his training. He would expect and deserve praise."

"Thank you. Now regarding his future danger to society, what is your view on that?"

She hesitates. "Well, if the person who trained him had control and directed him to steal in the same fashion, he would do that."

"What if he were under my control, and I gave no such instructions?"

"Then he wouldn't do it."

"Are you sure?"

"I'm positive."

I turn Juliet over to Eli, who gets her to admit that dogs don't always behave in completely predictable ways. It's not exactly a stunning admission, and doesn't harm our case in any appreciable way, unless the judge is predisposed against us.

Eli has put in an uncharacteristically weak effort. I attribute this to a basic indifference to whether Milo is kept in the shelter or not, and perhaps to some annoyance about being kept in the dark regarding the armed guard. The feds obviously saw fit to deal with the police but not the prosecutor. This is not the best tack to take when the issue could wind up in court.

Eli and I make closing statements, and then I expect Judge Catchings to defer his ruling for at least a few days.

He doesn't. "It is the opinion of this court that the county has not made a compelling case for depriving this dog of his liberty. I direct the defense to present to the court a statement stipulating how Milo will be cared for, and what arrangements and precautions will be made to guarantee that he will not participate in any further actions contrary to the public good.

"Once that statement has been approved by the court, I will order him released to your custody, Mr. Carpenter."

"Your Honor, can I request that the guard remain on duty at the shelter until you have approved my submitted statement?"

"So ordered. My opinion in its entirety will be posted on the court Web site."

Game, set, and match.

• • • • •

I GO STRAIGHT from the office to the county
jail to tell Billy the good news. It's generally very easy
for an attorney to see his client, and no previous appointment is necessary. This is especially true during the phase
in which the accused has not yet gone to trial or been
convicted. This is the time when contact between lawyer
and client is most crucial, and there are few roadblocks to
overcome.

I'm therefore surprised and annoyed at having to wait
an hour before anyone comes out to escort me inside.
When they finally arrive, it's not a uniformed guard, but
rather a civilian employee.

This is unusual, but is partially explained when the
man says, "The warden wants to see you."

"Why?" I ask.

"He should be the one to tell you that."

I'm ushered directly to the warden's office. His name is Daniel Maddow, and I've met him a few times over the years, mostly when I've been dissatisfied with the hospitality his people have shown to my clients. He's been in the job for a while, at least ten years, though he's no older than forty. He seems to present himself as something of a contradiction; while he has the demeanor of a grizzled veteran who's seen it all, he talks carefully, in a refined, almost delicate manner.

Maddow gets up from his desk when I come in, and we shake hands. "I'm afraid I have some distressing news," he says.

"Oh?"

"Mr. Zimmerman was attacked in the lavatory early this morning. He was badly injured."

"How badly?"

"Three broken ribs, broken clavicle, minor concussion, knife wound on his arm, possibly some internal injuries. My understanding is that none of it is considered life threatening."

"Who did it?" I ask.

"We believe there were three assailants. We've identified one of them, which was fairly easy, because he's dead."

"As a result of the same fight?"

"Yes. The man suffered a broken neck. Let's just say Mr. Zimmerman put up more than a token resistance."

"How did they get to him? I thought he was in a separate area for protection?"

Maddow nods, clearly uncomfortable with the situation. "He was. There seems to have been some cooperation between the assailants and one or more guards, though we haven't been able to identify those culpable yet."

"That is terrible," I say. "Inexcusable."

He nods. "Yes, but I'm afraid it reflects the realities of modern prison conditions. We of course have zero tolerance for this type of thing, but unfortunately our level of tolerance is not always a deterrent."

"Can I see him?"

"I'm sure that can be arranged, but he's not here at the moment," he says. "He was transferred to Saint Joseph's Hospital, where I am told he is in intensive care."

"What's going to happen when he comes back here?"

"Believe me, that is a matter that will be intensely analyzed, and adequate security will be provided."

"You'll understand if I'm not completely confident with that?" I ask.

He nods. "Certainly."

Once I leave, I call the hospital and learn that if all goes well, Billy should be out of intensive care by early evening, and I can see him then. I ask for the head nurse on the floor, who in my experience is the person in the hospital who basically runs the place and knows everything that's going on. I ask her if Billy is being protected, and she assures me that a police officer is there to guard him.

It's taken a while, but Billy's finally attained the same status as Milo.

When I get back to the office, I'm surprised to find that Hike is there. "Hey, we won," I say. "It couldn't have gone better."

"For now. If they appeal, who knows?"

"You trying to cheer me up?" I ask.

"Nah, I just came to drop off my bill."

He hands me a bill for the time he put into writing the brief. It's lower than I expected; he certainly didn't pad the hours.

"Great. If you can wait a minute, I'll give you a check."

"Where am I going?" he asks. This is obviously a guy who likes to be paid on time.

I write out the check, realizing as I'm doing so that Milo and I never negotiated a fee structure. If he gives me a problem, I'll just withhold his kibble until he pays, or maybe I'll send Hike around to collect.

Before Hike leaves, he asks the obvious question. "What are you going to do with the dog when you get him?"

"I'm not sure. You got any ideas?"

"Nope," he says, and leaves.

Thanks, Hike.

• • • • •

BILLY DOESN'T LEAVE intensive care until the morning, so I'm at the hospital at nine AM.

The decision has already been made to keep him in the hospital for at least the next few days, rather than transferring him to the prison infirmary. I support the decision and would have fought for it if there was resistance. If solitary confinement in the prison couldn't prevent this attack, the infirmary would be a shooting gallery.

There are two guards outside Billy's room when I arrive. He looks like he's been through a meat grinder, but he does not seem the type to complain about it. "You okay?" I ask. "Are they treating you well?"

"No problem, although what the hell is the deal with this male nurse thing?"

"You've got a male nurse?"

"Damn straight; he's gotta be six foot two. He wanted to sponge me down. I told him if he tried it, he'd be taking my bed in intensive care."

"Do you need anything?"

He nods. "Yeah. I need you to get me out of here."

"The hospital?" I ask.

"No...prison. But first tell me about Milo. I heard you got him off."

"Yes. We prevailed."

"Man, Pete was right. You must be good. Where's Milo now?"

"Still at the shelter. I should have him out by tomorrow. Which brings up the question of what I should do with him."

"Can you hold on to him until you get me out?"

"What makes you think you're getting out?"

"If you go to the prosecutor, I think he'll be willing to make a deal."

"You're going to plead?"

He shakes his head. "I'm going to trade."

"Billy, I don't think you get it. First of all, I'm not your lawyer; I only represented you for the purpose of getting Milo out. Second of all, if I was your lawyer, I wouldn't put up with this cryptic bullshit."

He is aware that I'm angry, and backs off immediately. "Okay, I'm sorry, you're right. I need you to be my lawyer, full-time. I want you to do for me what you did for Milo."

"No thanks. I've got all the clients I need."

"Do it as a favor for Pete."

"Been there, done that. Besides, he hasn't asked me to represent you," I point out.

"He will." When I don't respond, he says, "Come on, man, I'm a wounded veteran. Don't you care about your country? What do I have to do?" he asks. "Sing 'God Bless America'?"

There's something obnoxiously charming about Billy, but I've always been able to resist obnoxious charm. Maybe it's because I possess so much of it myself. The truth is, I don't want this case; in fact, I don't want any case. But I also can't leave him confined to this hospital bed with no one to help him.

"All right," I say. "I'll compromise with you. I'll handle your plea bargain—"

He interrupts to correct me. "Trade."

I nod. "Trade. But you're going to tell me what it is you have to trade. I'm not going in there unless I know what I'm talking about."

He thinks for a moment, weighing his options, and then nods. "Okay. Jack Erskine...the guy that was killed...if there was ever someone on this planet who deserved to die, it was him."

• • • • •

ALAN LANDON WAS listening to the most boring speech ever delivered when his cell phone rang. More accurately, it didn't ring; it vibrated. And it wasn't his cell phone, at least not his main one. It was his second phone; the one he always answered, no matter what.

Since he was sitting on the dais next to the mayor of New York, and it was the same mayor who was giving the boring speech, answering the phone took some delicate maneuvering. He quietly got up and walked off the stage, hoping that everyone would assume he was going to the restroom. Since the mayor was twenty minutes into a talk on the intricacies of educational reform, the likelihood was that the audience was so close to comatose that they wouldn't have noticed a hand grenade going off on stage.

As Landon was walking, he opened the phone in his

pocket so that the call would go through without cutting to voice mail. He knew the caller would be smart enough to hold on and wait for Landon to answer.

Actually, there was no doubt that Marvin Emerson would hold on. M had called Landon at least thirty times in the last year, and Landon had answered every single time. He also always knew that it was M calling even before he said a word, yet M's phone ID was blocked. It could only mean one thing: He was the only one who called on that particular phone.

When Landon reached an area in the hallway that afforded him some privacy, he took the phone out of his pocket and spoke into it. "You have news?"

"I do," said M. "The lawyer pulled it off. The dog is going to be released from the shelter."

Landon couldn't help but smile. "Justice triumphs. When will this take place?"

"I'm told tomorrow."

"Where will it be taken?" Landon asked.

"I don't have that information yet. But I will. Our people will be there, waiting to follow whoever takes him."

"Make sure that you are personally involved in that process. But don't take any action yet. Just keep track of his whereabouts."

"Will do," M said.

"Is that all?"

"No, and the other news is not as good."

Landon hated statements like that. He didn't need anyone to characterize news in advance; he could certainly figure out for himself whether it was good or not. Those were wasted words, which amounted to wasted time. "Speak."

"The operation in the prison was not successful. And one of our three people was killed."

"The other two?"

"Don't worry, they can't implicate anyone. They don't know where the orders or money came from."

"I trust you'll take other steps to rectify their failure?" Landon asked, though it was more a statement than a question.

"I will, but it'll be much harder now."

"That's why I pay you the big bucks," Landon said before cutting off the call and heading back to his seat on the dais. He got there just in time to catch the last five minutes of the speech, and to lead the applause.

Like everyone else in the room, he was applauding the fact that it was over.

• • • • •

I HAVE NO idea if Billy's opinion of the late Jack
Erskine is fair or accurate. But I do know that his opinion
can prove extremely damaging to Billy's chances of ever
getting out of prison.

Major Erskine was stationed in Baghdad, and was in
charge of security in that city. It was a uniquely important
position, especially as the war slowly wound down and
police, rather than strictly military, action became dominant.

Many commanders earn and inspire respect from their
rank and file. It doesn't mean that they are soft on disci-
pline, or that they act like one of the guys. All it means is
that they have paid their dues, and are tough but fair.

Jack Erskine had earned no such respect, at least not
according to Billy. While Erskine had little contact with

anyone other than his direct reports, he had been widely disliked by virtually every soldier under his command. They had watched his willingness to throw subordinates under the bus and behave in a manner designed to curry personal favor with his bosses and Washington.

There were also the rumors that Erskine was corrupt, that he and a small coterie of his men used their power within the country to enrich themselves. Billy had no reason to believe it or doubt it, but with what he had seen in Iraq, nothing would have surprised him.

Not that Erskine really affected Billy's life one way or the other. Billy enlisted to protect and serve; that was why he became a cop, and why he became a soldier. His father had done the same, as had his two uncles. But it didn't take long for him to regret his decision, and he had resigned himself to putting in his time and going home. Erskine had no role in that decision one way or the other.

Then came that summer day and an event that was unusual for a number of reasons. The United States, eager to demonstrate what it called a return to normalcy of the country, had invited a number of major players in American private business and finance to meet with Iraqi leaders, in and out of the government.

Nothing of enormous consequence was to be discussed; those things generally got decided in far more private settings. This was for show, and was held outside the safety and security of the Green Zone as a symbolic way of telling the world that Iraq was ready to take its place in the world community.

A brief part of the event was to be held outdoors. That brevity was dictated by the oppressive heat, as well as the obvious fact that security was more difficult to maintain outdoors. But the authorities wanted the citizenry to be there and be a part of it, and more important, they wanted television to beam pictures of those participating Iraqi citizens around the world.

Security was jointly planned and executed by the American military and Iraqi police, with Erskine in charge of the American end of things. It was understood but unspoken that he would therefore be in the lead position for the entire operation.

Billy, like just about every other soldier or MP stationed there, was assigned a role in the operation. He was not at one of the checkpoints through which citizens were admitted into the area; his task was a more general one of being on patrol inside and looking for anything suspicious.

"I saw this girl," he says. "She couldn't have been more than sixteen, although I'm usually not that good a judge of age. There was something about her that caught my attention."

"What was it?" I ask.

He shrugs. "I don't know. Maybe something about the eyes. They were afraid, but fear is something you saw a lot of over there. Anyway, I wasn't too worried, because if she had a weapon, she would have been stopped at the checkpoint."

"So what did you do?"

"I watched her for a while. That was really the only job I had that day, to watch for something suspicious, and I thought that she qualified. She walked pretty close to the stand that was set up, where the dignitaries were. But that wasn't unusual, because that's what everybody was there to see."

He's talking slowly, carefully and with emotion, and I wonder if this is the first time he's told the story out loud.

"I watched her for about five minutes, and she was just standing there. She didn't seem to have any interest in what was going on, and it wasn't like she was there with any friends. After a while I stopped watching, because if she was going to do anything, by that point she would have done it already.

"Anyway, I walked away from her, which is the only reason I'm alive today. A few minutes later I looked back in her direction, but I couldn't see her. All I saw was a wall of flame shooting up, and these bleachers that had been constructed were coming down on me. They pinned me down and landed on what used to be my leg, but I don't remember much of it."

"How many people were killed?" I ask.

"Eighteen, with another seventy-one badly wounded. The Iraqi oil minister was killed, a guy by the name of Yasir al-Hakim. He was most likely the target. Two of the dead were American businessmen."

"Where does Erskine fit in?"

He shrugs. "You want to know what I know? Or what I think?"

"Start with what you know," I say.

"Nothing."

"Then let's try what you think."

"The Iraqi that was killed...the oil minister, al-Hakim...he was new to that job, and the word was that he was going to clean up the corruption. And believe me, there was plenty of corruption to clean up. And I think Erskine was in position to have a piece of it."

"So you think Erskine was in on having this guy killed?"

He nods. "I do. There's no way that girl should have been able to get in there with a bomb that size strapped to her. It had to be a setup, and Erskine was one of the people in a perfect position to make that happen."

"Was there an investigation?"

He laughs. "Sure. Went nowhere."

"Could it have been an Iraqi that let the girl in?"

"No way. There were American MPs and soldiers everywhere. It just doesn't ring true. Anyway, Erskine didn't get off scot-free. The incident at least put him out of favor, and he left the army." He shakes his head. "The son of a bitch. He lost his command, eighteen people lost their lives, and I lost my leg."

"So you've been watching him since he got back?" I ask.

He nods. "On and off."

"And you were at the club that night because he was there."

"Right. And I don't know what was in that envelope, but the way he was acting, it had to be something important. Something that everyone will want."

"And you think the prosecutor will trade your freedom for the chance to get it back?"

"I think he'll be instructed to."

"Have you told other people your feelings about Erskine?" I ask.

"You mean that I hated his guts? I would say a number of people know that."

"That will be used against you," I say.

"Only if I go to trial."

There's a lot more for me to learn, but I don't need to ask those questions now. He's given me enough to bargain on his behalf, or at least to discover if we have a bargaining position at all.

It's time to find that out.

• • • • •

ELI SEEMS FAR less willing to meet with me this time, but he finally agrees.

"Let me guess" is how he greets me when I arrive at his office. "You're representing a goldfish in a paternity suit."

"Nope."

"Okay. You're handling a probate matter for a ferret."

"You're a bitter loser," I say.

His mood suddenly seems to change and he laughs. "Not this time. This time I actually thought it was pretty funny. Did you get the dog?"

"No, I filed the paper with the court, but it hasn't been approved yet. Should hear anytime."

"So what do you want now?"

"I'm representing Billy Zimmerman for the purpose of plea bargaining."

"Then this will be a short meeting. Which plea bargain are you talking about?"

"The one we're about to have."

He frowns. "Okay, I'll start. He cops to first degree, forty years minimum."

"You must be bitter," I say. "Because that's ridiculous."

"Andy, he robbed and killed a former high-ranking army officer, just returned from a tour of duty in Iraq. We have eyewitnesses, patrons from the bar. We also have the gun with his prints all over it, and gunpowder residue on his hands. This is not exactly a whodunit; why would we possibly take less?"

This is not going well. "Eli, during the trial there were references made to federal agents involved with the dog. Have you checked into that?"

"You think I'm going to share that with you?"

"I have reason to believe that they might have a point of view on my client's situation."

"Andy, I've talked to them, and as far as I can tell they don't give a shit what happens to your client. And to tell you the truth, neither do I."

This represents proof that Billy has completely misjudged his situation, which does not surprise me. If Eli was under any pressure, federal or otherwise, to make a deal, he wouldn't be rejecting my overtures so definitively. And Billy's idea that he can trade for his freedom is clearly not on any table I can find.

What continues to surprise me is the hands-off attitude the feds are taking. They were so anxious to hang on to Milo that they installed an armed guard on his cage, but they didn't try to prevent my getting him at the hearing. Now they seem to show no interest in Billy at all.

I decide to change the subject, since this particular subject is going nowhere. "Did you find out why they were guarding Milo?" I ask.

"Andy, I must have missed that day in law school when they taught how before a case the prosecutor is supposed to tell the defense everything he knows."

"Where did you go to law school, the University of Mars? It's called discovery."

"Discovery relates to evidence. Any conversations that I may or may not have had with federal authorities are not evidence. Which reminds me, are you Zimmerman's attorney? Because there is a lot of actual discoverable material to turn over when and if he gets himself a lawyer."

This is the moment of truth, at least for me. "Yeah. Send it over."

He nods. "Will do. And unless he's willing to accept the forty years, I'll see you in court, counselor."

As soon as I leave Eli's office, I get a call from Rita Gordon telling me that Judge Catchings has approved the release of Milo to me.

Within the space of five minutes, I've added a klepto German shepherd and a client to my life.

Oh, happy day.

• • • • •

WILLIE, FRED, AND I come up with an in-genious plan to spring Milo from the shelter.

Actually, "ingenious" may be too strong a word. We're not talking *Mission: Impossible* here, but for us it qualifies as high-level tactical maneuvering. And because the media have jumped on the case, we want to make sure that it goes off without a hitch. Since a dog getting out of prison is a surefire ratings and circulation booster, members of the press will certainly be there in full force. We want to get Milo out safely while keeping his future whereabouts a secret, so in this case the media must be seen as the enemy.

The plan is for Willie to arrive at the shelter at least twenty minutes before me. The assembled reporters will pay little attention to him, but will wait and mob me when I arrive.

Fred will keep them out of the shelter and give me a different German shepherd, one who was found stray two weeks ago, for me to take out through the front door. This other dog and I will go out, I'll talk to the press for a couple of minutes, and then we'll make our way to my car and drive off. I'm certain the reporters will then either follow me home or disperse to cover another earth-shattering news event.

This will allow Willie to slip out the back with Milo, and once he's safely gone, he'll call me. I'll then return my German shepherd to the shelter, so that the media will know Milo is not at my house. We'll then re-rescue the stand-in shepherd in a couple of days, and find him a good home through our Tara Foundation.

It's a win-win for everybody.

Unfortunately, the plan works better on paper than it does in real life. When I arrive at the shelter, Willie is nowhere to be found, and I ask Fred what happened to him.

"He called and said he was going to be twenty minutes late," Fred says. "I was supposed to call you and tell you, but I didn't have your cell number."

"Is Milo okay?"

Fred nods. "He's fine. They pulled the guard off this morning, but nothing seems to be happening."

We wait for Willie to arrive, and finally I see his car pull up in the back. "What happened to you?" I ask.

"I stopped to get Milo some biscuits and a few really cool chew toys. Didn't Fred tell you?"

I don't want to keep talking about this; I just want to get Milo safely out of here. Fred gets me the other German shepherd, named Snickers, and I gear myself up to take him through the crowd. "Is Snickers okay?" I ask. "I mean, he's not going to bite any reporters, is he?"

"How the hell do I know?" Fred asks. "He's only been here two weeks, and he's been stuck in a cage. As far as I know, this is going to be his first press conference."

I once again tell Willie that he is to wait ten minutes after I leave, make sure the press has followed me, and then sneak out the back with Milo. "No problem, Andy. I'm cool with the whole plan."

I leave with Snickers, who seems perfectly happy to get out of his cage and play a role in this production. Just before we go outside, I tell him, "If anybody asks, your name is Milo, your lawyer is brilliant, and you have full confidence in the justice system. Beyond that, you have no comment."

When we get outside, I stop to briefly answer some questions. In my experience, down deep everyone likes to talk to the press, for various reasons, but nobody will admit it.

People can watch their forty-five closest relatives killed by lightning, and the next morning they're on the *Today* show gabbing about it. Of course, if you ask them why, they don't admit that they think it's really cool to be on television. Instead they'll say that they just want to make sure a tragedy like this doesn't happen to anyone else, and please, everyone, stay indoors if it rains.

My reason for talking to the press is that I want to accomplish something: I want to get a specific message out. But of course I don't want to reveal my purpose, so I act guarded and let them draw it out of me.

"Andy, where is Milo going to live?" is the first question I'm asked, and the only one I really want to answer.

"That's something I can't share with you," I say. "If the police saw fit to station an armed guard outside his cage, then we'll assume there's reason to worry about his safety. So I won't be disclosing his location. But if you want to send him biscuits or toys, send them to me and I'll make sure he gets them."

This gets some laughs, which is what the press is hoping for. They view this as a feel-good story, while I see it as part of a very serious murder investigation.

"Will you have him guarded as well?"

I shake my head. "I really can't go too deeply into this, but I can tell you that Milo will live in a secluded place very far away from here," I lie as I pet the fake Milo's head.

"Out of state?" a reporter asks.

I grimace, as if the questions are torturing me, but finally I sigh, nod, and lie again. "Out of state. But that's all I'm saying about it."

I answer a few more frivolous questions about Milo, but when the reporters turn their attention to the murder and Billy's defense, I deflect them and leave with Snickers, who has played his part to perfection.

Fifteen minutes later Willie calls me on my cell. "Okay, man. Milo and I are on the road."

"The press were all out of there?"

"Yup. Five minutes after you took off, the place was empty."

"And you're sure you're okay with keeping him?"

"Absolutely. Sondra and Cash are cool with it." Sondra is Willie's wife, and Cash is his dog, a Lab mix whom Willie and I found on the street.

"Okay. Keep in touch if anything unusual happens."

"Anything happens, I'll deal with it." Willie grew up in the toughest of Paterson neighborhoods, and he can take very good care of himself. He's a black belt in karate, though that won't help against someone armed, unless the bullet happens to hit him in the belt.

Getting Milo out was enjoyable and satisfying. Now comes the tough part. I have to tell Billy he's not quite so lucky.

• • • • •

M WATCHED AS Willie Miller and Milo left the shelter through the back door. He saw Willie put Milo in the back of his car, and then look around to make sure he wasn't being watched. M was at a well-concealed vantage point, so he wasn't worried that Willie would see him.

M had been smart enough to realize that the lawyer might try to come up with a diversion. That was why he stationed himself in the back. Not taking any chances, he had some people covering the front and following the lawyer as he left, but M was right that the whole thing was a fake.

The fact that Landon had told him not to take any action other than following the dog seemed to M a mistake. It would be the easiest thing in the world to kill the dog right now, or to kill Willie Miller and grab the dog.

M wasn't pleased that Landon seemed to have taken over day-to-day control of the matter. Such operational issues were often military in nature, and this was not Landon's area of expertise. Yet for the moment, it was not M's job to question it.

M followed Willie's car at a distance. As always, he had done his homework, and he knew about Willie's partnership with Carpenter in the animal shelter that they ran. So he knew where Willie lived, and he knew where the shelter was. There was little doubt that the dog would wind up in one of those places.

Once Willie got on Route 46, M knew that he was taking Milo to his home in Montclair. It didn't surprise him; M knew that the property was secluded and fenced in, an ideal place to keep Milo hidden from public view.

M also knew that he would have no trouble getting to Milo whenever he wanted. As soon as Landon gave him the word—and M hoped that would be soon—M would do what had to be done.

M picked up his cell phone and called Landon at the number he always answered.

"Speak," Landon said.

"The dog has been taken out of the shelter, and I'm following him."

"Does the lawyer have him?"

"No."

"Are there any reasons for me to be concerned?" asked Landon.

"None."

"Good."

Click. Landon hung up without saying good-bye. M didn't take offense. Not with the money he was making.

• • • • •

"THERE'S NO DEAL to be made." I have a tendency to be direct with my clients, which they sometimes find jarring. But it's the only way I know how to do it, and as bad as it might feel for them in the moment, in the long run they're better off. In my view there is nothing, absolutely nothing, worse for someone in prison than false hope.

If Billy finds my announcement upsetting, he hides it well. "This is coming from the prosecutor?" he asks. His tone is mild curiosity, as if I just told him the Mets split a doubleheader.

I nod. "It is, but he says he has spoken to everyone involved, including the feds. Nobody has put the slightest bit of pressure on him to make a deal."

"So where does that leave us?" he asks. Still no panic, no arguments, just a desire to focus on what needs to be done. You can't ask for much more from a client in this situation.

"We go to trial and get a jury to take our side. That's as soon as we get a side."

"You mean other than I didn't do it?"

"That goes without saying," I say. "But I like to tell the jury who else at least might have done it. If A is their only choice, they have a tendency to pick A. We need to give them a B and maybe a C."

"I saw the guy who did it," he says. "It was dark, but I might be able to ID him. And he was at least six foot five. When I kneed him in the balls, I almost went too low and missed."

"That might come in handy, but we have to find him first."

"There was a lot of commotion after it happened, and there were a couple of guys, maybe three, who got to the scene really quickly. I don't think they were cops, because I never saw them again."

"Can you ID them?" I ask.

"No chance. But I got a license plate number off the shooter's car."

This revelation, while certainly a positive, annoys me in that it wasn't made before. "When were you going to let me know that?" I ask.

"Now," he says, and then softens it with, "No more holding back, I promise."

"So is there anything else?" I ask.

"Maybe. I've been thinking about that night. When Erskine took out the envelope, the killer reached into his own inside jacket pocket for the gun. Like this." He demonstrates how it was done.

"So?"

"So that's not where someone would ordinarily carry a gun, which I imagine was designed to fool Erskine."

"Sounds like it did," I say.

Billy shakes his head. "I think there was more to it. Erskine was tough and smart; he would have reacted if he thought there was any danger at all. And that guy reaching into his pocket should have meant danger, unless Erskine thought he was reaching for something else."

"Like an envelope of his own?"

Billy nods. "Right. I think Erskine believed they were going to trade."

"Blackmail," I say. We're far from knowing that for sure, but it's certainly a possibility. It's also quite possible that Erskine just expected to be paid for whatever was in the envelope.

"You have investigators?" Billy asks.

I nod. "I do, but I need to figure out what direction to send them in. What are the chances Milo can lead me to that envelope?"

"No way; he was pretty freaked out from the gunshot. I could probably get him to lead me to it, but I doubt he'd do it for you. You'd have to build up a lot of trust first, which takes time."

"Could he have been so scared he just dropped it somewhere?"

He shakes his head. "I wouldn't think so. Milo knew that the things I had him take were important; he wouldn't be careless with them."

I hadn't had much confidence that I could get Milo to retrieve the envelope for me, so I'm not surprised by what

Billy is saying. "We can get by without the envelope, as long as we can learn what was in it."

"Why?" he asks.

"Because there's a good chance Erskine was killed for it. If we know why it was so important to someone, we're a hell of a lot closer to figuring out who that someone is."

We kick this around a little longer, and I tell Billy to write down everything he knows about Erskine. "Even if it's a rumor and you have no idea if it's true, write it down and tell me that."

He nods. "Okay, I'll get right on it. How's Milo doing?"

"He's fine and somewhere safe."

"Thanks for doing that," he says. "I was feeling awful that I put him in that situation."

Every time Billy says something like that, I like him a little more, and regret my taking on a new client a little less. "Starting right now you have to worry about yourself."

"So you're going to do this?" he asks.

I nod. "Yeah. I am, if you still want me."

"I absolutely do. But we need to talk about your fee," he says. "The problem is, no matter how much it is, I can't pay it."

I shrug. "Then we need to get you and Milo back out there stealing again."

He laughs. "Sounds good to me."

I leave and reflect on what has been a long day at work. I take less satisfaction in that than other people might, because I hate long days at work. I hate short days at work also, just not as much.

The truth is, today wasn't so bad, especially getting

Milo sprung. It pains me to admit it, even to myself, but Laurie was probably right that I ought to be back in the action occasionally; that I need to intellectually engage in that fashion to stay sharp.

Now that I think of it, I hope she was right. Because a murder trial requires a lot of very long, very stressful workdays, and there will be little time to think of anything else if we hope to win.

And there's nothing, absolutely nothing, worse than losing.

• • • • •

TRIALS, LIKE FOOTBALL games, are won or lost by teams, not individuals. The lawyers, the investigators, the expert witnesses, and the client are all integral to the process, and must function smoothly together. It is much more difficult than it sounds.

Teamwork is, in fact, one of the many built-in advantages that the prosecution side generally has in its favor. The same people, all employed by the government, work together on many cases throughout the year. There is usually a substantial familiarity among the lawyers, police, forensics people, and expert witnesses on the prosecution side, and they don't have to waste time trying to develop a cohesive unit.

This morning I am convening a meeting of the team that will attempt to earn an acquittal and release for Billy Zimmerman. The only newcomer to the team, meaning someone who hasn't worked with this group previously, is Hike Lynch. He'll share the lawyering duties with me, though I'll be in first position.

Laurie will run the investigative unit, with Marcus Clark supporting her. Sam Willis, my accountant and an absolute computer genius, will provide all of us any information we need that can be found online. Which is a valuable resource, since everything that has ever taken place in recorded human history can be found online, especially if the person sitting at the computer is a brilliant hacker with no concern for legalities.

Providing further support will be Willie Miller, who brings no particular talent to the operation other than a desire to help out and the toughness and fearlessness to tackle any task I give him. Then there is Edna, reluctantly prepared to do whatever it is that Edna does.

The meeting is scheduled to start at ten o'clock, and at the appointed time everybody is here except for Marcus and Edna. Willie and Laurie already met Hike at the wedding, so I introduce him to Sam.

Sam and Hike inhabit opposite ends of the emotional spectrum. It's not that Sam is an out-and-out optimist. It's more that he's enthusiastic about tackling new projects, especially those that involve investigative work on my criminal cases. Hike approaches each task as if it's a root canal, and one that ultimately will fail to avert the extraction of the offending tooth.

"Let's get started," I say. "Laurie, you can fill Marcus in on whatever he misses." This is already a plus of allowing Laurie to participate in the case. She is pretty much the only person I know who has always demonstrated an ability to effectively communicate with Marcus, and who isn't petrified to do so.

I go over the parameters of the case as I know them, which doesn't take very long, since there's not a hell of a lot that I know. "The discovery material should be here this afternoon," I say. "Hike and I will go over it, and then we'll be able to plan our initial strategy."

"Have you traced the license plate yet?" Laurie asks. She's talking about the plate Billy saw on the murderer's car.

"Not yet. But I'll take care of it."

"Where does the dog fit in?" she asks.

"At this point he doesn't. I just want to keep him hidden and protected."

There isn't that much for me to say, at least not until we've gone through the discovery. All I want is for everybody to be on the same page as we get started. I'm about to end the meeting when the door opens and Marcus comes in.

He doesn't say a word, which for Marcus is business as usual. The only sounds in the room are his footsteps as he moves toward a chair, and the involuntary gasp from Hike at seeing him.

I can't remember the first time I met Marcus. I'm sure my subconscious has blocked it rather than allow me to relive it in my mind. I would guess there is about a 70 percent chance I pissed in my pants; either that or I ran away.

Marcus is the most powerful, most menacing-looking human being I have ever seen. His entire manner is uncompromising; to look at him is not only to know that he could kill you, but also to know that it wouldn't faze him.

"Hike, this is Marcus," I say.

"Unh," says Marcus.

At first Hike doesn't say a word; he just stares at Marcus, openmouthed for at least twenty seconds. Then he manages a feeble, "Hey."

"Marcus, Laurie will bring you up to date on where we stand, and you'll get your assignments from her as well."

He nods at Laurie, the hint of a smile on his face. She is the only person I have ever seen him show any warmth toward.

"Great. We're done here," I say.

I ask Hike to stay as the others leave, because I want him to go over the discovery material with me when it arrives. I need to know how far his abilities extend, and whether I can expect him to help in strategy or just be a legal mechanic. I can deal with it either way; I just have to know.

"Kevin told me about him," Hike says.

"Marcus?"

He nods. "Kevin says he got used to him. That after a while he wasn't so scared to be in the same room with him."

"I agree," I say. "I'm not nearly as afraid as I used to be. My teeth don't even chatter anymore. You just have to remember that he's on our side."

Hike nods. "That's a good thing."

"And the other thing is, if he bothers you, just smack him around a little, and he backs off."

Hike doesn't say anything, possibly pondering this concept.

"That's a joke," I say, just in case.

He nods. "I picked up on that."

While we're waiting, I call Pete Stanton. "I'm taking your friend's case," I say.

"More than just the dog?"

"More than just the dog. I'm defending Billy on the murder charge."

"That doesn't count as a favor," he says. "I didn't ask you to do that."

"It counts," I say.

"It does not."

"Do you want to start buying your own beer, effective immediately?"

"Okay," he says. "It counts."

"Glad we cleared that up. Now here's a chance for you to return the favor."

"I don't like where this is going."

"It's no big deal," I say. "I just want you to trace a license plate."

"I'm supposed to use city resources, provided by the taxpayers, to do your work?"

"You want to get your friend out of prison?"

"Give me the plate number."

I do so, and Pete tells me he'll have the information within twenty-four hours. "Is that it, I hope?" he asks.

"Almost. Billy says the shooter was six foot five, maybe taller. That ring any bells for you?"

"Maybe we should arrest the Knicks," he says.

"You're a pain in the ass, you know?"

"Of course I know. But once I get you the plate number, we're even," he says.

"We are not even. We're not close to even. I am putting in months of my life on this, and you're tracing a license plate. That is not in the same ballpark as even."

"Okay," he says. "But you're still buying the beer."

• • • • •

JEREMY IVERSON HAD no idea that one of his partners was dead. He and Donovan Chambers had dropped out of touch and gone their separate ways after returning home from the war. Chambers had never told him he was going to live in the Caribbean, and the truth was that Jeremy wouldn't have cared anyway. They had done a job together; it wasn't like they were best friends.

Jeremy was aware that Erskine was dead; he had seen that on television, when they were talking about that dog. The news didn't come as a surprise to him. Pretty much everybody he knew hated Erskine, so it made sense that eventually somebody would take a shot at him. Jeremy just hoped it had nothing to do with the Iraq operation. If it did, it could have ominous consequences for himself, although he was well hidden from the world.

Jeremy basically hadn't touched the money, other

than to provide for some basics like a place to live, some decent civilian clothes, and three hunting rifles. He realized that he was in a state of emotional limbo, unable to decide in which direction he should go. He instinctively knew that whatever first steps he took, they would influence his life forever.

The only real decision Jeremy had made since returning was to make a clean break with his past. It wasn't a great sacrifice; all that was left back home in Missoula was an alcoholic mother and an ex-wife whom he learned had filed for divorce while he was in Iraq. Mail call wasn't much fun that day.

Jeremy had rented a cabin about thirty miles from Jackson Hole, Wyoming. He drove through the town on the way out there, and was struck by how the rich people had taken over the place. He found it pretty funny to realize that he could afford to live there if he wanted to.

He didn't want to.

Except for occasional trips into town for food and other supplies, Jeremy pretty much stayed to himself at the cabin. He had some success at the bar with the local women; money even helped at that. But he had no interest in establishing any relationships, at least not until he felt more ready to face the world.

So like every other day, Jeremy woke up that morning with the choice of going hunting or hanging out in the cabin and watching television. The only sports on were baseball games, and Jeremy wasn't that big a fan. He was more into football and basketball. So Jeremy made the decision he had been making almost every day, to go hunting.

He found it strange how much he enjoyed hunting,

since he'd never particularly liked it growing up. But now it was something about the solitude; he could get lost in it and love doing so.

It was around eleven o'clock that Jeremy happened upon another hunter, a large but seemingly agreeable man, alone and dressed in orange hunting garb like Jeremy.

"Mornin'," said Jeremy. "Any luck so far?"

The man grinned and held up a bag that was obviously empty. "Not a bit. But that's okay; just being out here is enough for me."

"I know what you mean." He reached out his hand to shake. "Name's Jeremy."

"John. John Burney."

Jeremy had no way of knowing, and no inclination to suspect, that the man was lying about his name. Even if the man had given his real name, Marvin Emerson, or his nickname, M, it would have meant nothing to Jeremy.

"You live around here, John?"

"Nope. Visiting friends, about ten miles outside Jackson Hole."

"They don't hunt?"

M laughed. "They're from New York."

M didn't ask Jeremy where he lived, since he had already searched Jeremy's cabin. In the process he found and took twenty-five thousand dollars in cash, which made it a rather profitable morning—almost worth coming out to the middle of nowhere.

Instead he asked gentle questions about Jeremy's time in the army, claiming to have been a veteran himself. He wanted to assure himself that Jeremy was not the type to talk about his time in Iraq or what got him discharged.

Jeremy was tight-lipped about it, though he was willing to discuss his private life. After an hour, M felt reasonably certain that Jeremy had not revealed anything about the time in Iraq, and that there was no one he would have confided in.

It was just past noon, and M figured it was time to kill Jeremy. That would give him time to bury the body, get back to town, and get the last flight out.

He had decided to shoot Jeremy in the back. It wasn't out of cowardice, though M was aware that as a former soldier Jeremy could be a worthy and dangerous adversary. It was basically unfair to Jeremy to do it from the front, and thereby have him experience the fear of knowing death was imminent. M didn't want him to suffer; Jeremy had only been doing his job.

Just like M was now doing his.

He took out his handgun. He had equipped it with a silencer, more through force of habit and extra carefulness than anything else. Certainly the sound of a gunshot out here during hunting season would not attract attention.

But Jeremy turned around, possibly a result of instinct, possibly by happenstance. As soon as he saw the gun, he knew what was coming. And he knew why.

"You don't have to do this," Jeremy said.

"I'm afraid I do."

M fired three times, though Jeremy was certainly dead from the first shot.

On the way to the airport he called Landon to report on the successful trip. "I'm on my way to Albuquerque now for number three."

"Have you got somebody back here you can rely on?" Landon asked.

"Of course. What do you need?"

Landon had been disconcerted by the amount of press coverage Milo was getting, and that morning's paper had carried the news that Andy Carpenter had signed on to represent Zimmerman. Publicity was not in any way desirable; before long the entire world would be looking for the dog, and maybe the envelope.

"I want the dog," Landon said.

"Now?" M asked. "I thought you wanted to wait."

"I'm finished waiting. Get me the dog now."

• • • • •

IF WE EVER lose our democratic, personal freedoms, discovery will be among the first things to go. For someone accused of a crime, I consider it among the most important rights. To tell you the truth, it makes Miranda look like an aging flamenco dancer.

Discovery is the process by which the prosecutor is forced to share the evidence he has, and that he will rely upon at trial, with the defense. It takes away the element of surprise and allows often underfunded defense attorneys to properly prepare their cases.

The discovery documents Eli sends us in the Zimmerman case are limited in scope. That's not to say they're not substantial, because they are. They include all the direct evidence against Billy, including very damaging forensics and eyewitness accounts. It is no wonder that

Eli has no desire to offer a deal; he must correctly assume that his case is overwhelming.

But what the documents don't include is background information on Erskine, or any information about the envelope or its possible contents. That is for the defense to probe; the prosecution does not need to dig out those facts to prove its case.

While there is no necessity for the prosecution to prove motive, I'm sure Eli will tell the jury that Billy was seeking revenge against Erskine, blaming him for his devastating injury. Eli will not go near any possibility that Erskine was corrupt, or that other people might have had reason to kill him. That is our job.

I ask Hike to prepare a request for information related to the bombing in Iraq. We could present it to the Defense Department, which would likely take forever to give it to us. Rather than go that route, I'll ask the court to issue an order that it be provided.

I call Eli and ask that he stipulate no objection to our getting the information. He agrees to do so, not because he wants to be helpful, but because he knows we'll eventually get it anyway. This way he avoids the possibility that it could lead to a delay in the court proceedings. Except for acquittals and hung juries, delays are the things prosecutors hate most in the world.

Hike and I spend three hours going over the discovery material, exchanging documents after we've read them so that we'll each be sure to see all of it. This is just the beginning; we'll be reviewing these same documents many times, in addition to others that are sure to follow. There is absolutely no excuse for a lawyer not to be totally knowledgeable about every aspect of the case. If there were I would have found it long ago.

Spending three hours with Hike reminds me of a scene from *Take the Money and Run,* one of Woody Allen's earliest and funniest movies. Woody plays Virgil Starkwell, a small-time criminal who unsuccessfully attempts to escape from prison. As punishment, he is locked in a small, underground room with an insurance salesman, who shakes his hand and starts trying to sell him various policies before they are even locked away.

Hike has no interest in selling me insurance, but he has the unerring ability to focus on all that is wrong with the world, combining it with the certain knowledge that nothing can be done to fix it.

"This is not good," Hike says when we are about to wrap it up for the night.

I nod. "Not so far."

"You going to recommend he plead it out?"

"Eli already turned me down when I brought it up. I don't think our client would go for it anyway."

Hike frowns. "He's an ex-cop; he must know what he's up against."

"He does."

"You think he did it?"

"No. If he hated Erskine enough to kill him, he wouldn't have done it this way."

"Why not?" Hike asks.

"Because it put Milo in danger, and there would have been no reason to. He could have left Milo home, followed Erskine to the club, or anywhere else, and shot him. And if he wanted the envelope, he could have just taken it."

"No jury is going to buy the he-wouldn't-put-his-dog-in-danger argument. Unless you get twelve dog nuts like you."

I nod. "The good news is, there are a lot of dog nuts out there."

He smiles. "I'll research if we can challenge a juror for cause based on the fact that he's sane as it relates to dogs."

"We'll break new ground." I'm stunned to realize that for the first time, I'm enjoying my conversation with Hike. He's being pessimistic about our chances at trial, but that's okay, because it's logical. With what we know right now, we have very little chance.

"You ever have a murder one case?" I ask. "As lead counsel?"

He nods. "Once. I lost. It was the worst experience of my life."

"Because you lost?"

"No. Because I don't think he did it. The prosecution had a strong case, but I don't think he did it. I still work the case; I don't think a week goes by that I don't look through the file."

"And your client...he's in prison now?"

Hike shakes his head slowly. "He was...for four years. Then he hung himself in his cell."

"I'm sorry," I say, because I am. There is no worse feeling imaginable to me than losing a murder case that could have been won.

He nods. "Thanks. Me too. I wouldn't trade places with you on this case for anything."

"Why?"

"I believe my client was innocent, and he depended

on me to prove it, and now he's dead. And you could be headed toward a similar result."

I nod.

"I'll help you however I can," he says. "You just tell me what to do, and it's done."

•   •   •   •   •

FOR ME, A murder case officially begins when I go to the scene. It gives me a feel, a context, for what happened, and I find that invaluable. It's the difference between sitting on the fifty-yard line at a football game and reading a newspaper account of the same game.

When Laurie was my full-time investigator, we would go to the scene together. She would view it through the eyes of a trained detective and was able to provide insights that I could never come up with on my own.

This time Laurie asks if she can go along, and I'm delighted to have her. It feels like old times, and there's nothing wrong with that.

We go there at midnight, since that's when the murder took place. It gives us more of a feel for what happened, for how it might have looked to both the participants in the crime and the witnesses to it.

As we're driving toward the club, I look over at Laurie

in the passenger seat and see that she is struggling to keep her eyes open. It's evidence of the lingering effects of her injury; she still tires far more easily than she used to.

When I see her eyes open, I ask, "You okay?"

"I'm completely fine," she says. "Why?" She asks the question in a challenging way, not wanting to admit to any weaknesses.

"You just seem tired, and it's late," I say.

"I'm not tired, and it's not late," she says.

I nod. "Right. You're fresh and it's no wonder, since it's so early. But you said last week, and I quote, 'I need to start listening to the doctor and stop pushing myself.'"

"Do you remember every word of every conversation you've ever had?" she asks.

I smile. "It's a gift." That's actually the truth; for some reason words stick in my mind. I'm verbal rather than visual. I could go to the Grand Canyon and forget what it looked like, but I would remember every word I heard while I was there.

I know I shouldn't push this, but my concern for Laurie overwhelms my self-preservation instinct. "I just don't want you to overdo it."

"Riding in a car is overdoing it?"

I can tell she's really annoyed, so I back down, belatedly but in characteristic fashion. "Nope. It's definitely not overdoing it. If anything, it's underdoing it. Way under."

She still has a slight frown on her face, so I hold up my hand, palm down, near the inside roof of the car. "Overdoing it is up here." I move my hand down toward the floor. "Your doing-it level is down here. Way, way under."

We reach the Skybar on River Road and park across the street. The place is very active at this hour, with quite a few people going in and out, and the music from inside spills out onto the street.

I point to the front of the bar, just to the right of the door. "According to Billy, Erskine was standing there for more than an hour. A couple of witnesses confirmed that he was there, but they didn't know for how long."

"Where was Billy?" she asks.

I point across the street. "Over there. And Milo was by that tree to the left of the bar."

"What were they waiting for?"

"An opportunity for Milo to take something," I say.

"How did he know he'd have the chance?"

I shrug. "Billy said he didn't know, but he was hopeful. He said, and I quote, 'A slimeball like Erskine wouldn't have been standing there for so long for his health. Something had to be going down.'"

She frowns. "He could have been meeting a date who was late showing up."

I point down the street. "So Billy's version is that a car drove slowly from that direction, and that Erskine saw him and started walking the other way. The car passed the bar and Erskine met him down there. Billy said the man parked near the corner and came back to meet Erskine."

We walk to the place where Erskine and the man spoke, and where the murder took place. "Erskine wasn't running away?" Laurie asks.

I shake my head. "No, it was obviously a prearranged meeting. Billy is positive that Erskine was waiting for this guy to show up."

The trees and buildings combine to make it particularly dark at the spot of the murder, and I mention that to Laurie. "I'm sure it was by design," she says. "Otherwise they would have met closer to the bar. Erskine clearly did not realize he had something to fear."

"So he takes out the envelope, Billy gives Milo the signal, and he springs into action. Then the killer reaches into his inside jacket pocket, and Billy's surprised to see that it's a gun."

"How did he see it?" she says.

"He says there was a gleam of light off the barrel."

"You see much light here?"

I shake my head; that could be a problem at trial. "No, but it's possible. It's pretty cloudy tonight; maybe it was clear the night of the murder. I'll check that out."

"Let me check that," she says.

I nod. "Great. Anyway, Billy says he thought the killer was taking out an envelope or something like that of his own, since bad guys don't usually carry guns in that pocket."

"Maybe Erskine thought he was there to make a trade," she says.

"If it was a trade, he got the bad end of the deal. So Milo jumps into the picture and grabs the envelope out of the killer's hand as Erskine's hitting the ground. Billy gets there as the guy is trying to shoot Milo, who's taking off down the street. Billy grabs the gun as it goes off, knees the guy in the groin, and the guy doubles over. Billy goes to Erskine, and in the meantime the killer jumps up and runs to his car before Billy can see him and react."

"You ever get kneed in the groin?" she asks. "I would imagine that would slow you down."

"I haven't, and this is not the time for a reenactment. I take it you don't believe Billy's story?"

"I have my doubts," she says. "But it's going to be tough to prove. What about the witnesses?"

"A few came running when they heard the shot, but all they saw was Erskine lying there with Billy holding the gun. Nobody noticed the guy getting away, but they did see Milo running by them with the envelope in his mouth. Scared the shit out of them."

"And they connected Milo to the shooting?" she asks.

"No, the cops did that once they knew Billy was involved. There were a couple of similar robberies in the general area the month before, and they put two and two together. They caught Milo a couple of hours later, without the envelope."

After we've spent about twenty minutes on the scene, placing ourselves at both Billy's and Erskine's vantage points, we've learned all we're going to learn. "Seen enough?" Laurie asks.

"I think so," I say. I point to the bar, which is still going strong. "You want to go inside and have a drink?"

She shakes her head and smiles. "I don't think so. I don't want to overdo it."

On the way home Laurie says, "Thanks for letting me come, Andy. It felt good."

"I know what you mean," I say. "When I'm feeling down, there's nothing like a murder scene to cheer me up. For some reason I don't get the same emotional boost from robbery and assault scenes."

"You know what I'm talking about," she says.

"Yes, I do."

SONDRA AND MILO left the house at six thirty in the morning. That was standard procedure on the days that the foundation was open. There were always at least twenty-five dogs in runs, waiting their turn to be adopted, so there was much to be done. Feeding, walking, cleaning up...it all had to be done before prospective adopters started showing up at ten o'clock.

The foundation had grown considerably in size and reputation since its inception three years before, and had attracted a number of unpaid, dog-loving volunteers to help with the work. But for most of them, their dog loving didn't kick in until at least nine AM, and Sondra was always in long before that.

Sondra loved the work and felt that there was nothing more rewarding than seeing a dog who had recently been in the shelter going off to a new, loving home. The only part she didn't relish was the process by which she and Willie had to determine if that home was dog-friendly enough. They weren't about to send a dog off to be tied to a tree in some backyard, or used as a guard. But telling people that they could not adopt one of the dogs still made Sondra uncomfortable.

Willie couldn't care less about offending anyone. If they weren't offering the kind of home for the dog that Willie felt acceptable, he had no qualms in letting them know it, often in graphic terms.

Since Milo had come to their home, Sondra had been taking him to the foundation each morning. He stayed in a back room, unseen by the volunteers or potential adopters, to protect his safety and security, just in case.

Sondra spent as much time with him back there as she could. Not because he needed the company; he could amuse himself quite well with a chew toy, and he was happy to sleep the day away or play with dogs who were brought back there to keep him company. It was because she had already grown to love him, as had Willie, in the brief time he'd lived with them.

Not only was Milo playful, affectionate, and hysterically funny, but he was as smart as any dog they had ever been around. He had already learned to manipulate their dog Cash, and Cash had clearly accepted him as his leader.

When Willie and Sondra would sit on the couch watching television, Cash would be up there between them, accepting petting from both. Since there was then no room for Milo, Milo would suddenly start to bark and move toward the doggy door to the outside as if he had heard something out there.

An excited Cash would run outside to see what was going on, whereupon Milo would immediately take Cash's position on the couch. When Cash returned, disappointed by the lack of action outdoors, he would be relegated to a place on the floor, or another chair, with no one to pet him.

As Willie had directed her, Sondra pulled up to the back of the foundation building, so that Milo would not be seen by cars passing by on the street. She got out of the car and looked briefly around, then reached into her bag for the keys to the building.

Once she had them in hand, she opened the door to let Milo out. He jumped out of the car, tail wagging, since he enjoyed his time there. She didn't put him on a leash; it would have been unnecessary and maybe even a little demeaning. Milo was not a dog to run off or disobey commands.

"I'll take the dog."

Sondra heard the words and whirled around to see Ray Childress, all six foot two and 230 pounds of him, holding a gun on her and not looking too pleased to be there. Dog-napping was beneath his dignity as a hit man, Childress felt, though the money he was getting for it certainly was more than enough to soothe his ego.

Unfortunately for Childress, Milo also whirled around and saw the gun, and he immediately sprang into action. Without hesitation, he raced the four strides toward Ray and launched himself into the air.

Childress was blessed with very quick reactions, and physically he would have had the time to point the gun and shoot it at Milo. His hesitation was mental, as he had been specifically told to take the dog, not to kill him.

But Childress would be damned if he'd let the dog bite him; he'd rather kill him first, no matter what the instructions.

Sondra watched Milo as he moved, so she didn't see the other activity that rendered moot any decision making by Childress. As he raised the gun, and before Milo arrived, the left side of his skull was crushed by the side of Willie Miller's hand, much in the way Willie used to break bricks at the end of his karate instruction classes.

Childress was dead before he hit the ground. Milo, recognizing that there was no longer a live assailant to disarm, immediately paused and waited for further instructions, though none were forthcoming.

Sondra was sobbing softly, and Willie put his arm around her. "I'm gonna go in and call nine-one-one," he said.

"What if he gets up?"

Willie took a look at the fallen Childress and shook his head. "He ain't getting up."

• • • • •

I AM THE second call Willie makes, right after 911. I dress quickly and drive down to the foundation; Laurie is at the gym, and though I call her, I don't want to wait for her. I'm worried about Willie; since he's an ex-con, even an exonerated one, I'm concerned about the treatment he will get.

When I get there, I find that Pete Stanton is on the scene and has already taken over the investigation, which pleases me greatly. Pete knows Willie well, and will not have a knee-jerk reaction against him.

Laurie pulls up as I get out of the car, and we go straight over to Willie and Sondra, who are in the office. Once we make sure that Sondra is okay, I ask Willie to describe what happened, which he does.

"Was he going to shoot Milo?" I ask.

Willie shakes his head. "I don't think so. If he were

gonna do that, he wouldn't have had to hold the gun on Sondra, or even come out in the open. The worm could have hidden in the bushes and shot Milo."

"What were you doing here?" I ask.

"Watching Sondra and Milo, just in case." He goes on to say that he hadn't even told Sondra about it, because he didn't want to make her nervous.

"Have you told the story to Pete?"

Willie nods. "Yeah, but he said he wants to question us more, and that we should wait here. He's acting like a cop."

"He is a cop." Willie and Pete are friends, and Willie expects special treatment. I know that Pete is first and foremost a terrific cop who will do his job the way it is supposed to be done. Dead people with crushed heads and guns make cops very careful.

I go over to Pete, walking by the body still lying on the ground. The medical people and the coroner have arrived, and they will no doubt be removing it in a few minutes. It is not a pretty sight; the deceased man's head looks like a cantaloupe that came in second in an argument with a bazooka.

I have to wait ten minutes while Pete talks to his forensics people, who are photographing the scene and looking for physical evidence. When he's finished, he comes over to me.

"What's going on?" I ask, leaving the question open-ended.

"What's going on? Your partner killed a guy with a sledgehammer that's attached to his shoulder."

"A guy who was attempting a kidnapping with a deadly weapon," I point out.

Pete nods. "Don't worry; you don't have another client on your hands. Willie's clean on this."

I'm surprised that he's making such a definitive statement so early in a situation like this. "Who's the dead guy?" I ask.

"Name is Ray Childress."

"Doesn't ring a bell," I say.

"It rings plenty of bells," Pete says. "You just can't hear them."

"Enlighten me."

"He is, or was, available for hire. Not usually for kidnappings, almost always for hits. And believe me, he didn't come cheap."

That explains why Willie is finding a receptive audience for his recounting of the events. It's completely credible that Childress had bad intentions, and Willie's reactions were perfectly logical and legal. "Any idea who hired him this time?" I ask.

"I could ask you the same thing. You know more about this situation with the dog than I do."

I shrug. "Anything I might know is protected by attorney–client privilege."

"I got you the damn client," he points out.

I nod. "I know; I'm so grateful my eyes are filled with tears. You can take comfort in the fact that I don't have a clue what's going on."

"What a surprise," he says, and goes back to work.

It's another three hours until I can get Willie and Sondra out of there. We spend the time taking care of the dogs, which is especially important since the volunteers are turned away from the crime scene.

As we're getting ready to leave, I tell Willie that I'm

going to keep Milo at my house for a while. "He can stay there without having to leave, and the backyard is fenced in and protected."

"Andy, I want to be a part of this," Willie says.

"Part of what?"

"Finding out what the hell is going on. Somebody sent that piece of shit to hold a gun on Sondra; I want to find out who that is and deal with him."

I'm not sure I've ever seen the look on Willie's face that I see now. If I don't get him involved, he's going to go off on his own. "I hear you," I say. "You can be a big part of it."

He nods. "Good. Damn good."

• • • • •

LAURIE AND I head home with a new problem. It's not just how to successfully defend Billy, or figure out what the hell is going on. This particular problem is sitting in the backseat, head out the half-opened window, smiling as if he's the Grand Shepherd in the Rose Bowl Parade.

"How are we going to take care of and protect Milo without all of us getting killed in the process?" I ask. "The floor is open to suggestions."

"I think you should work out of the house for now," Laurie says. "That way we'll be around more to watch him."

"Good idea."

"And we need to get Marcus. He should be Milo's bodyguard."

"Been there, done that," I say. Marcus had watched

over a show dog that I was involved with in a previous case, and who was also in danger, though for very different reasons. The major drawback was that feeding Marcus proved to be a full-time job; his capacity to eat is stunning, and he does it at all hours of the day and night.

"It's either Marcus or you have to bring in a marine battalion," Laurie says.

"They would probably eat less."

"Andy, this is a serious threat we're dealing with. Sondra could have been killed today, to say nothing about Milo."

I know that she's right, but since it makes me somewhat uncomfortable that Marcus and I even occupy the same planet, the idea of once again having him as a housemate is daunting. "Don't you need him as an investigator?"

"Not right now; if I can't handle things on my own I'll bring somebody else in."

"What about Willie? He wants to help catch the bad guys."

I know Laurie isn't thrilled with that idea. She loves Willie and respects his physical ability and street smarts, but she believes that investigators should be professionals. "If I can use him I will," she says.

I spend the next few minutes pondering the recent changes in my life. I've got a new client that I don't want, a murder trial that I dread, a new dog that's a direct descendant of Jesse James, and a full-time houseguest that could kick the shit out of Godzilla.

And then there's another problem. "Who's going to tell Tara about Milo?" I ask.

"She'll be fine," Laurie says. "She loved having

Waggy around." She's referring to a show dog who
stayed with us, a wild puppy with whom Tara showed incredible patience.

"I'm telling her that it's your fault," I say.

When we get home, we bring Tara around to the backyard and do the introduction there, since we've had good
luck with that in the past. It is rather uneventful; Tara and
Milo spend a few minutes sniffing various parts of each
other's bodies before Tara lies down.

Milo, for his part, seems more interested in exploring
his new surroundings. Once he's done so, we bring them
both inside. They lie down near each other and go to
sleep.

"See?" Laurie asks. "I told you there would be no
problem."

"So far, so good." My admission is grudging, because
I know what's coming.

"Do you want to call Marcus, or should I?" she asks.

"You should."

Laurie nods, picks up the phone, and dials the number. What follows is a perfectly normal situation; in a
million years I would never guess that she was talking to
Marcus.

When she hangs up, she says, "He'll be here at four
o'clock."

"Okay. I'll go rent a moving van."

"What for?"

"Food."

Before I start making the rounds of grocery stores, I
turn my attention to the impact that today's events will
have on Billy's case.

My initial goal is becoming more clear each day.

While Eli will attempt to portray Erskine's death as a simple robbery-murder, I must find a way to introduce the outside elements into the case. Included in this will be the mysterious envelope and what it might say about Erskine's past and shady dealings.

It will not be easy to get evidence like this admitted, and I'll have to learn much more before I have a chance. But events like today's can only help. A hit man trying to steal or kill Milo shows that there are other bad people and motives involved in this case. If I can present this kind of evidence to a jury, with a credible theory behind it, it can't help but introduce some element of reasonable doubt.

I tell all this to Laurie, after which she says, "And he knows something important." She's pointing across the room at Milo, now sharing a dog bed with Tara. "It's hard to imagine, but under those great ears lies the secret to the case."

I nod. "But he's not talking. I called Juliet Corsinita, the dog trainer, and she has some ideas, but warned it will be tough."

"You'll figure it out."

I shrug. "Maybe. As long as Marcus is able to keep him from getting killed first."

"They're not trying to kill him," Laurie says. "Willie was right about that. Hit men don't behave the way this one did if the goal is to kill. They take their best shot the moment it presents itself, and that would have been as soon as Milo got out of the car."

Laurie and Willie are both clearly right. The area behind the foundation building was secluded and the perfect spot for Childress to have shot Milo, if that was his intent.

There would have been no reason to take him somewhere else to do it.

"Childress is a key," I say.

"Or he would have been if Willie hadn't smashed in his skull."

"That's unfortunate, but it still leaves us an area to pursue. At the risk of a bad pun, Childress had no dog in this fight. Somebody bought him, and the person who did that is the one we want."

"Those kind of people don't leave tracks," Laurie says. "They don't make these kinds of purchases with credit cards."

"That's why investigators like you exist," I say. "That's why I pay you the big bucks."

"You aren't paying me a dime."

"You're forgetting room and board, use of a car, sexual favors..."

"I think we need to renegotiate the terms," she says.

I nod. "Okay, everything is on the table except the sexual favors. That's a deal breaker."

• • • • •

PETE STANTON CALLS and invites me to lunch, as long as he picks the place and I pay. He chooses a steak house in Fort Lee, probably the most expensive one in New Jersey. I don't think that Pete is jealous of my wealth; he doesn't seem the type to want things that he can't afford. It's not that he wants more money; it's simply that he wants me to have less.

But he says that he has information for me on the case, and he knows that's something I can't ignore, regardless of the size of the lunch check.

For some reason, the more expensive the restaurant, the more cloying the service. We spend the first ten minutes at the table answering questions about our preferences from the various waiters, when my first preference is for them to ask us what we want, serve the food, and leave us alone.

Even the water provokes an inquisition. Do we want bottled water or tap? Flat or sparkling? What about ice? In exasperation I finally say that I want sparkling tap water with flat ice, which results in an "I'm sorry, sir, I don't understand," and more questions.

We finally order our food, though Pete's ordering his steak well done causes some apoplexy from the waiter. He tries to talk Pete out of it, but gives up when Pete says, "When the cook thinks it's just right, cook it another ten minutes. And cook the french fries another twenty."

"The *pommes frites*?" the waiter asked, in some confusion.

Pete nods. "Sure, throw some of those in, too."

Pete asks for the wine list, and orders an expensive bottle of "Château-something." "But don't open it," he says to the waiter, staring at me as he talks. "I'm going to take it home."

When the waiter finally leaves, I say, "What the hell was that about?"

He shrugs. "I can't drink when I'm on duty."

I decide to let that non sequitur die an ignored death. "So what information do you have for me?"

He waits to finish chewing his third piece of bread before saying, "I ran a check on the license plate."

"And?"

"It was stolen off a car in South Jersey."

"That's it?"

"Yup."

"I've learned more about water options from the waiter than I've learned about the case from you."

"Hey, you asked me to run the plate and I ran it."

"Right. Great job," I say. "Where do you stand on Childress?"

"He's dead."

Pete is starting to annoy me, which is not a major departure from the status quo. "I'm aware of that. Who hired him?"

"How the hell should I know?"

"You're a detective, so I was hoping you could detect something."

He shrugs. "Not so far."

"Who's hired him in the past? Petrone?" Vincent Petrone is the unchallenged head of organized crime in North Jersey. I've had a number of dealings with him in the past. It's uncomfortable for me, because at any moment he could decide to have me killed. That doesn't make for a particularly close and trusting relationship.

"Maybe, but I have nothing to connect him to this. It doesn't seem to fit."

"Why not?" I ask.

"Well, besides the fact that Petrone has never done much dog-napping, he pretty much sticks to North Jersey. Erskine wasn't local, and whatever was going on feels much bigger, probably international, especially if the Childress piece is a part of it."

"Why do you say that?"

"Because a hundred grand was wired into Childress's bank account the day before Willie nailed him. From a Swiss account."

I'm surprised to hear this. "Traceable?"

"Of course not. If they were okay with it being traced, they could have sent it from a bank in New Jersey. What the hell would they need Switzerland for?"

"How do you know about the wire transfer?" I ask.

He looks insulted. "Hey, I'm a detective. I detected it."

"What else haven't you told me?"

He points to my mouth. "Well, I didn't want to say anything, but you've got a bread seed or something stuck between your teeth."

"Anybody making any progress on Erskine or the envelope?" I ask.

He shrugs. "Not my case."

"I know, but you would be aware if something developed. Your friend is in jail, remember?"

"Which is why nothing is likely to happen. I don't know if you've noticed this, but once we detectives think a murderer is in jail, we tend to focus on other cases."

I know this is true; it's human police nature to consider a case closed when the arrest is made. If Billy is behind bars and guilty, why not work on something else? There is certainly never a shortage of unsolved crimes.

"I need you to get me something," I say. "I could go through the court, but I might not get it, and it would take too long if I did."

He stares at me, as if trying to intimidate me from even asking the favor. "What might that be?" he says.

"I need a piece of Erskine's unwashed clothing. Something with his scent on it."

"You are a sicko," he says. "Maybe you want his underwear?"

"The dog trainer says it may help in getting Milo to lead us to the envelope."

"And you think I have Erskine's clothes lying around?"

"I think you know people who can get a piece."

It takes a while, but he promises to see what he can do. The only thing I get out of the rest of the lunch is the check, which includes a two-hundred-dollar charge for the bottle of chardonnay.

I tell Pete the price, and he shakes his head. "At that price, if it's not any good, I'm going to be pissed."

"You're into fine wines, are you?"

"You better believe it. I pour it into ice trays and freeze it, then suck on the cubes. I call them wine-sicles."

"I hope you choke on them."

• • • • •

LAURIE, MARCUS, MILO, and I get in my car and head for the crime scene. We make quite the little family. We don't bring Tara on the outing, because Juliet Corsinita says she would be a distraction for Milo, and we don't bring a picnic lunch, because this is a business trip.

Juliet meets us in the parking lot of the Skybar, but she instructs us to stay in the car. All she wants to come out is Milo, along with the article of Erskine's clothing that Pete has provided us. I was relieved to discover it was a shirt rather than underwear.

I understand she wants to have as few distractions as possible while she works, but her conditions are not acceptable. Marcus has to be nearby, in case another attempt is made to kidnap Milo. And Laurie and I want to be in position to see what is going on.

We work out an arrangement where Marcus is nearby, but remaining as unobtrusive as Marcus can remain, which is pretty low on the unobtrusive scale. Laurie and I will park down the street in our car, with the motor running. If Milo takes off, we want to be able to follow him.

Just in case he runs and manages to lose us, Laurie has attached a small GPS device to his collar, which we can follow from a monitor in the car.

I think we're set up as well as we can be.

Unfortunately, our high-tech operation is delayed by the fact that we can't find an acceptable parking space, and it's impossible to double-park on this street. James Bond never seemed to have these problems.

Fortunately a young couple walks up the street and gets in their car, so we wait behind them to pull in when they pull out. Then we experience a phenomenon that is becoming more and more common, and which drives me crazy. It takes them a full five minutes to pull out.

I have no idea what people do in this situation. Are they running through a checklist, like an airplane pilot? "Seat belts...check. Key in the ignition...check. Radio tuned to FM...check." They're probably driving to Teaneck, but they act like they're flying to Tel Aviv.

Finally they pull out, and we pull in behind them. Things are really cooking now.

Juliet had told me to keep Erskine's shirt in an airtight plastic bag, so that Milo would not smell it in advance. When Laurie and I leave, I give her the bag, but she doesn't open it.

Once Laurie, Marcus, and I are in our respective positions, I see Juliet get out of the car with Milo, leading him on a leash. I've gone over the mechanics of the night of the murder with her, so she knows the various land-marks.

Juliet takes Milo to the tree where he sat that night, waiting for Billy to signal him that he should make his move on Erskine. I can't hear what she is saying to him, but she makes a motion for him to sit, and he does so willingly. He seems to respond to her well, and is allow-ing her to control him. I would think that's a good sign.

With Milo sitting there out in the open, I see Marcus nearby, looking around warily. If there is any suspicious occurrence, be it from a pedestrian or a car coming down the street, I know Marcus will intervene and end the demonstration.

Juliet walks over to the front of the building, where Erskine stood that night, and Milo watches her. She just stands there for five minutes, and then walks slowly to the spot down the street where the murder took place. Milo does not take his eyes off her as she walks.

Once she reaches the murder spot, she waits another few minutes, and then takes the shirt out of the bag. She motions to Milo and calls out something I can't hear. Milo jumps up from his spot and races toward Juliet, and for a moment I'm afraid he's going to attack her. But she seems unconcerned, holding the shirt in front of her and not backing away at all.

Milo leaps in the air and grabs the shirt, and Laurie and I get ready, hoping that Milo will now do what we want, which is take the shirt to the same place he took the envelope. With the shirt in his mouth, he comes to a graceful landing and then…

Nothing.

Milo just sits where he landed, holding the shirt in his

mouth in triumph, offering it to Juliet and not moving a muscle. I see her talking to him, but all he does is look up at her, the shirt in his mouth not concealing the smile on his face.

She pets him, complimenting him on a job well done, which I assume is a simultaneous admission of defeat. His tail is wagging a mile a minute at the praise.

Laurie, Marcus, and I walk over to them, and Juliet says, "It's not happening. He doesn't completely trust me."

I nod. "Billy said it would be a trust issue."

"You'd have a better chance than me," she says. "Because he's living with you. I could teach you the technique, but it will take a while."

"Might as well try it," I say, and then turn to Milo. "You trust me, right, big guy?"

Milo just sits there, not committing one way or the other.

"Talk to Tara; she'll vouch for me. But if she tells you about the time I ran out of biscuits, it wasn't my fault."

● ● ● ● ●

CHAPLIN AND FREEMAN, INC., obviously never got the memo about the financial crisis. While most of Wall Street has made something of a show of cutting back on extravagant spending, C&F Investments, as the medium-size hedge fund is known on the street, has opted not to be a part of that particular show.

Admittedly, so far my only frame of reference is the lobby, which is modern and very expensively furnished. There is a large painting on the wall signed by Picasso, and unless it's Freddie Picasso from Parsippany, New Jersey, it has to be worth a fortune.

If there is blame to be assigned for this ostentatiousness, it will have to be laid at the feet of Jonathan Chaplin, the man I am here to see. Stanley Freeman, the other founding partner, is off the hook, since he was killed in the blast that took Billy Zimmerman's leg in Iraq.

The receptionist is a woman, probably in her early twenties, who is absolutely beautiful. Maybe it's just based on my limited experience, but I find that upscale firms, be they legal or financial, always have great-looking young receptionists. Downscale firms like mine have Edna.

Whenever I approach receptionists like this I reflect on the fact that I spent my early twenties in bars, trying to meet women, when I should have been hanging out in lobbies. Who knew?

Before I say a word, she says, "Mr. Carpenter?" Either they don't have many visitors, or her efficiency matches her looks.

"Yes."

"Welcome to Chaplin and Freeman. Mr. Chaplin is available to see you now. May I offer you something to drink?"

I decline the offer, and another young woman instantly appears to escort me back to Chaplin's office. It is a study in chrome and black leather, with what I'm sure is even more expensive art on the wall than was in the lobby. I don't look too hard to check out the signatures, because they're probably paintings somebody sophisticated should recognize instantly, and I don't want to look like an uneducated peasant.

The place is so clean that it looks like it's been detailed. This includes Chaplin's glass desk, which has only a computer and a phone on it. There isn't a piece of paper to be seen anywhere. Nor is there any in drawers, since there are no drawers.

Chaplin is around fifty, and probably twenty pounds heavier than he was when he was forty. His hair is jet black, a likely giveaway that it's really gray. "Mr. Carpenter, it's a pleasure to meet you," he says. "I'm a fan of yours."

"Really? I haven't seen you at club meetings."

He smiles tolerantly. "I'm sort of a courtroom junkie. Not that I attend, but I like to follow legal cases...read about the trials. I think if I had to do it over again I would become a defense attorney."

"That makes one of us."

He smiles, a little more condescendingly than before. "What would your choice be?"

"Super Bowl–winning quarterback for the New York Giants, after which I would become a network analyst."

"Sounds like Phil Simms."

I nod. "Bastard beat me to it."

Another smile, moving even farther up the condescending scale, and then, "So how can I help you? Looking to invest your millions?"

I must look surprised, because he says, "I believe in being prepared. I like to check out people I'm going to meet with, and in this case I learned of your inheritance."

"Thanks, but I'm pleased with the way my money is being handled," I say.

"May I ask who helps you with your estate?"

"Edna's nephew Freddie."

"I don't believe I'm familiar with him." He says it in an annoying, pompous way, probably because he is an annoying, pompous guy.

"Really? He's five ten, maybe a hundred sixty pounds, a small mole on the side of his neck...his mother is Edna's sister Doris."

"So why are you here, Mr. Carpenter?"

I have no doubt that he knows why I'm here, since I believe him when he says he checked me out thoroughly before my arrival. However, I play along and tell him that I'm representing Billy. "Two of your colleagues were killed in the same explosion that cost my client his leg."

He nods solemnly. "We are still grieving that loss."

"Stanley Freeman was the co-founder with you of this company?" Freeman and Chaplin are considered pioneers in the hedge fund industry.

"Yes," he says. "And my best friend in the world."

"What about the other man killed? Alex Bryant."

"Alex was twenty-nine years old. Much too young...much too young. I'm still dealing with the guilt."

"Guilt?"

"Yes. I was supposed to go on the trip with Stanley, but I was taken ill. Alex went in my stead." He shakes his head sadly. "I wound up going to his funeral."

"What was his position here?" I ask.

"He was an investment analyst. One of our brightest stars. Definitely could have been sitting in this chair one day. What does this have to do with your client?"

I shrug. "Probably nothing; I'm just checking boxes. After they died, did you follow the investigation that the army conducted?"

"As best I could," he says. "They weren't very forthcoming with information, especially since I wasn't family."

"Anything strike you as unusual, maybe cause you concern?"

"I don't think so, other than my annoyance that they could let something like that happen."

"Did you feel security measures were lax?" It's a stupid question, since eighteen people getting killed by a sixteen-year-old girl is by definition less-than-impressive security.

"I did, and I do. But they simply said that sometimes these things are impossible to prevent."

"Were Mr. Freeman and Mr. Bryant married?"

He hesitates a moment before answering. "No. Stanley had been recently divorced. I don't believe Alex was married. Is there anything else, Mr. Carpenter? I'm quite busy."

I stand. "I know how it is; Freddie is the same way. Sometimes Edna can't even get him on the phone."

He doesn't seem to find this particularly amusing, and we just say good-bye.

I hadn't expected much from this meeting, and I got what I expected.

• • • • •

KEVIN BACON IS at least four degrees behind
Vince Sanders. There simply isn't anyone that Vince either doesn't know or can't instantly get to. Sometime I
would like to test him, just for the fun of it. The problem
is that Vince isn't familiar with the concept of fun.

But I do know that if I asked him whether he could
get me in to see the Dalai Lama, he would say, "Now you
ask me? I just got off the phone with him." Or maybe, "I
don't know him, but I can set it up through his sister-in-
law, Shirley Lama."

Of course, in real life it's not that easy. First Vince has
to show his obnoxious side, which is not a problem for
him, since that is the only side he has.

I call Vince at home, and he answers with "What do
you want now?"

"Did you ever consider the possibility that I might be just calling my good friend to say, *Hope you had a good day*?"

"That is not something I considered, no," he says. "I feel so ashamed."

"I forgive you, old friend. In fact, there may be a way you can make it up to me."

"I'm all tingly at the prospect."

"I need to talk to someone who understands the world oil market."

"Why?" he asks.

"It's in connection with a case," I say, knowing what is coming next.

"A case that might prove to be newsworthy?"

"Yes, and if there's a story that comes out of it, you will get the exclusive."

"You got a pen?" he asks.

"Sure."

"Call the Institute for Energy…"

"Hold on, I need to get the pen," I say.

"You thought when I asked if you had a pen, I meant did you own one? I was asking if you had it ready."

"Vince…Okay, I'm ready."

"Call the Institute for Energy Independence, it's in Manhattan on West Forty-eighth Street, and ask for Eliot Conyers. He's the director."

"And he's knowledgeable about the oil market?" I ask, instantly regretting it.

"No, I just thought you two would make a nice couple. In case Laurie wises up and goes back to Wisconsin."

Vince gives me the phone number of the institute, so after we hang up I wait ten minutes, and then call it.

Three minutes after that I have an appointment for tomorrow morning with Eliot Conyers.

Vince is amazing.

I've been focusing my energies on the explosion in Iraq for a couple of reasons. For one thing, the prosecution is going to use it as evidence of Billy's motive, claiming that he was getting revenge for what he thought was Erskine's culpability that day in Iraq.

In addition, there is always the chance that what happened that day ultimately led to Erskine's murder. According to Billy, the death of the newly appointed Iraqi oil minister enabled corruption to go on unchecked, with billions of dollars the prize. If Erskine was truly involved in that world, certainly subsequent violence could be expected for a variety of reasons.

But there is of course another possibility: that I am spinning my wheels, that the explosion in Iraq has nothing whatsoever to do with Erskine's death. I won't know that until it's over, and maybe not even then, but it's something I have to pursue.

Besides, it gives me something to do.

IT PAINS ME to do it, but I turn off the Mets game. It's in the fourth inning of a scoreless game, but it's time for one of the "trust sessions" that I've been doing with Milo every night. Juliet Corsinita told me I should try to hold them as close to the same time as possible, and even though I don't have a clue why that would be important, I'm following her advice. .

She also told me not to have a television on, and to limit the distractions. The only thing I wouldn't go along with is her suggestion to keep Tara out of the room. As the song sort of goes, "If being with Tara is wrong, I don't want to be right."

Trust sessions with dogs are different than I imagine they would be with people. There is no endless and cloying talk about "feelings," and nobody is falling backward, counting on the other party to catch them before they hit the ground. Instead it's all about basic commands and consistency.

I have never been a practitioner of commands with dogs. In my mind it seems demeaning to the dog to force him to obey commands or do tricks. Even the "sit" and "come" orders irritate me; if somebody tried to get me to do that stuff I'd be pissed and would refuse.

Unless, of course, it was Laurie doing the commanding, or Marcus.

But with Milo I have to make an exception, since Juliet and Billy agree that trust will be the key if we're to have a chance of getting Milo to lead us to the envelope.

So Milo takes his position on the floor, me standing beside him. Tara reclines on the couch, watching the action. Occasionally she looks around, maybe for a biscuit vendor, but mostly she just enjoys the show.

"Sit, Milo, sit!" I say, followed by "Good boy!" when he performs the task. Unfortunately, I'm forced to say this and all other praising comments in a ridiculous, high-pitched voice that Juliet says will somehow remind him of his time in the womb.

I am supposed to ask minor, easy things of him, like sitting, coming to me, and walking obediently on a leash.

Once he does these things, which he's smart enough to do in his sleep, I've been told to reward him with these special treats, which Billy said he loves. I've been stuffing him with so many treats that he's going to be too fat to lead us anywhere.

The one who's enjoying this process the most is Tara on the couch. Since I can't give treats to Milo without giving them to her, she's got it made. She's sucking down the treats without having to do anything to earn them. If

I know Tara, when I'm not around she's counseling Milo against finding the envelope, since that would effectively shut off the treat faucet.

I occasionally interrupt the sessions to go over and pet Tara. I'm concerned that she might be jealous of the personal attention I'm giving Milo. Tara and I have never had similar sessions, and I don't want her to think I prefer him.

She doesn't let on whether or not she's feeling any resentment, probably because she fears that if I realize she isn't jealous, I might cancel the biscuit parade.

As we're nearing the end, Laurie comes in and watches with a bemused expression. "You know. I don't completely trust you, either."

"Is that right?" I ask. "Anything I can do to change that?"

She nods. "I'm thinking chocolate-covered strawberries."

I have no idea if any of this stuff with Milo is working, since Juliet has instructed me to wait a good while before trying to get him to find the envelope. But I don't really mind, since I'd rather hang out with dogs than people anyway.

Milo and Tara are better company than Pete and Vince, and I don't have to buy the beer.

When the session ends, I quickly turn on the Mets game. While I've been gone the Braves have taken a six-run lead.

Can't trust those Mets.

M WAS MORE than a little tired of his road trip. He had arrived in Albuquerque three days ago, only to find that Tyler Lawson had gone to Las Vegas that morning. It was not a difficult thing to discover; Lawson had always been a compulsive talker, and he told at least five people, who related it to M when he arrived.

M had said he was an old army buddy of Tyler, but any excuse would have done. Tyler's new friends in Albuquerque were not particularly suspicious, and they were quite willing to share with M what little they knew about Tyler.

M recognized the possibility that Tyler had heard about the deaths of his partners and run off in a panic, planting false information about going to Vegas to throw off his pursuers. M doubted this was the case, though. Tyler was so dumb that M thought he should be watered twice a day, and it was unlikely he had read a newspaper in the past decade.

If Tyler said he was going to Vegas, he was likely going to Vegas.

But Vegas is a big place, far bigger than it had been fourteen years earlier, the last time M had been there. Coincidentally, he had followed someone that time as well, but had managed to murder him and get out of town within twelve hours. Tyler would prove a lot tougher to find.

M was anxious to get it over with. Landon was very unhappy, and rightfully so, with the botched attempt to kidnap that dog. The fact that Childress was killed in the process was a plus; being dead made him substantially less likely to talk.

M checked into Caesars Palace, choosing it mainly because it was one of the few really nice hotels that had been there the last time he was in Vegas. In fact, he had gunned down his target in the Caesars parking lot, so the place held a sentimental attachment for him.

Once he checked in, M called room service for dinner and set about calling the hundreds of hotels in Vegas where Tyler could conceivably be staying. Since Tyler was newly wealthy, M started with the high-class hotels and worked his way down.

After calling twenty hotels and dealing with what he considered to be twenty idiots on the switchboards, he had not found the hotel that Tyler was registered at. There was always the chance that he was there under a different name, but M doubted it. If he had told the truth to his friends about going to Vegas, then he wouldn't try to hide once he got there. He was there under his own name, or he wasn't there.

M decided to go to sleep and continue the process in the morning. He never considered going to the casino; gambling had never interested him. Besides, with the money he was going to make, winning or losing at gambling would have no effect on him whatsoever, and therefore would provide no excitement.

It took another fifteen calls to learn that Tyler was staying at Circus Circus. It figured; the man was an idiot, child-like in many respects, and the name alone would have appealed to him.

M went to the hotel and walked around the casino, hoping to see him. He had the advantage of knowing what Tyler looked like, without Tyler knowing him. M was somewhat concerned about the ubiquitous security cameras, but if the operation went according to plan, there would be no reason for law enforcement ever to view the tapes.

M was there for eight hours, walking around and occasionally playing fifteen minutes of blackjack or roulette. He never gambled more than fifteen dollars at a time, careful not to call attention to himself. Gambling serious money in a place like this would be like shining a klieg light on himself.

Tyler finally showed up and sat down at a twenty-five-dollar blackjack table. M waited ten minutes, and then took the chair next to him. There was only one player at the table other than the two men. M handed the dealer a fake ID, so that the pit bosses could track his gambling, in case he was looking for comped meals later.

Tyler was the talkative type at the table, telling M and the other player whether they should draw or stand, and yelling loudly in support when any of them won. He also

ordered and drank three scotch and waters in the first fifteen minutes that M was there, prompting M to reflect on
the fact that it might not be necessary to kill Tyler, that
perhaps he should just wait a few minutes for his liver to
explode.

When the table was in the middle of a hot streak, the
dealer having busted three hands in a row, M stood up.
"Well, that's enough for me." He pushed his chips to the
dealer, to change them for larger ones.

"Where you goin'?" asked Tyler. "We're hot."

"Believe me, I got someplace better to go."

Tyler's interest was clearly piqued. "Yeah? Where?"

M hesitated, as if thinking whether he should say
something. "It ain't for you."

"What do you mean? Try me."

M pretended to consider this again, and then finally
leaned in to Tyler and whispered, "Meet me in front of
the hotel in ten minutes. Near valet parking."

"Ten minutes? I'm winnin' here."

M smiled. "Then stay and keep winning." He got up
and walked toward the front of the hotel.

Ten minutes later, just as M's rented Mercedes was
being brought up by the valet, Tyler appeared. M pretended that he didn't see him, and took the keys from the
attendant, as if preparing to drive off.

"Hey, where you goin'?" Tyler asked, then stepped
back and assessed the car. "Nice wheels."

"To a party," M said.

"I'm always up for a party," Tyler said.

M thought for a moment, as if weighing an idea, and
then smiled. "Get in."

They drove on US 15 South, toward Los Angeles. M

said they were going to a place near Primm, which was a small group of three casino hotels designed to attract drivers from LA before and after they went to Vegas. He told a story about the cocktail waitresses throwing a party once a month, admission one thousand dollars, making it sound like a sexual Disneyland.

The story did not have to be particularly well formed or believable, since Tyler was too drunk and stupid to judge its credibility. "A thousand? No problem, man."

They exited about five miles before Primm, pulling off on a small road that seemed to lead to nowhere but desert. By then Tyler had fallen asleep, and M would have preferred to shoot him then. Unfortunately, that would have gotten blood all over the rental car, so M had to force him out of the car before putting a bullet in his head.

By the time he buried him, it was too late to get a flight out of town, so that had to wait until the next morning.

At which point the road trip would be over, which would allow him to get back and deal with the dog, and the lawyer.

• • • • •

THE INSTITUTE FOR Energy Independence's motto is "the future is happening all around us." Which may be true, but the directors chose a building that stopped representing the future around 1908. It's old and run-down, with an elevator that has to make rest stops on its way up to the sixth-floor offices.

My only-rich-companies-have-good-looking-receptionists theory takes a hit when the young woman sitting at the lobby desk is an absolute knockout. She brings me back to Eliot Conyers's office, and on the way there I only see three other employees. This does not appear to be a thriving institute.

Conyers has the look of a guy who works for a living, complete with loosened tie and rolled-up sleeves. He has an earnestness about him, the type who really cares and thinks he can make a difference. But if he's been working on energy independence, he doesn't have that much to show for it. If George Washington had the same independence-achieving record, we'd all be eating fish-and-chips.

He welcomes me with a smile and an offer of a Diet Pepsi, which I gratefully accept.

"Thanks for seeing me," I say.

"I was afraid that if I didn't, Vince would be pissed at me. Life is too short for that."

I laugh. "Believe me, I know what you mean."

"So what can I do for you?"

"I'm working on a case that—"

He interrupts. "I know. The Erskine murder."

"You're familiar with it?" I ask.

He nods. "Only because it's tied to the al-Hakim killing. That was a rather major event in my world."

"How so?"

"When we invaded Iraq, the media talked about how people were looting stores, museums, even ammunition depots from the previous regime. Unfortunately, that was kid stuff compared with the way the country's oil was being stolen. The corruption in the oil ministry was mind-boggling, and it continued for years. On some level it's continuing now."

"How much money are we talking about?"

He smiles. "Many billions. Many, many billions."

"And we couldn't stop it?"

"That depends on who you mean by 'we.' If you mean the American government, we could have stopped a lot of it if we put our mind to it. But if you remember, our troops were otherwise engaged. And we farmed out a great deal of what we did to private contractors, many of whom saw a chance to become unbelievably wealthy in a very short time."

"Where does al-Hakim fit in?" I ask.

"As the military situation got better, we started putting pressure on the Iraqi government to get the corrupt oil system under control. When the pressure became too great to resist, Yasir al-Hakim was appointed to head up the oil ministry. He was the man we insisted on."

"Because he was honest."

He shrugs. "That was his reputation going in, but of course you never know until someone is put into the position. He didn't get a chance to deliver on his promise, which was to go through the industry with a scrub brush."

"Which made him a target."

"I figured that if he was for real, his life expectancy would be about a week. He lasted six, but three of them were in a coma after the explosion."

"And his death has had a major impact?"

Conyers nods vigorously. "In a couple of ways. In the long term, it's had a chilling effect on other potential reformers; martyrdom in that part of the world is limited mostly to religion, not business or government."

"And in the short term?"

"It sent the price of oil way up. The market doesn't like instability and uncertainty, so the explosion was a major event. Since then the price has gone down considerably, mostly because of economic conditions."

"So who killed al-Hakim?" I ask.

"I can't give you names, but you can be sure it was the people whose profit al-Hakim was preparing to eliminate." He shakes his head sadly. "They took a sixteen-year-old girl, probably convinced her she was on a mission from God, and sent her in to blow herself up."

"But she couldn't have gotten there on her own, which is where Erskine came in."

He nods. "Do I have proof of that? No. But that would be my first, second, and third guesses. And his murder makes it even more likely."

"Any idea why they waited until the foreign business-men were there for that conference?"

He shrugs. "Al-Hakim knew he was a target, so he was almost never out in public. But for this event, he was probably assured by the Americans that we had his back. How'd that work out?"

We talk a little more, but Conyers has no more infor-mation to offer. I thank him, and as I'm leaving I ask, "So are we going to get energy independence?"

He smiles. "Not this week."

• • • • •

PATIENCE WAS NEVER something Willie Miller ever really had patience for. It made sense, seeing as he had wasted seven years sitting in a prison for a murder he didn't commit. He certainly wouldn't want to waste more of his life waiting or sitting around. But the truth was that Willie was an impatient person long before he ever went to prison, and that trait simply continued afterward.

Yet Willie's lack of patience was never quite as pronounced as in the days after he killed Ray Childress. He had told both Andy and Laurie that he wanted to be involved in the investigation, that he was anxious to help in any way he could.

They had both assured him that he would get his wish, but he felt they were just putting him off, and in the days since they hadn't come to him with anything.

He didn't want to keep bothering them, but he had this problem: Somebody had paid Ray Childress to hold a gun on Sondra, and that somebody was still walking around free. That was simply intolerable.

It was time to talk to Joseph Russo.

Joseph Russo had been convicted on a weapons charge just before Willie's retrial, and their stay in prison had overlapped for almost three months. One day Russo was attacked by three other inmates in the prison yard, men who either didn't know who Russo was or who were trying to make a name for themselves.

Russo was a top lieutenant in the Vincent Petrone crime family, which considered New Jersey its personal playground. But that didn't help him that day in the prison yard, alone and facing three men with makeshift knives.

What helped him was Willie Miller. Russo and Willie weren't friends, but they had conversed a few times and developed a prison form of respect. What Willie did not respect was what was about to happen to Russo. Three against one, especially when the three had weapons, was not the kind of competition that Willie would look favorably on. And it was certainly not the kind of thing he would look away from.

The whole thing took about forty seconds, and an hour after that Willie and Russo were back in their cells, and the three men were in the hospital. No action was subsequently taken against either Willie or Russo, mainly because the entire incident was captured by the prison surveillance cameras.

Russo was appropriately grateful, and vowed that if Willie ever needed anything, all he had to do was ask.

Now was the time to ask.

The problem was that Willie had no real idea how to do that. He hadn't seen or spoken to Russo in years, though he had heard Russo had only spent eight months in prison. It wasn't like he had his address or phone number, but it was going to take much more than that little glitch to stop him.

It was pretty well known that the Petrone family used the Riverside area of Paterson as their base of operations. It was a collection of unassuming streets and houses, rather old-fashioned, and completely free of crime. Kids played out front without parental supervision, secure in the knowledge that no one in their right mind would dare harm anyone in that neighborhood.

Willie went down there at six PM, a time when he figured a lot of people would be out and about. He parked in front of a diner and started walking. To everybody he saw he said the same thing: "Hey, my name is Willie Miller, and I'm looking for Joseph Russo. You know him?"

Every single person said they did not know Russo, so Willie smiled and said, "If you meet him, please tell him I'll be at the diner, waiting to talk to him." Most people in Willie's situation would have been nervous, but Willie had been born with a defective anxiety gene.

After half an hour of spreading the word, Willie went back to the diner, ordered a burger and french fries, and waited.

He didn't have to wait very long. Two men, one large and the other larger, came in and the diner immediately felt crowded. They walked over to Willie's table, and the smaller of the two said, "Let's go."

Willie stuffed the last few french fries into his mouth

and followed them. They walked down the street, and the smaller man dropped behind Willie, so that Willie was in the middle. Willie noticed kids in the street and on the porches staring at them, and he waved as if he were in a parade.

The unlikely threesome went three blocks, ending at a house that looked no more expensive or impressive than any of the others. The larger man went up the steps and opened the door without knocking, then signaled for Willie and the other man to follow.

Willie heard the sound of a television, which seemed to come from upstairs. He was led into a den, where Joseph Russo was shooting pool with another man. Willie was struck by how much weight Russo had gained since getting off prison food. Back then he was maybe 160 pounds, which looked appropriate for his five-foot-ten frame. Looking at him now, Willie figured him for more than two hundred.

Russo looked up, saw Willie, and broke into a broad grin. "My man," he said, then put down the cue stick and walked over, wrapping Willie in a bear hug. "How ya doin'?"

"Still cool," said Willie. "Stayin' cool."

Willie suddenly realized that they were alone; his two escorts and the other pool player had seemed to vanish in thin air. He wanted to get to the reason he was there right away, but Russo wanted to drink beer and reminisce about the old days, as if they had been fraternity brothers for four years rather than casually acquainted inmates for three months.

Russo only briefly referred to the attack that day in the prison yard, but did mention that the three men regretted what they did "until the day they died," which was only two months later.

"So," Russo finally said, "what can I do for you?"

"I killed a guy last week," Willie said, but Russo showed no reaction at all. "His name was Ray Childress."

"That was you?" Russo asked, and then laughed. "Childress was messing with you? I always knew he was an asshole. Man, I've been telling my people for years about how you could handle yourself."

Willie was pleased that Russo knew Childress. "He held a gun on my wife and tried to steal my dog."

"Your dog?"

"Yeah. I need to know why he did that, and who sent him, so I can make sure it doesn't happen again."

"You think I know?" Russo asked.

Willie shrugged. "I figured you could find out. Especially if Petrone is involved."

Russo reacted quickly to the mention of his boss. "This had nothing to do with Mr. Petrone," he said, then softened and laughed. "He don't even like dogs."

Russo stood up, hand extended to shake, a signal that the meeting was over. "Let me see what I can find out, okay? I'll call you."

"Thanks, man." He handed Russo a business card, which he'd had made when he and Andy started the Tara Foundation.

Russo looked at it. "Dog rescue? What the hell is it with this dog stuff? You and that lawyer friend of yours."

The reference to Andy was a sign that Russo had checked Willie out, which surprised him. "You should get one," Willie said. "A dog will never bullshit you."

Russo smiled. "Nobody bullshits me."

● ● ● ● ●

THE DEFENSE DEPARTMENT must pay its investigators by the page. Hike and I are going over their report on the "incident" in Iraq, which took five months to prepare and an entire forestful of paper to print. It arrived from the office of the court clerk in eight boxes, each filled with documents.

I randomly choose four boxes and Hike takes the other four, and as we go through it we occasionally stop to discuss what we're reading. The writers of the report were clearly operating under a mandate to conclude nothing, and then use as many words as possible to support that conclusion.

"Shit. Crap. Garbage," says Hike as he closes his last book. There's a lot of Winston Churchill in Hike, and this particular pronouncement has to rank up there with the "Blood, sweat and tears" speech. "How do they get away with this stuff?" he asks.

I've been waiting for Hike to finish, mainly because by the time I got to my third book I switched to reading-every-fourth-paragraph mode. I don't think I missed much.

"I take it you didn't find anything that would be helpful?" I ask.

"Only if we want to put the jury to sleep."

The problem for us is that the investigators clearly had as a goal the management of political fallout from the incident. To that end, they predetermined that personnel were lax in their implementation of procedures, without criticizing the procedures themselves.

More significantly, the investigators, or at least the authors of the report, never considered intent as a possibility. That is to say that they never looked at whether or not the people in charge of security, or those implementing it, wanted the explosion to happen. And when you're not at least open to something, it makes it a lot harder to find it.

Pretty much everybody in the Middle East was interviewed for the report, in an obvious effort to be able to claim that no stone was left unturned in pursuit of the truth. It's not a total loss for us, in that at least we get the names of everybody involved, especially the soldiers assigned to security.

There were seventy-one assigned that day, including Billy. One was killed, and fourteen others besides Billy were injured. While no specific blame has been laid, five soldiers were reprimanded and discharged from the army. Their names are Donovan Chambers, Jason Greer, Tyler Lawson, Jeremy Iverson, and Raymond Santiago.

Erskine was not specifically implicated in the fiasco,

but the report refers to a general weakness in the command structure. The report does not speak to his military fate, but we know that he was at least viewed less favorably afterward, and he seems to have chosen resignation. It was a relatively graceful exit, only to end somewhat less gracefully on the street in front of a bar.

"If I ever commit a felony," Hike says, "I want these guys investigating the case."

"They found exactly what they wanted to find…nothing."

"Leaves us in a pretty big hole."

I nod. "Although we do have the names of the five soldiers who were discharged. We can find them and talk to them; at least it'll give us something to do."

"How are you going to find them?"

"I'll give it to Laurie, and she'll probably put Sam Willis on the case. Ten minutes at his computer and he'll be able to tell us where these guys are, what they had for breakfast, who they've called in the past three months, and who they're sleeping with."

"Is all that legal?" he asks.

"It wasn't last time I checked, but I haven't checked in a while."

He nods. "Makes sense. Checking stuff like that can be a hassle."

"Maybe I'll put it on Edna's list of things to do."

"What have you got on my list?" he asks.

"Are you knowledgeable about investments, commodities, rich people's stuff like that?"

He shrugs. "I've got an MBA, for what little that's worth."

"You've got an MBA and a law degree?" Hike is a constant surprise to me. "From where?"

"Harvard and Yale," he says. "I'm a walking rivalry. So what have you got for me?"

"I want you to find out everything you can about the hedge fund C and F Investments."

"Because of the two guys that got killed? I thought you went over there and talked to the top guy."

"I did." I point to the books. "But I just read in one of those books that Alex Bryant, the younger and lower-ranked of the two victims, was married for a year when he died."

"So?"

"So Jonathan Chaplin, his boss, told me he didn't think Bryant was married."

"At the risk of repeating myself...so? Maybe he didn't even know the guy. That's a big company; they've got offices all over the country."

"He said he's racked with guilt because Bryant took his place on the trip, and that he went to his funeral. I would have to assume his widow would have been hard not to notice there."

"Maybe he just signed his name at the funeral and left. Or maybe he met the wife and forgot. Or maybe he's been nailing the wife for two years and doesn't want anyone to know," Hike says.

"Or maybe he's lying because he doesn't want me to talk to Bryant's wife."

"Either way, it's got nothing to do with our case," he says.

"Or maybe it does."

I put in a phone call to Colonel Franklin Prentice, Kevin's brother-in-law, who has been very helpful to us on a couple of previous cases. He used to be stationed in

South Carolina, but I saw him briefly at the wedding, and I think he said he was transferred to Washington, DC.

I have no idea how to reach him, so I call the Pentagon's main number. "I'm trying to reach Colonel Franklin Prentice," I say.

"Do you mean General Prentice?"

"That'll work."

Within a couple of minutes he gets on the line, which is a surprise to me. I didn't realize generals were so easy to reach. I identify myself, and he assures me he remembers me quite well.

"You're the partner of my crazy brother-in-law," he says.

"Not anymore," I say. "He's off saving the world. Have you talked to him?"

"Last week. I heard some kind of jungle music in the background, so I asked him about it. He said that was actual jungle."

Prentice seems inclined to chat, and we do so for about ten minutes. If there are any longer minutes in the world than "chat minutes," I don't know what they are, and these ten seem to take about six months. The pauses are so pregnant they feel like they originated in a fertility clinic.

I hate chatting, and it's particularly hard to avoid when you're the "chattee," needing help from the "chatter." I'm usually good at cutting it off, and I keep throwing in a "Well, I don't want to keep you..." and a "So listen, the reason I'm calling...," but I guess generals are used to making chat-ending decisions.

He seems to have nothing but time. Aren't there any wars he should be trying to win? Finally I manage to steer the conversation to why I am calling, and I tell him about Billy's case.

"I'm very familiar with the incident," he says. "Have you seen the inspector general's report?"

"Yes...fascinating reading."

He laughs. "Covered the army's ass pretty well, huh?"

"I need to know what was known but not written down, off the record if need be."

"Hmmm," he says. "That's a tough one."

"What if I talked to Erskine's boss?" I ask, looking through the report for the name as I talk. I find it. "Colonel William Mickelson."

"That I can do," he says.

"Where is he stationed?"

"Right down the hall from me. Call him tomorrow."

"Thanks," I say. "Will do."

"You know, I'd never say this to Kevin, but I think what he and Kelly are doing is pretty amazing."

"So do I," I say. "Maybe we should tell him."

He pauses for a moment, probably considering it. "No, I don't think so. He might keep doing it."

"We don't want to encourage that."

• • • • •

"ANDY WANTS TO talk to you," Laurie says. She says this at the end of a forty-five-minute conversation with Cindy Spodek, the result of my asking her to make the call. During all of this time she has ignored the fact that I was pacing and looking at my watch as a way of letting her know I was impatient to get on the phone.

After a pause, Laurie says, "He said to tell you that he just wants to chat with a dear old friend, but between you and me there's a one hundred percent chance that he's lying."

After another pause, Laurie turns to me and says, "Cindy said to tell her dear old friend to kiss her dear old ass."

I walk over and take the phone from Laurie. "Cindy, how are you?"

"Do you realize the only time you ever talk to me is when you want something?" she asks.

Cindy is an FBI agent, working out of the Boston office. We've crossed paths on a couple of cases over the years, and in the process she, Laurie, and I have become good friends. She has also become a person I frequently call for information. "Do you have any idea how unfair that is? Or how much it hurts?"

"What do you want, Andy?"

"I didn't want anything, but now that you've unfairly attacked me like this, I feel a need to lash back at you."

"By asking me for information."

"Exactly. There was an explosion in Iraq last year in which eighteen people, including the Iraqi oil minister and two American businessmen, were killed."

"Iraq?" she asks. "Now you're becoming an international pain in the ass?"

"I'm a citizen of the world. I just read the Defense Department's investigative report on the incident, which takes almost seven thousand pages to say nothing."

"So?"

"So I'm assuming there's an FBI report on it as well. It's standard operating procedure for the bureau to be called in when American citizens are murdered, no matter where it happens. I want to know what it says."

"You think I'm going to turn over an FBI report to you?" she asks. "You've got balls the size of ocean liners."

"And you're a delicate flower. Come on, Cindy, I can get it anyway by petitioning the court, but it will take too long. And I'm fine if you read it and give me the highlights."

"That's big of you," she says.

"And that's a transparent attempt to get back on my

good side. Which may or may not work, depending on what you come up with."

"Good-bye, Andy."

"Good-bye, dear old friend."

I hang up, and Laurie says, "You really do take unfair advantage of her friendship, you know."

I nod. "True, but she gets something out of it as well. She gets to insult me."

She smiles. "You almost ready for bed?"

"Is that a serious question?" Nothing could be happening in my life that could make me say no to Laurie when she asks that question. The Super Bowl could be about to start, or I could be standing to give my closing argument to the jury...I'd still say yes and start to take my clothes off.

"Let's go upstairs."

We start heading up the steps, followed by Tara and Milo. "I obviously grow more irresistible by the day."

"I must have a thing for older men," she says. "The older you get, the sexier I find you."

"Makes me glad I'm not Benjamin Button," I say, and then stop halfway up the stairs. "Wait a minute."

"What is it?"

"I just realized that it's been a couple of hours since I heard the sound of chewing. Where's Marcus?"

"He's not here," she says. "I gave him an assignment."

"I thought we agreed he would guard the house while Milo is here?"

"I know, but he's an investigator, Andy, and we need him doing that. I can guard the house; I was a cop, remember?"

I'm not thrilled with this. "But what if you're otherwise engaged, like you're going to be in about five minutes?"

"I can multitask, remember?"

I could continue to argue about this, pressing my point that we are better off with Marcus guarding the house. Or I can shut my mouth and get into bed with Laurie.

End of conversation.

• • • • •

I'VE NEVER MET her, or seen her picture, but I recognize Kathy Bryant immediately. Her twenty-seven-year-old face is grief-stricken. Not the kind that you feel in the first hours and days and weeks after hearing terrible news, but rather the kind etched by months of unrelenting pain. She has learned to publicly keep her emotions under control, but the effort of it must wear on her, and make it more difficult to summon the energy to suppress hellish private moments.

I had called Kathy to discuss her husband's death in Iraq, and at first she tried to deflect me by giving me the name of her own lawyer. He is representing her in dealing with Alex's estate, and in settlement negotiations with the US government regarding a possible negligence lawsuit she might file.

I finally persuaded her that I was more interested in

the cause of the explosion than in the financial entan-
glements that have followed it, and she agreed to meet
with me. Her chosen location was here, at the food court
of the Garden State Plaza Mall in Paramus, a large area
of fast-food restaurants that collectively contain more
cholesterol than your average third-world country.

I'm a few minutes late, since I don't know where in
the mall the food court is, and I wind up parking as far
away as is possible. Then I have to decipher the mall di-
rectory, which helpfully tells me with an arrow where I
am, which would be good news if where I am is where we
are meeting. It's not, and by the time I figure out where
I'm going, and then trek over there, I'm late.

She's sitting at a table when I arrive, and after we say our
hellos, I get us a couple of coffees from the Coffee Bean.
"Thanks for seeing me," I say when finally settled in.

"I'm not sure what it is you want."

I smile my charming Carpenter smile, a guaranteed
funk remover if ever one was invented. "I'm not, either,"
I say. "I'm just asking questions until someone gives me
an answer that I can use."

"Okay."

"I'm afraid I'll be asking you about the circumstances
surrounding your husband's death. I hope that's okay."

"When you think about something twenty-four seven,
talking about it doesn't really make it any worse."

I nod my understanding, even though it's hard for
me to relate to what she has been through. When I was
twenty-seven, pretty much the most tragic event in my
life was when the Giants lost a play-off game.

"Has anyone in the government given you an explanation for how it happened?"

She nods. "Yes, someone from the State Department called the first week, and then again after the investigation was completed."

"What did they say?"

"That this teenager blew herself up trying to kill the oil minister, and that Alex and Mr. Freeman were in the wrong place at the wrong time. And that while every effort was made to prevent it, it's a dangerous country, and not every lunatic can be stopped."

"So they didn't admit negligence?"

"No. My lawyer said they wouldn't, and they didn't. They didn't say much more than I could read in the paper." She pauses, then, "Not that I read the papers."

"Why did Alex go on that trip?"

"Because Mr. Freeman asked him to; Alex worshipped Mr. Freeman," she says.

"Do you know why Mr. Freeman asked him? There were other people in the company higher than Alex."

She shrugs. "I don't really know, other than it was a late decision. For some reason the spot opened up. And since Alex's job included dealing with the oil markets, I guess he was a logical choice. Mr. Freeman seemed to think of him as a protégé. Alex was on the fast track."

She says this with a hint of scorn, so I ask her about it. "You didn't approve of Alex's job?"

"I guess I had mixed feelings about it. It was incredibly stressful, and I could see the effect it had on him. He had trouble sleeping... stomach problems... especially in the last couple of months. It's tough when his health and the quality of our lives seemed to depend on the price of things like oil or gold."

"Your feelings don't sound particularly mixed," I point out.

"Now they're not; losing the person you loved more than anything in the world at twenty-seven has a way of clearing things up. But back then, Alex was making a lot of money, and we had this vision of him retiring early, so I bought into it. Mr. Freeman wasn't even fifty, and Alex said he was going to quit soon and sail around the world. That sounded so appealing…"

"What about Jonathan Chaplin?"

"I don't really know him. I met him a couple of times at a company Christmas party, and then again at the funeral. He was really very nice…said all the right things."

"Have you had contact with the company since then?"

"Oh, yes. The HR person called me a number of times, to see if I needed anything, or if there was anything they could do for me. And they needed Alex's papers dealing with work, so they could transfer it on to someone else."

"You gave them everything?" I ask.

"Whatever I had. He took some things with him on the trip, so I don't know where they are, and I didn't give them his personal papers, of course. That's something I need to go through when I'm ready."

"Was Alex nervous about going on the trip?"

She shakes her head. "Very. I told him not to go, but I don't think he ever considered it. He would never turn down Mr. Freeman."

We talk a little while longer, but she really has nothing to tell me that can help Billy, and I don't have the sensitivity or the power to help her. The only consolation she can seem to find on her own is in the fact that Alex

and Freeman were killed instantly. She thanks God that
they didn't suffer, but doesn't seem to ask Him why they
died.

I'm sure she'll eventually move on, but it's going to
take a while, and involve a lot more pain.

When we say our good-byes, she says she hopes she's
been of some help.

"Absolutely," I lie.

When I get back to the office, I call Colonel William
Mickelson, Erskine's immediate superior back when
Erskine was alive enough to have one. General Prentice
had told him I was going to call and cleared the way,
so he gets on the phone right away. Having a general on
your side is like having a military genie.

I tell him why I'm calling and offer to come down
to Washington at his convenience, providing I'm not in
court. He doesn't seem thrilled by that, and mutters about
how busy he is. But he tells me he's going to be in New
York next week for a speaking engagement, so we make
arrangements to meet then.

I doubt that I'll learn much more than what was in
the report, but it can't hurt to try. If he's evasive, I'll just
keep mentioning how close I am with the general.

●　●　●　●　●

"I'M TEMPTED TO say we caught a break." Laurie says this as soon as I walk in the house. I didn't even have a chance to say, *Honey, I'm home,* or ask how little Ricky's soccer practice went.

"So go ahead and say it," I say. "Actually, you can say it over dinner."

"There is no dinner. I've been working. I thought you could bring in Taco Bell."

"You clearly don't have this domestic-bliss thing worked out yet. Tell me the break."

"Sam's been trying to find the soldiers who were discharged as a result of the explosion in Iraq. It's been hard, which is probably revealing by itself. But he managed to trace down one of them, Tyler Lawson, to a condo in Albuquerque, New Mexico."

"Good."

"So I used a few connections, and wound up talking to a detective out there. It seems Lawson went to Vegas a couple of weeks ago, checked into a hotel, and played some blackjack."

"Why are you only 'tempted' to call it a break? Sounds like a full-fledged one to me."

"Because he might be another murder victim. The first night he was there, he disappeared. Security cameras in front of the hotel showed him getting into the passenger seat of a car with a guy, and they drove off. That's the last anyone has seen of Lawson."

The story isn't making perfect sense to me. "Why would Vegas cops have checked the security tapes? People leave those hotels early all the time, usually because they've lost money. Did they suspect foul play?"

"When Lawson never checked out, they went into his room. All his stuff was there, and the safe was locked. So they opened it and found two hundred thousand dollars in cash. With that kind of money involved they obviously became suspicious, which is why they checked the tapes."

"Any idea who the driver was?"

"No. He seemed to know where the cameras were, and never gave them a good shot at his face. They traced the plate number on the car; it was rented at Avis with a fake driver's license and credit card."

"But Lawson got in the car willingly?"

"According to this detective, yes."

This is a potentially big development, though "potentially" is the key word. Five soldiers left the army as a direct result of negligence that day in Iraq, and one an indirect result; if two of those six, Erskine and Lawson, were subsequently murdered within a short period of time, then that would be way beyond an enormous coincidence. And it would be great for Billy, since he was an involuntary guest of the county when Lawson disappeared.

Of course, there's no proof that Lawson was murdered; for all we know he may be at the Cathouse Ranch. On the other hand, it's a fact that people don't generally leave two hundred grand behind in hotel safes.

We're also very far from certain that we will be able to introduce any of this as evidence. My hope is that Eli will open the door to our doing so, by bringing in testimony about the alleged grudge Billy was holding against Erskine for his injury in the explosion. But Eli may stick strictly to the physical and eyewitness evidence, and then it'll be much harder to bring in all this Iraq stuff.

"We need to find the other four soldiers," I say.

Laurie nods. "I know. Sam's working on it; he's got more things he can try. But for the moment they've disappeared."

"That's significant by itself. The average guy being discharged from the army wouldn't likely be wealthy enough to go on a round-the-world cruise. He'd have to make a living, unless he had money from some other source."

"The kind of money Tyler Lawson had."

"Right."

Although it doesn't change the effort I'll put into defending him, my confidence in Billy's innocence is starting to increase. If Lawson was murdered, my theory would be that there was a conspiracy to make the explosion happen, and now the conspirators are being silenced.

It's the kind of story juries like to hear, but unfortunately judges don't allow stories. They allow evidence.

I'm feeling guilty that Tara and Milo have been cooped up in the house. It's way too dangerous to take Milo outside for a walk, and I haven't been taking Tara very often, because I don't want to make Milo feel bad.

Laurie and I bring them into the backyard and throw tennis balls to them, but there isn't that much room to run. Milo is amazing; he jumps and grabs the balls in midair and never misses. Tara, on the other hand, is content to amble over and pick up the balls after they roll to a stop. She unfortunately has inherited my energy level.

All this activity makes me hungry, so I head over to Taco Bell to get dinner. I'm back with a bunch of burritos and quesadillas within fifteen minutes, and we chow down immediately.

We're finished by eight thirty, at which point I make a terrible mistake. I pour us some wine and then turn on the television without knowing in advance what channel it is tuned to. This is like a lawyer asking a witness a question that he doesn't already know the answer to.

Major faux pas.

What comes on the screen is a black-and-white movie. Worse yet, it's the *beginning* of a black-and-white movie, and Laurie sees it before I can turn it off. Laurie is constitutionally incapable of not watching a black-and-white movie; it could be the worst film ever made, but if it's in black and white it has a built-in status that demands her reverence. If they filmed *Santa Claus Slasher* in black and white, Laurie would consider it a work of art.

I don't have to be a math major to know that if the movie lasts two hours, we're not going to bed until at least ten thirty. That would be much later than my planned schedule, which had me in a sexually satisfied sleep by ten o'clock.

"Haven't we seen this one already?" I ask.

"Of course. It's Tracy and Hepburn."

"As I recall, they argue and are completely incompatible for ninety percent of the movie, and then they fall in love. I hope I didn't spoil the ending for you."

"The ending is my favorite part," she says. "Let's watch this, okay? We can talk later."

The last thing I want to do after this is over is talk. "Okay, sure. You want to watch a love story without nudity... hey, I'm all for it."

"Keep it up and there's not going to be any nudity at all tonight. On television or off."

This sounds like a threat, and Andy Carpenter does not take kindly to threats. "I'll go make the popcorn," I say.

That'll teach her.

●　●　●　●　●

JURY SELECTION IS the pits. I think the technical legal term for it is Pitsius Corpus, but "pits" sums it
up nicely.

Eli and I spend seemingly endless hours questioning
people, trying to figure out which ones are more likely to
take our side in a future verdict.

This is difficult enough on its face, but the problem is
vastly compounded by the fact that most of the people we
talk to are bullshitting us. The direction of the bullshitting
is generally determined by whether or not they want to sit
on the jury in the first place. Depending on their point of
view, they'll say either what they think we want to hear,
or the opposite.

Of course, we don't know what we want to hear. We
have our theories, and our general idea about the right juror for a particular case, but basically we're just guessing.

And we won't know if we've guessed right until the verdict comes in.

The court has summoned a total of eighty-one citizens from whom we are to choose our panel of twelve, with four alternates. That will be more than enough, though there is an endless supply of people to call upon if it isn't.

I have never finished jury selection with any idea how our side has done, and I would be just fine picking the jury by lottery, with no questioning at all.

Today's questioning is no different from any others. I'm basically looking to get people with above-average intelligence, who might be more likely to grasp and accept more than the obvious evidence put before them. To this end, six of the first eight accepted by both sides are college graduates, so I guess I'm doing okay.

At least twenty of the prospective selections are eager to say that they have predispositions about the case, are related to a cop, or are strongly pro- or anti-military. They believe these are factors that will get them sent home, and they're right.

The ninth juror selected is in his forties, sells medical supplies, is a college graduate, and clearly wants on this panel. He answers everything earnestly, and takes every chance to show how open-minded he is.

Of course, open-minded isn't my first choice; biased in our favor would be my preference. But I have no reason to turn him down, other than a slightly uncomfortable feeling that he is too anxious to be chosen. Salesmen generally work on commission, and spending two weeks in a courtroom therefore cuts down on income. But if number nine isn't concerned with that, then I guess I'm not, either.

We plow through until the end of the day; Judge Catchings obviously wants to get this over with. It's almost five o'clock when we empanel the fourth alternate, and the lucky group is asked to be here first thing tomorrow morning.

All in all, I'm happy with the group.

Or not.

I'll let you know when I know.

• • • • •

.

WILLIE SAW THEM as soon as they entered. Joseph Russo and his two bodyguards came in the front door of the Tara Foundation and checked out the place as if they were setting foot on Mars.

Of course, they looked upside down to Willie, since he was seeing them while lying on his back in the center of the foundation's play area. He was participating in an energetic wrestling match with eleven dogs, and loving every minute of it.

It took him a while to get to his feet, since there were probably four hundred pounds of dogs on his chest. The largest of these was a Newfie, who insisted on licking Willie's face during the entire process.

Finally Willie was able to make it over to Joseph and his men, all of whom seemed pleased to be behind the fence separating the main area from the play area.

"Hey, man. I didn't expect you to come by," Willie said.

"This is what you do?" Russo asked, not bothering to hide his incredulity.

"Yup. Every day."

"Whose dogs are these?"

"Ours," Willie said. "Until people adopt them; then we go out and get more."

"You're a fucking whacko."

Willie nodded. "You got that right. Your friends want to come in here?" he asks, referring to the play area.

Russo looked at his bodyguards, whose expressions clearly conveyed the fact that they had no inclination whatsoever to enter the madhouse. He laughed. "I don't think so. Is there someplace we can talk?"

Willie led Russo into the office, and the bodyguards waited just outside the door. "So, did you find out who hired Childress?"

"I did."

"What's his name?" Willie asks.

"He don't have a name. They just call him M."

"M like the letter M?" Willie asks.

"Yeah. He used to work out of Chicago; only handled big-time hits. Then he dropped out, but the word is he's working for serious money people."

"You know who they are?"

Russo shook his head. "No."

"So how do I find this M guy?"

"Willie, this is not somebody you want to find. We're not talking about a guy in a prison yard with a knife. We're talking about bad news."

Willie wasn't about to back down. "I want to find him."

Russo looked at Willie and knew he wasn't going to be talked out of it. "Okay, I got the word out, but it won't be easy. The cops have been looking for him for years. Every once in a while there's a rumor he's dead, like that Osama asshole. But he ain't. He makes other people dead."

"Thanks, Joseph. I appreciate this."

"No sweat. So maybe I'll get myself a dog. One of the big ones."

"Yeah?" Willie said, showing no enthusiasm whatsoever.

"You don't think that's a good idea?"

"Do you like dogs?"

Russo shrugged. "Yeah. As long as they shit where they're supposed to."

"Where would you keep it?"

"What do you mean?"

"Where would it sleep?"

"In the backyard. I'd get one of those doghouses. A real nice one."

Willie shook his head. "Sorry, can't help you. The dogs we adopt out live in houses with the people. Hanging outside is a pretty crummy life, you know?"

"So you're telling me I'm not good enough for one of your dogs?"

"No, I'm saying that you're good, and the dogs are good, but you ain't good together."

Russo didn't say anything for ten seconds, trying to digest what he'd just heard. Then he smiled. "Your balls haven't gotten any smaller, have they?"

Willie returned the smile. "Hope not."

• • • • •

"HOW THE HELL did you find that out?"

"What's the difference?" Willie asks. "I told you I wanted to help out, and that I wanted to know who hired Childress. So I did both."

"M? That's the guy's name?"

"That's what they call him."

"Willie, I need to know where this came from."

"Why?"

"So I can judge how reliable it is. No offense, I trust you completely, but anyone can be wrong."

So Willie reluctantly tells me about his friend Joseph Russo, and how he is sure Russo is correct about this. I have no doubt he's telling me the straight scoop, and I'm also sure that Russo is the type of guy in position to have access to this information. As search engines go, the Vincent Petrone crime family has the power of about six Googles.

"You took a big chance, Willie."

"The piece of shit held a gun on Sondra. M sent him, so M is going down, no matter what kind of chances I have to take. Besides, I told you, Russo is a friend, and he thinks he owes me."

"Why does he think that?"

"Because I took care of three guys that were trying to kill him in prison."

"You took care of them?" I ask. "How did you do that?"

"They were coming at him with knives, and I didn't think that was fair, so I stopped them and put them in the hospital."

"Oh." I'm amazed that such a momentous event could have happened, yet Willie is so nonchalant about it that he never told me. If I heroically thwarted a murder, I would have a book deal and a *Today* show appearance within an hour. I would also walk around wearing a sandwich board proclaiming myself a "hero" sandwich.

"Russo's going to put out the word to try and find him," Willie says. "And I want to help as well."

Obviously Willie is going to be active in this hunt whether Laurie and I want him to or not, so I can't say no. Nor do I want to; he's learned more in a few days than I have since I got on the case.

"Okay. We'll—" I'm interrupted by the ringing of the phone. Since Edna is off somewhere being Edna, I answer it myself.

"Hello," I say, using a clever phone conversation opening that I've perfected over time.

"Hello, Andy." It's Cindy Spodek; the first time I've

spoken to her since I asked if she could get the FBI report on the Iraq explosion.

"I hope you're not calling for another favor," I say. "I'm starting to feel taken advantage of."

"Don't push it, old friend. I tried to get a look at the report you asked about."

Her use of the word "tried" doesn't exactly fill me with optimism. "And?"

"And there is no way. I'd have an easier time getting my hands on the nuclear codes."

"Sorry to hear that," I say. "Is that to be expected in a situation like this? Is it standard operating procedure?"

"Even without seeing it, I can tell you that there's nothing standard about that report. It's classified in the extreme; Homeland Security is all over it."

"Homeland Security? This happened in Iraq, not Iowa."

"Andy, think of the world as one big happy homeland."

This is confusing to me, which means it gets added to the list. "Thanks, Cindy. I appreciate your trying. And while I have you..."

"Uh-oh," she says.

"If I say 'M,' what does it mean to you?"

"I hope you mean, like in Mary."

"No, I mean like in criminal or hit man," I say.

The next ten seconds defines the phrase "ominous silence." "Cindy?"

"Andy, this is someone you don't want to have anything to do with, in any form."

"So you know of him?"

"I've been chasing him for six months."

"Why?"

"He's a murderer, Andy. And one of his murders is part of a case I'm working on."

"Which one?" I ask.

"I'm not at liberty to say. Sorry."

"Is it mob-related?"

I can just about see her frowning into the phone. "I'm not going to play twenty questions with you, but no, it's not mob-related, depending on your definition of mob."

"That's a little cryptic for me," I say.

"That's the best I can do, other than to tell you to be very careful with this guy. And I can also send you the sketch we're working with; we don't have a picture."

I ask her to send it to me right away, and then I get off the phone and tell Willie about the conversation, and he nods confirmation. "Russo said he was bad news."

Which is pretty significant, because I imagine Russo is a pretty good judge of bad news.

• • • • •

"WE ARE A nation of laws." Eli Morrison has chosen to begin his opening statement with a sentence that everyone can agree with. It is probably the last sentence he will say during the entire trial that doesn't get an argument from me.

"Some of those laws are complicated; anyone who has ever gotten a look at the tax code can attest to that. But some are simple, like the one the State of New Jersey has accused William Zimmerman of breaking."

Eli is calling Billy "William" in an effort to dehumanize him. Regular guys have nicknames, would be Eli's theory, and murderers are not regular guys.

"This particular law says that one person cannot murder another. It doesn't matter if the murderer has a grudge against his victim. It wouldn't even matter if that grudge was legitimate, if the killer considered it vigilante justice. That is just a name killers use; the real name for it is murder.

"William Zimmerman killed Major Jack Erskine, against whom he held a grudge. A man whom he blamed for destroying his life. So he stalked Major Erskine and then gunned him down in cold blood, at point-blank range, on an Edgewater street. The forensics evidence, the eyewitness testimony, will prove this conclusively to you, beyond a reasonable doubt."

Eli has answered one question for me; he has quite willingly opened the door to testimony about Billy's grudge against Erskine, and will no doubt introduce evidence of it during the trial. I'm pleased about that, but it doesn't go far enough for me. I want to be able to show that other people had a reason and a desire to kill Erskine, but it's problematic at this point whether that testimony will be admitted.

"The defense will try to cloud the issue and, if I know Mr. Carpenter, will cloud it very creatively. They will advance wild theories about alleged conspiracies hatched thousands of miles away, about shadowy villains who murder and then disappear into the night. It will all be very interesting, even fascinating, but it will be irrelevant.

"Your job, and Judge Catchings will instruct you as to this, is to focus on the evidence that is presented to you. Not theory, not speculation, just evidence. That is all I ask you to do, and I know you will."

During Eli's statement, I glance over a few times at the people sharing the defense table with me. Billy sits impassively, showing no emotion whatsoever. Having an ex-cop as a client presents some challenges, but a significant advantage is his familiarity with this process.

Billy knows what to show the jury, and what not to show them. They should see dignity, and thoughtfulness, and courage in the face of adversity. They should not see emotion, especially in this case. Billy is being accused of letting emotion and a desire for revenge cause him to murder; his acting emotionally now would only feed into that.

Emotion can also be easily misinterpreted. Tears of anguish can be construed as tears of guilt; outrage at a witness's falsehoods can be taken as anger that the truth is being revealed.

I discussed this desired code of conduct with Billy before the trial, but he already knew it, and I am confident he will continue to act accordingly.

Farther down the table is Hike, who looks far more unhappy with things than Billy. Unfortunately, this is the natural state of affairs; Hike is in fact unhappier than Billy. There are prisoners in CIA black-hole rendition prisons who are positively giddy compared with Hike.

Hopefully, as the trial goes on, the jury will realize that Hike's demeanor is a permanent affliction, and that he naturally looks miserable even when things are going our way.

Eli has done an excellent job on his opening, and it's not because he was particularly eloquent. The strength of his argument rested in the fact that he was telling the truth; the evidence is overwhelmingly on the prosecution's side, and if the jury isn't led astray, Billy is history.

Which means I have to lead them astray.

"Ladies and gentlemen, there will be very few instances in which Mr. Morrison and I will be in complete agreement, but here is one of them: We both want you to focus on the facts.

"So let's start with some background facts. Billy Zimmerman is a hero, a public servant worthy of our respect and admiration. He has spent his entire adult life protecting our laws, protecting me, protecting you.

"After graduating from college, he went directly to the police academy, as his father did, and as his grandfather did before that. He spent the next eight years in dedicated service, receiving multiple commendations, and earning the rank of detective. He is the eighth youngest person to achieve that rank in Passaic County in the last fifty years.

"Had he continued in that role, progressing at that pace, he would no doubt be an even higher-ranking officer in the department today. The only problem was that there was this war going on, on the other side of the globe, and Billy felt he was needed there even more than here.

"So he volunteered for active duty and became a military policeman, putting his life on hold so he could go to Iraq and protect us again. And he received three commendations for his efforts.

"Until one day his life took a turn. A sixteen-year-old girl strapped bombs to her waist and blew herself to bits, killing eighteen people in the process. Bill Zimmerman lost his leg that day, and at the same time he lost his opportunity, but not his ability, to protect us.

"He was considered physically unable to remain in the army, and when he came home, instead of being greeted as the hero he was, he faced the stupid, heartless treat-

ment so many of our veterans are subjected to. Quality
medical care was difficult to come by, and his job at the
police department was no longer his for the retaking.

"By a curious coincidence, Milo, the dog that Billy
worked with on the force, was also finding himself suddenly unwelcome, because he had reached the ripe old
age of seven. So Billy took custody of Milo, with few options and the need to provide for both of them. So what
did he do?

"He became a thief."

I can see the surprise in the jurors' eyes when I say
this, but it was an easy call for me. Billy's new "profes-
sion" was going to come out in this trial no matter what,
so it should come from me. This way I can present it in
the best possible light, while not looking like I am trying
to hide it. If handled right and we get lucky, it could even
play as a positive for us.

"Yes, Billy Zimmerman became a thief; in fact, Milo
did as well. They used the same technique that Milo
learned in disarming dangerous criminals to steal items
that they could then sell for money. In the course of six
months they did this three times, not enriching themselves in the process, but earning enough to keep them
fed and sheltered.

"And then one night he saw Mr. Erskine, a man in
charge of security the day that Billy was injured. He saw
him acting suspiciously, so he watched and waited to see
what was going on. And when the opportunity presented
itself, he and Milo tried to steal something that Mr. Erskine had that seemed to have possible value.

"But the evidence will show that Mr. Erskine had his
own agenda that night; he was meeting someone to make

what seems to have been a sinister exchange. And the person he was meeting proved to be his killer.

"But here's what you need to know: In that horrible moment, Billy Zimmerman once again became a protector. He rushed to protect Mr. Erskine, but he was too late. The evidence will show that because he made that effort, and only because he made that effort, he sits here before you today, accused of the murder he tried to prevent.

"Those are the facts, and I join Mr. Morrison in asking you to please follow them."

• • • • •

MY OPENING STATEMENT isn't over until four o'clock in the afternoon. The good news is that Judge Catchings then decides to put off Eli's first witness until tomorrow. The bad news is that there is likely to be a tomorrow.

The presentation of the prosecution's case is not surprisingly always the toughest part of the trial for the defense. Cases aren't even brought unless there is deemed to be probable cause, which means that by definition the prosecution has substantial evidence of the defendant's guilt.

So I can be sure that witness after witness will be called, creating a barrage effect that has the danger of overwhelming our defense before we have our turn at bat.

All we have during this time is cross-examination, where I will try to pick apart their witnesses and find inconsistencies in their testimony. I will try to create doubt, not necessarily reasonable doubt, but enough for the jury not to make up their minds too quickly.

Ordinarily, this time includes an eagerness on my part to get it over with so that I can go on offense and present our case. That impatience doesn't exist here, because at this point we don't have a case.

During a trial I am in work-intensive mode, which is my least favorite mode to be in. I spend all my spare time reading and rereading the case file, paying particular attention to the witnesses I will be dealing with the next day. There is simply no substitute for preparation, and much as I hate it, I really do pride myself on not being outprepared by anyone I face.

My nightly ritual during this case is slightly different, since I have to include my ridiculous hour-long trust-building sessions with Milo. I swear, Milo and Tara have started not finishing their dinners because they want to save room for the better-tasting treats they will receive during these sessions.

We do it in the den, and once they're finished with dinner they start hanging around in the hallway outside the den, impatiently waiting to get started. Tara's got an especially good deal. She already trusts me and has no idea where the envelope is, so she has no significant role to play. All she has to do is lie there and inhale the treats.

Laurie hasn't been joining me for these sessions; she's busy working the phones trying to gather information that we can use. She's been working ridiculously long hours, since she also has her teaching responsibilities at the college. But she's thriving at it, and the aftereffects of her injury are becoming harder and harder to notice.

Actually, I feel like I'm making pretty good progress with Milo. Using the techniques Billy and Juliet have taught me, I can get him to take objects out of my hand and go hide them, yet lead me to the hiding place on command. Of course, I have no idea if this will result in him leading me to an envelope he took long ago without me around. For all I know, he doesn't even remember where the envelope is.

"Milo, old buddy, pretty soon it's going to be your chance to shine."

He looks at me quizzically, tilting his head slightly. The head tilt is something that Tara mastered long ago; it simultaneously makes her look cute and interested in what I'm saying. Milo isn't as good at it as she is, but he's learning.

"Don't give me that head-tilt crap; you know what I'm talking about."

"I do hate to interrupt this meeting of the minds," Laurie says, having entered the room without me realizing it.

"He's trying to pull the old head tilt on me," I say. "I'm calling him on it."

"I'm impressed," she says. "You want to call me when you're finished? Because I've got some big news."

"Good big news?"

She nods, so I end the trust session early to give her my full attention.

"Sam found a plane reservation made six weeks ago by Donovan Chambers," she says. "It was Nassau in the Bahamas, to San Juan, to Cancún. He made it in the evening for a flight that was to leave at seven o'clock the next morning."

I recognize the name instantly; Donovan Chambers is one of the soldiers discharged from the army as a result of the explosion in Iraq.

"Sounds like he was in a hurry. Has Sam found any traces of him in Cancún?"

She shakes her head. "He hasn't even looked; Chambers never got on the plane in the first place."

"Do we know why?" I ask.

"No, and neither do the authorities in Nassau. A friend of mine in the Miami PD put me in touch with someone down there. Chambers hasn't been seen since that day; all his clothes and possessions were there, including seventy-five grand in a hidden safe."

The same thing happened with Tyler Lawson in Vegas; there seems to be a run on ex-soldiers disappearing and leaving large sums of money behind.

"Have they got any leads?"

"None. And I doubt that they care a lot, him being a foreigner and all. If they had a body, that would be a different story. But they don't."

"Can we depose them?" I ask. "I need something tangible to give me any shot at introducing this at trial."

"We can definitely depose them," she says. "I can go down there and do it myself."

If there's a worse idea than Laurie going off to Nassau, I'm not aware of it. "It should be a lawyer," I say.

"What about Hike?"

"I really don't want to be responsible for depressing an entire country. I think we have international treaties prohibiting stuff like that."

"Well, you can't go, and it's not like you have a whole staff of lawyers," she points out.

"Too bad it's not Bangladesh; I could have Kevin do it."

I pick up the phone and call Hike, who never answers before the fifth ring. It's like he's hoping the caller will hang up and he won't have to be bothered.

He finally answers, and I tell him the situation and ask him if he would be willing to go.

"To Nassau?" he asks.

"Yes. Have you ever been there?"

"Of course not. Twenty minutes in that sun and I'd be peeling my skin off with a squeegee."

"You can put suntan lotion on your expense account," I say.

"What about bug repellent? On those islands they have mosquitoes the size of Volkswagens."

"No problem."

"Are there direct flights?" he asks.

"I don't think so. I think you fly to Miami and then switch planes."

"To one of those little puddle jumpers? You know what the crash rate is on those? It's like forty percent."

"Hike…"

"Look at just the singers that have been killed on those things. Buddy Holly, Ritchie Valens, Patsy Cline, Ricky Nelson, John Denver, Jim Croce, Otis Redding, the Big Bopper…if I were a singer, I wouldn't even drive by a damn airport."

"But you're not a singer, Hike."

"So? Half of them had their lawyers on the plane with them."

"I need you to do this, Hike. At double your hourly rate."

"On the other hand, plenty of singers have landed safely," he says. "But what if it's dangerous once I get there?"

"You mean sunburn?" I ask.

"No, I mean murder. Isn't that what we think happened to this Chambers guy?"

"There's no reason to think that whoever did it would still be on the island."

"Unless he is," Hike says.

We agree that I'll ask Willie to go along as protection. That way Willie can play detective, and Hike can get the depositions done.

The exhausting negotiation is finally over, and it's proven one thing: Milo trusts me more than Hike does.

• • • • •

ALAN LANDON WAS getting worried. Ever since he'd received the call from M while listening to the mayor's speech, things had not gone nearly as smoothly as he wanted...as he demanded. Perhaps he was spoiled, since the previous operations had gone off without anything resembling a hitch.

Anxiety was a sensation so unusual for him that he was actually struck by it. Landon had spent his entire life being smart enough to think two steps ahead of anyone else, and rich and ruthless enough to deal with any impediments to those steps. The occasions where worry was called for were few and far between.

From the beginning, he wanted the envelope that Erskine had, and that the dog had run off with. But he had always been a patient man, and he was willing to let matters unfold, and wait to make a move when it presented itself.

Landon prided himself on that willingness to be patient. Back in his basketball-playing days as a point guard for Dartmouth, he had learned the wisdom of what coaches referred to as letting the game come to you. The trick was to see the entire court, to know the game well enough to anticipate, and to take advantage of openings when they presented themselves.

And until now, the game had always come to Alan Landon.

But this situation was different. So far his patience had not been rewarded, and outside pressures were getting greater. He couldn't pull this operation off on his own; he literally did not have, and could not get, the necessary device to do the job. And the person who did have it was getting worried, and threatening to withhold it.

It was becoming clear that the only way to eliminate that pressure was to get the envelope, and the time left to get it was decreasing.

Landon knew that M was getting impatient as well. M was a man of action, they had that in common, and he was disenchanted with the lack of momentum to this operation. But M knew very little of what was really going on, and Landon had no desire to fill him in. M would have a very specific role to perform, and when Landon gave him the go-ahead, he would perform it in devastating fashion.

The truth was that Landon was right in assuming that M was frustrated, but if anything he was underestimating that frustration. M thought that Landon was getting indecisive, perhaps even soft, and it surprised him. With what they were doing, and with what they had already done, there was no room for that.

M knew that the dog was at Carpenter's house. He hadn't seen him, but he knew it as certainly as if he had. And he knew he could go in and get him whenever he wanted to. It wouldn't be the easiest thing to do; M was aware that Marcus Clark was lurking around, guarding the place. He had checked out Clark, now knew him by reputation, and respected him as a force to be reckoned with.

But not as much of a force as M.

Clark could be handled, especially since M had the advantage of surprise and timing. He could take him out whenever he wanted. And then there would be nothing to stop him from walking in and taking the dog.

After that M knew that Landon was on his own. M knew nothing about dogs, other than the fact that he didn't like them. If they were going to get the mutt to lead them to the envelope, Landon would have to figure out how.

So M was frustrated that he wasn't taking action, and he was frustrated that he could do nothing to change the situation. Landon was calling the shots for the time being, because Landon had the money, and if there was one constant in life it was that money ruled.

When it came time to kill Clark, and Carpenter, and Carpenter's girlfriend, none of it would be personal. It was simply about getting the dog, because getting the dog meant getting the money.

•   •   •   •   •

SCIENCE HAS ITS place in a trial, but prosecutors differ on where that place is. Their varying opinions on how juries receive scientific evidence especially impact on the order of the witnesses they call, and that decision can set the tone for the entire trial to follow.

Scientific testimony is drier than eyewitness or motive testimony, and some prosecutors believe it should therefore come first, when jurors are eager and alert. It also provides a more compelling proof, harder to refute, and introducing it first might render a juror more receptive to the "why" and "how" testimony to follow.

The majority of prosecutors take a differing view. They want their case to be an unfolding story, told in the same general chronological order as the crime was committed. Therefore, since forensic proof by definition must follow the crime, the witnesses who present it should bring up the rear.

If the eyewitness and motive evidence in this latter approach is compelling, the prosecutor can demonstrate the defendant's guilt independent of the forensics. When the science is finally introduced, it serves as ironclad confirmation of what the jury already knows, and it is therefore even more unassailable by the pathetically weak defense, in this case me.

Eli is a proponent of the second approach, as I would be if I were in his shoes. As his first witness he calls Kenny Parker, a twenty-three-year-old law student who recently finished his second year at Seton Hall.

Once Eli sets the stage with some questions establishing Parker as a fine, upstanding young man, he brings out that he was present at the Skybar the night of the murder. He also has Parker admit that he had been drinking a bit, but that he was sober and clearheaded when he left.

"Please describe what happened and what you saw as you left the bar," Eli says.

"Well, I was standing there, and I heard this loud noise, I thought it was a firecracker or something, coming from down the block. I started to turn that way, and all of a sudden this big dog comes running right toward me, with something in his mouth."

"What did you do next?" Eli asks.

"I backed up a little, because I thought the dog was coming at me. But he ran right by, and then I heard another loud noise. Then there was all this yelling, and a lot of people running around. So I went down the street, and I saw a body on the ground, and someone standing over him."

"Can you identify that person?"

Parker nods. "Yeah...yes. It was him." He points to Billy to complete the identification. "And then he leaned over to the guy on the ground, and put his hand on his neck. It was like he was feeling for a pulse or something."

"Did you see anyone else there?"

"You mean by the body? No, there were a lot of people running around and yelling, but he was the only one by the body at that point."

Eli turns the witness over to me, and I ask Parker why he went to the bar that night.

"Just to have a little fun with some friends; there aren't that many places to go at night around here."

"So you were having fun," I say. "Playing Wiffle ball? Video games? Pin the tail on the donkey? That kind of fun?"

He laughs a little uncomfortably. "No, we had some drinks and talked. Danced a little."

"How many drinks did you have?"

"I think two," he says. "But I was there for almost three hours."

"What were you drinking?"

"I'm pretty sure it was vodka and tonic."

"How long does it take to drink one of those?"

He shrugs. "Maybe fifteen, twenty minutes. Depends on how long I want it to last."

"So you had two drinks, lasting maybe twenty minutes each, and you were there for three hours. Sounds like you had a lot of downtime, huh?"

Eli objects that I'm being argumentative, which I will continue to be throughout the trial. Judge Catchings sustains the objection.

"How much do they charge for a vodka and tonic?" I ask.

"I'm not sure. Maybe eight bucks."

I introduce as evidence a copy of his bar check that night, which totaled eighty-two dollars and seventy-five cents. He tells me that he bought a bunch of drinks for his friends.

"That's nice; you're obviously a generous guy. Ten of the eleven drinks listed on that check were vodka and tonics; sounds like you and your friends have similar taste."

"Sometimes the bartender just keeps writing down whatever the first drink was."

This makes no sense to me, and the jury will feel the same way, so I don't have to pursue it further.

"You testified that when you left the bar, you were standing there in front. Were you waiting for something?"

He looks worried as he says, "For my friend, Danny."

"Did Danny drive you there that night?"

"Yes."

"Why?"

At that moment, Parker has to decide whether to continue lying or tell the truth. He chooses the truth, probably because he assumes I already know it and will nail him with it. "He was the designated driver."

I could press and embarrass him on this for the rest of the day, but I don't. The jury is smart enough to know when designated drivers are required, and I don't want to be seen as badgering him.

I keep Parker on the stand for another twenty minutes, getting him to admit that it was dark down the street, and hard for him to see. I can't get him to retract anything that he testified to about the murder itself, mainly because it was all true.

He may have been drunk, but his recollections are accurate. And damaging.

When court ends I head home, have dinner with Laurie, put in a trust session with Milo, and then decide to take Tara for a walk. I haven't been doing enough of this lately, because of Milo's presence.

My walks with Tara are special times for both of us, and I think she's been missing them as much as I. I'm only a little embarrassed to say that I talk to her out loud, secure in the belief that she understands me, if not the actual words. I know I understand her, if not the actual barks.

Our timing is perfect, because we meet a neighbor walking Bernie, a five-year-old golden who lives two blocks away. Tara and Bernie love each other; their joy every time they meet is obvious and terrific to watch. I'm especially pleased because Willie and I rescued Bernie three years ago and placed him in his current home. He's a great dog.

When we get home, I swear Tara looks at me with gratitude, and with the silent message that we should do this more often.

We should. And we will.

• • • • •

I'M TRYING TO solve at least twenty-one murders at once. In addition to Erskine's murder, for which Billy is on trial, there are the eighteen deaths in the Iraq suicide bombing, and the likely murders of Tyler Lawson and Donovan Chambers. This doesn't include Jeremy Iverson, Raymond Santiago, and Jason Greer, the other discharged soldiers whom we haven't been able to trace at all yet. Even though we haven't gotten any information on them, it's safe to say that I'm glad I didn't write their life insurance policies.

I have no doubt that all these murders are connected, and solving one will put me on a path to solving them all. Unfortunately, all that I know right now is that it all started with the Iraqi oil minister, and that on some level it's all about money. Oil and money definitely do mix.

Solving a mass murder in Baghdad is difficult when you're sitting in a bed at one o'clock in the morning in Paterson, New Jersey. All I have is the file, so I'm going over it once more, having already prepared for tomorrow's witnesses.

Laurie is lying next to me, sleeping soundly, which is what I would like to be doing. Tara is lying across my feet, which for some reason I find incredibly comforting, and Milo is across the room, curled up asleep on a chair. If the big guy would just wake up and tell me where the damn envelope is, a lot of this aggravation might be avoided.

As a rule I hate relying on assumptions, but I have a tendency to violate that rule when I have no facts to take their place. So my basic assumption is that Erskine recruited five of the soldiers in his command to allow the suicide bomber proximity to the oil minister.

The money that Lawson and Chambers seem to have left behind indicates that they were well paid for their negligence, so much so that they felt they could disappear and live comfortably after their discharge.

The fact that they and Erskine were murdered obviously means that the people behind the explosion would not tolerate any witnesses to their efforts. Erskine, Lawson, and Chambers seem to have been murdered to ensure their silence.

In Erskine's case, there is a possibility that he was blackmailing his employer. Billy believes that Erskine was preparing to make a trade just before he was killed. If that is so, then his actions may have also precipitated the deaths of Lawson and Chambers. There is no way to know, but it's possible that the killer believed they were part of the blackmail as well, or might commit their own in the future.

One of my concerns is that our investigation into Erskine has so far failed to turn up any substantial sums of money. If the soldiers enriched themselves by their actions, then the same should be true of Erskine, who as the leader should have made even more. The jury is going to want evidence, but so far we don't have it to show them.

I have in the files many of the contemporaneous newspaper stories about the explosion. It was a major news event, despite the fact that suicide bombings have not exactly been unheard of in Iraq this decade. The critical injury to the oil minister, who was not expected to survive at the time, plus the collateral deaths of two American businessmen, elevated this to a higher news status than most.

Different angles were taken on the story, probably due to the political leanings of the individual reporters. Some of them were straightforward, reporting on the event and concluding that the oil minister was the target, so as to prevent him from reforming the corrupt system.

Others focused on the lax security, and the inability of the American and Iraqi military and police to prevent the bombing, despite the fact that they knew this would be a tempting target for the enemy. Speculation was that heads would roll, particularly among the American security authorities. That is of course what ultimately happened, though they were low-level heads.

More business-oriented publications focused on the future impact the event would have on the oil industry within Iraq, and the secondary impact on the world oil market in general. All concluded that the explosion would signal an instability and a future question of oil supply that would send prices skyrocketing in the short term. That prediction was validated within twenty-four hours, as oil prices immediately went up 11 percent.

At the time the stories were written, the oil minister was in a coma, listed in grave condition. There were rumors that he was brain-dead, and that the life-support machines could be disconnected at any time. This proved not to be the case; he lingered for eleven more days before succumbing.

For some reason this fact strikes me differently than it has before, and I look in the army file to see if I can find sketches that answer the question I am forming. The sketches are there, but they're confusing to me, and it's going to be at least tomorrow until I can find out what I need to know.

But now I'm anxious and frustrated, which prevents me from falling asleep. I start to fake-yawn and stretch, nudging against Laurie each time, hoping to wake her up without getting blamed for it.

This doesn't work, so I start to put some voice into the fake yawn, giving off an "aaaahhhhh" each time I do. She doesn't wake up, so I do it increasingly louder, until I'm yawning like Luciano Pavarotti. Still nothing.

My next trick is to pull on the covers in various directions and turn the lamp on and off. Still no luck, so I pull, turn, and yawn all at once. If the Iraqi oil minister were still in a coma and lying next to me right now, even he would wake up.

"Andy, if you wanted to wake me, why couldn't you gently touch me on the back and say, *Laurie, please wake up, I need to speak to you, sweetheart.*" She says all this without moving a muscle or opening her eyes.

"Oh, sorry," I say. "Did I wake you?"

"Andy, be careful. I'm licensed to carry a gun under my pillow."

"Oh. Laurie, please wake up, I need to speak to you, sweetheart."

For the first time she moves, half sitting up, supported by her elbow. "Okay. Speak."

"Eighteen people were killed in Iraq that day. Sixteen of them died instantly, and two died days later."

"So?"

"So one of the two was the oil minister."

"I know that, Andy. We've both known that since day one."

"It was a powerful explosion, Laurie. If the girl was after the minister, why wasn't she close enough to him to kill him on the spot?"

Now she sits all the way up. "That's a good question. Maybe the girl got confused, and stood in the wrong place. She was sixteen years old, and she had to be scared."

I shake my head. "Maybe, but unlikely. Billy said she moved around for a long time before doing it. That's why he kept watching her."

"Then maybe she couldn't get close, because of the security."

"The security was set up to give her a free pass. This operation was planned perfectly; why go to all that trouble and then not give her access?"

"We need to check this out," she says.

I nod. "That's for sure. First thing in the morning."

I turn out the lights and lay my head down. "Good night."

"Andy, this could be important. I'm not sure I'm going to be able to sleep."

"Then just try to lie there quietly. I'm exhausted."

● ● ● ● ●

WILLIE AND HIKE were not the perfect traveling companions. They were in first class from New York to Miami, which Willie found to be "really, really, cool." The seats had elaborate entertainment systems, with a television, DVDs, and video games. The flight attendant seemed happy to quickly bring Willie pretty much anything he wanted, and in normal circumstances he would have been content if the flight went on much longer than it did.

That's if he hadn't been sitting next to Hike.

Hike thought the cabin was too cold, the chicken stringy, and the bloody Marys watered down. He mentioned all of this to Willie, who didn't share his viewpoints and told him so.

"It doesn't matter," said Hike. "We're going to die on the next flight anyway."

Once they boarded the small plane for the Miami-to-Nassau flight, Hike really kicked it into gear. His we're-going-to-die fear became a chant, annoying all the passengers and prompting a warning from the flight attendant.

By the time they landed in Nassau, Willie had decided that he would rather swim back to New York than fly with Hike. They got their bags, and then Willie rented a car while Hike covered himself in bug repellent and suntan lotion.

They went to the local headquarters of the Royal Bahamas Police, where they had an appointment with Inspector Brendan Christian. Christian had investigated Donovan Chambers's disappearance, and had spoken to Laurie on the phone.

Hike conducted the interview after getting Christian's permission to turn on his tape recorder. He took him through everything that Christian knew about the Chambers case, which was little more than he had already told Laurie. During the interview, Willie showed the sketch of M that Cindy had provided, but Christian had no recollection of seeing him.

When they were finished, they had four and a half hours until their flight, and Willie wondered to himself if he had time to buy a gun to shoot Hike during the flight back.

"I was just thinking about something," Willie said. "They say that this guy is a shooter only...that's how he hits. And Chambers was a combat soldier, so he could probably handle himself."

"So?" Hike asked.

"How did he get a gun onto the island? He wouldn't

try getting it through airport security, would he? That would be taking a chance."

Christian nodded. "And he wouldn't have purchased one on the island. That would call attention to himself, and we'd know about it."

"Which explains the fact that you haven't found a body," Hike said. "He came in by boat, and dropped the body at sea. And he would have needed a car to get around."

Christian held up the sketch. "I'll have this shown at all the rental car agencies and piers where the boat could have docked. But even if we get an ID, it doesn't help catch him. He's long gone."

"We can use it at trial," Hike said.

When they were back at the airport, Willie called Andy in New Jersey, while Hike went into the bathroom to wipe off the lotion and repellent.

Willie told him about the deposition, and the idea that M might well have come in by boat if he was there at all. "The cop is going to show the sketch around. Will it help if someone IDs him?"

"Absolutely," Andy said. "As long as I can figure out a way to get the judge to admit it."

"Cool."

"You're not half bad at this detective work," Andy said.

"Nah...I still don't know a lot of legal stuff."

"Like what?"

"Well, like...what if I throw Hike out of the plane between here and Miami? Which country would I be charged in?"

．　．　．　．　．

"I CAN'T BE sure where the oil minister was," says
Billy. We're meeting in a courthouse anteroom before the
start of today's trial session. "My job was to watch out
for what I thought might be threats, so I didn't see him at
all."

I take out the sketched map of the immediate area,
and point to specific spots on it. "She was here, and the
minister was here." There's a fairly substantial distance
between the two locations.

Billy stares at it for a few moments, then closes his
eyes. It's a sign of my sensitivity level that I hadn't anticipated he might react emotionally to this; he is revisiting
the time and place that cost him his leg. It also led him to
his current incarceration and plight.

Finally, he opens his eyes and nods. "Right. And I was

standing here, until I walked away. When the bomb went off, I was here." He points to the places on the sketch.

"Could she have gotten closer to the minister if she wanted to?" I ask.

"Absolutely. Once she got inside, there was really nothing to stop her."

"Any idea why she didn't?"

He shakes his head. "No. Not really."

"Could she have been nervous, and in a hurry?" I ask.

"She certainly should have been nervous; she was taking her own life. Even if she thought she was doing it for her God, it was still a big deal. But she was not in a hurry; I can tell you that. She walked and looked around for at least twenty minutes before she detonated the bomb. The length of time was why I stopped really paying much attention to her."

"The idea that the minister was the target...was that based on anything other than an assumption?"

"What do you mean?" he asks.

"I mean, did you have any advance warning that there was going to be an effort made to kill him? Did anyone claim credit after the fact?"

"No, none of that. You think there's a chance they weren't after him?"

"I certainly don't see any proof that they were."

"So who were they after?" he asks.

"I don't know. Maybe no one. Maybe they were just out to kill people and capture the attention of the world."

He nods. "Good old-fashioned terrorists. But let me ask you a question...so what? What's the difference who they were after or why they did it?"

"Because I'm operating under the assumption that the

explosion is somehow linked to Erskine's murder," I say. "If it isn't, it isn't. But I have to follow it as if it is, or we're nowhere."

"But even if it's linked, what does it matter? Even if someone paid Erskine and the other guys off to let it happen, and I'm sure someone did, how does that help defend me against Erskine's murder?"

"Because I believe the people who paid him off are the people who killed him. So if we solve that murder, we solve this one."

Unfortunately, we're not going to solve it before trial this morning, so we head into the courtroom. Eli's first witness is Marguerite Mooney, a young woman who lives across the street from the Skybar. She and her husband were sitting on their porch, enjoying the evening summer breeze.

She testifies that they saw Milo sitting slightly down the block, apparently tied to a tree. This upset them, because they thought he was abandoned.

"So what did you do?" asked Eli.

"I walked over to the dog, just to make sure he was okay," Ms. Mooney says.

"What happened next?"

"Well, when I got over there, he growled a little, so I backed off. Then a man who was standing about thirty feet away told me that it was his dog, and that I should leave him alone."

She identifies the man as Billy, and also mentions that she saw Erskine standing in front of the bar. She has set the scene perfectly for Eli, and the clear implication of her testimony is that Billy and Milo were stalking and lying in wait for Erskine.

There's not a hell of a lot I can do with her on cross-examination; everything she is testifying to is true, and she hadn't had nine vodka and tonics to cloud her memory.

"Ms. Mooney, you testified that Mr. Zimmerman is the person you saw that night, the man who told you to keep away from Milo."

"Yes."

"You had no trouble identifying him?" I ask.

"None. Where he was standing, there was a streetlight right nearby."

"So he wasn't hiding?" I ask. "He wasn't lurking in the shadows?"

She shakes her head. "No, he was down the street from the bar, so he was right in front of our house."

"So when he was standing in the light, talking to you, he didn't seem concerned that you could see his face?"

"No."

The implication is clear: If Billy was planning to murder someone, why would he be willing to be recognized? Of course, the truth is that Billy's conduct was overly risky—Milo was going to commit a crime, and Billy's actions could have tied him to it.

"And you said that Milo had growled at you?"

"Yes."

"Is it possible that Mr. Zimmerman was trying to protect you from Milo? That he was afraid Milo might bite you?"

"I suppose it's possible."

There's nothing left for me to do but reaffirm the testimony she gave to Eli that she and her husband were inside and asleep by the time the murder took place.

Her testimony has been damaging, but not fatal. She placed Billy and Milo at the scene of the crime, but we had already admitted they were there to commit a theft. Nothing she has said has disproven that.

The rest of the day is a succession of witnesses who also place Erskine in front of the bar, with Billy and Milo nearby. Some of them also saw Billy with the gun in his hand, or leaning over Erskine's body.

No one will admit to seeing the man Billy claims is the actual shooter, or to seeing him drive off. It's understandable, since the shooting happened down the block, in relative darkness, and they weren't drawn to walk down and look until after hearing the shots.

I get each witness to admit that it's possible that there was someone else there, but that will not be close to compelling for the jury.

The case being constructed against Billy will be very hard to tear down.

• • • • •

HE HASN'T FOUND the envelope, but Milo is still helping our case. He's not helping actively or intentionally; Milo clearly believes in stepping back and letting the justice system run its course. But his mere presence is having a positive effect.

The media always seems to bombard and depress the public with statistics chronicling all the bad things that happen to Americans. They dutifully report that there is a violent crime committed every twenty-two seconds, a cancer diagnosis every twenty-six seconds, an auto accident every five seconds, and an auto accident injury every ten seconds. It's the reason I no longer buy watches or clocks with second hands.

The point of this is that, with all the terrible things constantly happening, it's very difficult to break through the clutter. Certain crimes, for instance those involving JonBenét Ramsey, Natalee Holloway, Chandra Levy, and Laci Peterson, attract tremendous media attention; other, similar ones do not.

Milo is our clutter breaker. His notoriety as a canine thief has given this case a public forum. The fact that it all has roots in Iraq, and that the victim is a high-ranking military officer, would have attracted interest anyway, but nothing like that which Milo's involvement brings.

Dogs seem to have that effect on people. Rescue a person from a raging river, and you're on page four. Rescue a helpless dog from the same river, and you're on the *Today* show.

I'm taking advantage of this national canine fascination by appearing on Larry King tonight. It's not my favorite thing to do; the conversations always feel strained and stilted to me, and I feel like I need to rein in my normal obnoxious sarcasm.

I also dislike when Larry opens it up to phone-in questions; they have a tendency to be direct and on point, and thus more difficult to evade. All in all, the thirty minutes I have been allotted will feel like a month.

But we need to shake things up, and we simply don't have the resources to do so on our own. We need the public to know about our situation, and we need their help in dealing with it. And if the jurors are watching, despite the judge's admonition to avoid media coverage of the trial, so much the better.

I've handled a number of very high-profile cases in recent years, and I've made the media rounds on most of them. This is my third time doing the Larry King show, so Larry mercifully doesn't spend too much time introducing me to his audience.

We get right to the case at hand, and within five minutes I'm holding up the sketch of M. "There's no sense mincing words on this, Larry. This is the man that we think is the real killer, and this is not the only murder he is guilty of. I don't know his name, but he goes by the initial 'M.'"

"That's a pretty strong statement to make," Larry says, probably surprised, since strong, controversial statements are not exactly a staple of the show.

"Yes, it is. And if I held your picture up on national television and called you a murderer, you'd be suing me within the hour. If this man wants to come forward and take me to court, I would welcome it, but he won't."

"So what do you expect him to do?"

"To stay in the shadows and continue killing. That's why I am asking your viewers, if they have seen this man or know anything about him, to contact me or law enforcement. But please be careful: He is armed and very, very dangerous."

Larry then proceeds to ask me some semi-specific questions about Billy's trial, most of which I deflect, citing some vague confidentiality concerns. Finally I feign exasperation, and say what I've planned to say all along. "Larry, this case is about far more than a murder on an Edgewater street. It began when a young girl was sent in to blow up herself and a lot of innocent people, one of whom was my client."

"So what is your theory of the case?" he asks.

"That will all come out where it should, in front of the jury. But this is much bigger than one murder; it has huge national security implications. And my client has been an unfortunate, innocent bystander through all of it."

Before I leave, I show pictures of Jeremy Iverson, Jason Greer, and Raymond Santiago, the three soldiers we have been unable to locate at all. I realize that they may already be murder victims, though I don't mention this. Instead I call on the public to contact me if they have any knowledge about their whereabouts.

"I am not accusing them of anything. In fact, it's possible that they may already be victims. But if they are alive and well, I have reason to believe that they have information crucial to our case." My expectation is that the media, including CNN's own reporters, will pick this up and run with it. All of America will learn that the people I've mentioned are soldiers who were there that day in Iraq, and that were subsequently discharged.

Larry thanks me for coming, and obligingly gives me a chance to show the sketch of M again. I've accomplished my goals, which were to get these pictures out to the public, and also to reveal that we have an intriguing theory of the case. It's been worth half an hour of my time, even if it felt like a month.

When I get home, I have to delay getting into bed with Laurie in order to have a trust session with Milo. Suffice it to say that I'm not pleased.

After he and Tara chomp down a few treats, I ask Milo, "You starting to trust me yet?"

He just looks at me, noncommittal.

"You know, I could be upstairs in bed with Laurie, but instead I'm down here with you. Isn't that worth anything?"

Again no answer, and when I look over at Tara, she

looks away. She doesn't seem inclined to get into the middle of this.

"Tara, talk to him, will you? Put in a good word for me."

I guess my walk the other night with Tara didn't get me as many points as I'd hoped, because she's sticking with her new friend.

"Milo, if Laurie's asleep when I get up there, I'm not going to be pleased, and I'm going to blame you."

I swear, I think he shrugs his lack of concern.

"Just remember, pal, you may be neutered, but I'm not."

●　●　●　●　●

IT WAS A surreal moment for Raymond Santiago. For weeks he had been holed up in a motel room just outside Detroit, spending all his time watching television, venturing out only long enough to get food and newspapers. Ever since he heard about the Erskine killing, he had behaved like a man on the run, because running was what he believed necessary to survive.

It wasn't just Erskine's death that sent him into a panic. Erskine was an asshole; the kind of guy at whom many people would want to take a shot. And Greer had mentioned that Erskine might try a new scheme of his own as a way to get rich. What was more disconcerting to Santiago was his inability to reach the others, Lawson, Chambers, Iverson, and Greer.

They had agreed to keep in contact, so they could better monitor the situation. The army could not prove anything other than negligence in Iraq, and their subsequent discharge actually did them a favor. With the kind of money each of them received for their efforts, the last place they wanted to be was the army.

But Santiago was a man who trusted his gut instincts, and the combination of Erskine's murder and his inability to reach the others filled that gut with certainty and dread. So he went to Detroit, where he had no connections whatsoever, paid cash to stay in a dive of a motel, and almost never went out. There was no way anyone could find him.

That all changed the night that a stunned Raymond Santiago watched that lawyer show his picture and say his name on national television. Raymond was keenly aware that in that moment, his future was drastically altered. Now there were a million people, maybe more, looking for him. Now the supermarket cashier, the motel chambermaid, the guy selling newspaper on the corner...they were all enemies.

Raymond was going to be found, maybe by someone sent to kill him, but more likely by the public. They would locate him for the lawyer, and then his cover would be blown. He had no fear of the law at this point; he wasn't even charged with anything. He was afraid of exposure, because that could lead to the same fate for him that it had likely brought to his friends.

Staying underground was no longer an option for Raymond. He was going to come out of hiding, and was willing to reveal all that he knew, in return for iron-clad immunity and protections. The only question was whether to go to the authorities or that Carpenter guy.

He couldn't be sure what would happen to him if he

went to the authorities. He knew how high up the corruption went; in a way he would be walking into the enemy camp, and might never be heard from again.

Carpenter was another story. He only cared about getting his client off the hook on the Erskine murder. Raymond was a key to that, and Carpenter would want to protect him. And he obviously had the public visibility to expose anyone who got in his way.

Raymond was again going to trust his instincts. Carpenter was the way to go.

M watched the Larry King interview as well, hoping Carpenter would inadvertently say something he could use. His hope came to fruition, though it was a decidedly mixed bag.

He was not particularly concerned that the sketch of him was shown. It was far from an exact likeness when it was done, and he looked considerably different now. Then he had a mustache and small beard; now he was clean-shaven. He had also changed his hair color, and the overall effect was to make him unlikely to be recognized by the average citizen. Since law enforcement had been in possession of the sketch for a while, there was little about the televised release that was particularly threatening.

More concerning was that Carpenter had only shown photos of Greer, Iverson, and Santiago, and not Lawson or Chambers. Since he clearly was looking for them because of their potential involvement in the Iraqi explosion, the fact that he was not looking for the other two was a sign that he already knew their fate. That was unfortunate, but increased his level of respect for Carpenter as an adversary.

But outweighing all of this was M's pleasure that Carpenter had revealed Santiago's photograph to the world. He knew that Santiago was not particularly good under pressure, and this would likely panic him and draw him out. And when he came out, he would be committing suicide.

M's frustrating search for Santiago was soon to come to an end, courtesy of Andy Carpenter.

It took Raymond Santiago until ten o'clock the next morning to completely settle on his strategy for survival. Once he did, he drove forty miles outside of Detroit before stopping at a pay phone. If it didn't work out, he didn't want the call to be traced back to the motel.

He dialed the number that Carpenter had broadcast on the TV show, and it was answered on the third ring.

"Hello?"

He was surprised that it was a woman's voice, but didn't hang up. "I want to talk to the lawyer...Carpenter."

"He's in court. Who's calling?"

Santiago hesitated, not sure what to do.

"Is this Raymond Santiago?" Laurie asked.

Another hesitation, then, "Yeah."

"I can help you, Raymond."

• • • • •

DETECTIVE DONN SANFORD is very annoyed at having to testify. That is obvious by his body language and the short, curt answers he gives to Eli's questions. I have seen Detective Sanford testify a number of times, and he is ordinarily an outstanding witness, authoritative and confident. Not today.

Sanford is Billy's friend; they joined the police force in the same class. It is not part of his makeup to betray a friend—but neither is it part of that makeup to lie under oath. So he's here, but he's obviously not happy about it.

Hike has once again joined me at the defense table, having returned from his trip with Willie. I was glad to see him, both because he's a valuable trial resource for me to call on, and because his arrival means that Willie didn't drop him out of the airplane. The last thing I needed was another murder trial.

Eli leads Sanford to say that he and two other detectives went with Billy to a Knicks game at Madison Square Garden soon after Billy returned from Iraq, and afterward they went to a bar on West 35th Street.

"And the four of you had a conversation at the bar?" Eli asks.

"Yes."

"Did Erskine's name come up?"

"Yes."

"Who first mentioned him?" Eli asks.

"I believe it was Billy Zimmerman."

He barely whispers it, and Judge Catchings asks him to speak up, so he says it more loudly. I'm annoyed with Eli for putting Sanford through this. I know from the witness list that the other two detectives who were part of the conversation are going to testify. They are not friends of Billy, and have little compunction about doing so. Sanford is not necessary for Eli's case, but he probably wants to show the jury that even Billy's buddy has evidence against him.

Eli gets Sanford to say that Billy had some drinks in him, and talked about how it was Erskine's fault that he lost his leg, which in turn cost him his jobs with the army and then the police force when he got home.

"Did he say what he would like to do about it?" Eli asked.

"He didn't say anything. It was the alcohol doing the talking."

Eli objects and Catchings admonishes Sanford for the unresponsive answer. "He said he'd like to kill the son of a bitch," Sanford says. "That if he had the chance he'd strangle him with his bare hands."

On that dramatic note, Eli turns the witness over to me. Sanford and I have tangled quite a few times over the years, and there have been times he would admit he wanted to strangle me with his bare hands. But right now he's looking to me for help.

"Detective Sanford, when you heard Billy Zimmerman say those things about Mr. Erskine, did it worry you?"

"No."

"Did you caution him against taking violent action? Or contact Mr. Erskine and warn him his life was in danger?"

"No."

"Why not?"

"Because it was just talk," he says. "We were drinking and saying stupid things. I knew Billy well enough not to take it seriously."

I nod my agreement. "Detective, does the name Randall Brubaker mean anything to you?"

"Yes, it does." He just about lights up at the question, since he knows where this is going. I draw out of him the fact that Brubaker was a drug dealer who preyed on local high school kids. One of those kids, Joey Davidson, died of an overdose, and Brubaker was arrested in connection with it.

"Who was Joey Davidson?" I ask.

"He was Billy's nephew. His sister's kid."

"Was Brubaker convicted of that crime?"

"No, he got off on a technicality. Mishandling of evidence."

I frown, as if this is unpleasant news to me. "And how did Billy react?"

"He was very upset. He said he wanted to put a bullet in his head, so he couldn't destroy any more kids."

"And did he put a bullet in his head?"

"No. But he watched him, on his own time when he was off duty, and caught him doing it again."

"So he arrested him?"

"No, he called in backup to do it. That way Brubaker's lawyer couldn't claim that Billy set him up, and the case wouldn't be compromised."

"How did it turn out?"

"Brubaker got thirty years."

"Thank you."

This testimony from Sanford is a little risky. In truth it shows that Billy had a grudge against Brubaker, and it caused him to go above and beyond the call of duty to nail him. It could be thought by some to show that Billy acts on his grudges, and that in Erskine's case he just took it a major step further.

On the positive side, it showed that Billy operated within the law and did not commit violence against someone deserving of it. Billy could probably have killed Brubaker and gotten away with it, but he chose to risk the legal system messing up again.

I have less luck with the other two people at the bar that night, since they are not friends of Billy and have no reluctance to testify against him.

Eli has successfully conveyed to the jury that Billy had a grudge against Erskine, was at the scene of the murder, and had a gun in his hand.

It's getting ugly.

. . . . .

LAURIE IS AT the courthouse waiting for me when the afternoon session ends. This no doubt means big news, good or bad. Since 95 percent of all news has been bad lately, I'm not too thrilled to see her.

Once again, I'm wrong.

"I spoke to Santiago," she says. "He saw you on the show last night. He's willing to talk, but he wants immunity."

"Did you tell him I have no authority to do that?"

"Of course not."

"Good. Where is he now?"

"He wouldn't say, but caller ID showed he was at a pay phone outside Detroit. He'll be here tomorrow evening, so I would imagine he's driving."

"We could have sent someone to get him."

"I told him that, but he wanted to do it himself. He sounded really scared."

"Is he coming to the house?"

"He's meeting Marcus at seven o'clock at the corner of Broadway and Thirty-third, and Marcus will bring him to the house."

"Perfect. Did you describe Marcus to him? If he's going to be our witness, I'd just as soon he not have a heart attack."

"I tried, but Marcus is pretty hard to describe."

Laurie and I go back to the house, where Marcus has been standing guard on Milo. The dogs are in the kitchen, because that's where Marcus is. Marcus is in the kitchen because that's where the refrigerator is, though by the time we get home the refrigerator is empty.

Court is not in session tomorrow, so that Judge Catchings can attend to what he calls housekeeping issues. Mostly that means attending to matters on his docket that he has fallen behind on, and dealing with motions that Eli and I have filed along the way.

I am going to use this occasion to give Catchings and Eli a preview of our defense, and to obtain approval from Catchings for our approach. This will be one of the key moments in the trial; if Catchings rules against us, Billy might as well change his plea to guilty.

I continue to be impressed by both Hike's legal skills and his preparation. I had told him what we'd be talking about tonight, and he's researched the matter thoroughly. I have very little to do, basically just listen to him and try to remember the points he's making.

The meeting in Catchings's chambers is at two o'clock, which gives me time to keep an appointment with Colonel William Mickelson, Erskine's immediate superior. As promised, he's in New York for the day, and has offered me thirty minutes of his time.

To be more precise, the colonel's aide, Sergeant Brosnan, told me the colonel would "grant" me the thirty minutes. She said it in such a way that I should consider myself blessed, but for some reason I didn't.

New York's bridges are consistently underrated. The George Washington gets some props, and the Brooklyn gets included in jokes about con men trying to sell it to unsuspecting dupes, but that's pretty much it.

Yet New York has some spectacular bridges that surprisingly never get mentioned. Maybe it's a naming issue. "Throgs Neck" and "Tappan Zee" don't exactly roll off the tongue, and certainly don't evoke the image that "Golden Gate" does. But they're both actually spectacular, as is the one I'm currently under, the Verrazano-Narrows Bridge.

I'm at Fort Hamilton, which rests below the bridge in Brooklyn, and which serves as one of only two US Army bases in New York State. The other is Camp Drum, all the way up in frigid Watertown. If you are going to be stationed in New York and you like pizza, or civilization, you're considerably better off here.

Fort Hamilton basically exists as a home for the Army Corps of Engineers, but it is Hamilton that Colonel Mickelson is using as his base of operations while in New York. It doesn't really feel like an army post; certainly you don't see platoons jogging in lockstep and chanting, *I want to be an Airborne Ranger; I want to live a life of danger.*

Colonel Mickelson looks like he could defend Fort

Hamilton by himself if Staten Island ever declared war and invaded. About forty-five, he appears to be in as good a shape as someone twenty years younger. His face is chiseled in a young Kirk Douglas kind of way, and everything about him says, *Don't you dare bullshit me.*

If Jack Nicholson looked like this when he yelled that Tom Cruise couldn't handle the truth, Cruise would have said, *Yes, you're right, I'm sorry. My bad.*

"Carpenter, you've got fifteen minutes" is how he greets me, which I assume is army-talk for "Hello. Nice to meet you."

"I was granted half an hour," I say.

"Shit happens."

"Did General Prentice tell you what I wanted to discuss?" I ask.

"You trying to pull rank on me?"

"I was hoping he already did that."

He nods. "You want to talk about Erskine."

"Yes. What are the chances he conspired with the five soldiers under him to deliberately let that suicide bomber get by the checkpoint?"

"Somewhere between ninety-nine and a hundred and one percent."

That's the last thing I expected him to say, and I immediately shelve my next five questions, since they're now unnecessary. "Why did the investigative report not even mention the possibility of intent?"

"No proof. They put in those reports what they know, not what they suspect. Otherwise it's all downside."

"What do you mean?"

"If they say they think it was a crime, then they look incompetent for not arresting the bad guys, the overall publicity is a disaster, and they get sued by the families of the victims. You see much upside in that?"

"What about 'truth is its own reward'?" I ask.

"You're using your fifteen minutes to ask questions like that?"

"Are you familiar with the circumstances surrounding the explosion?"

"Of course. I was there," he says.

That surprises me; the report did not mention that Mickelson was at the scene that day. "What are the chances that the oil minister was not the target?"

He reacts slightly; the question has surprised him. "Why do you ask that?"

"You're using up my fifteen minutes to ask questions?" I ask.

"Don't be a wise-ass."

"I'm told that once the girl got inside the checkpoint, she could have gone anywhere. She took her time, but she didn't get near the minister. He almost survived, while most of the others were killed instantly."

He thinks about this for a solid one of my fifteen minutes. "So who was the target?"

I shrug. "I don't know; I'm not there yet." I don't bother to add that the obvious way to figure out who the target was just hit me. I make it a rule never to reveal anything to anyone until I know how it will play out for my client. "But I know about other targets," I say.

"That's a little cryptic for me," he says.

"I believe at least two of the discharged soldiers have been killed. Another is heading here even as we speak."

"To turn himself in?"

"To talk to me first."

"Make sure you provide adequate protection."

"That will be in the hands of the state police."

He ponders this for a few moments. "Looks like the army's version may undergo a slight revision." He doesn't seem thrilled at the prospect; if Santiago talks, it will make the army's whitewash version of a report seem inept. "We should talk to Santiago first," he says. "This is an army matter."

"Not anymore; he's been discharged. And the army had plenty of time to talk to him when they did their report."

He nods, recognizing the truth of that statement. "Maybe next time they'll be more thorough."

I use up the rest of my time asking him if he had any idea what might have been in the envelope that Erskine handed over to his killer before Milo swooped in and ran off with it.

He professes to have no idea, but adds, "If you find out, let me know."

"If I find out, I'll let the jury know."

"You know, I met your client on one of my trips over there. He's a first-class, stand-up guy. You think you can get him off?"

"If I can't get him off, nothing else matters."

"You mean the truth isn't its own reward?" he asks.

"Not even close."

• • • • •

"YOUR HONOR, WE believe the Erskine murder was just the beginning." That is how I begin the meeting with Judge Catchings and Eli in the judge's chambers. It's lead counsels only; Hike and Eli's three assistants have not been invited, at my request. This is going to be an argument I need to win, so I want it kept as focused as possible.

"It all goes back to that day in Iraq, when eighteen people were killed and my client lost his leg. After the conclusion of the army's investigation, Erskine quietly resigned his commission, and five other soldiers on duty that day were discharged.

"We have reason to believe that at least two of those soldiers have since been killed, we cannot trace two others, and the fifth is in fear of his life."

I can tell that Eli already does not like where this is

going. "You have reason to believe they've been killed," he repeats. "Does that mean you lack hard evidence? Like bodies?"

"We have evidence, compelling but not conclusive," I say. "Certainly we can demonstrate that they have disappeared under mysterious circumstances."

"I trust you'll be submitting this evidence to the court for consideration?" Catchings asks.

"We will, Your Honor, at the conclusion of this meeting. At the very least we believe it is sufficiently powerful and relevant to the Erskine murder to warrant presentation to the jury."

"I certainly look forward to seeing it as well," says Eli. "But the fact that two men may have disappeared does not seem on the surface to be significant. They all knew one another in the army; maybe they went off on a trip together. Or maybe they heard that Erskine was killed and feared that someone was trying to exact revenge on them for their apparent negligence in Iraq. That could have sent them all into hiding."

"I wish you would save this stuff for your closing argument, Eli. Because if the jury sees this evidence, they'll laugh you out of the courtroom."

"I haven't heard much laughter so far," Eli says.

"Relax, gentlemen. I'll examine the evidence and reserve judgment," Catchings says. "What about the fifth soldier, the one you said fears for his life?"

I nod. "Thank you, I was about to get to that. I should be speaking with him this evening. After I speak with him, I expect he will need protection, and I would appreciate it if you would order the state police to do that on a contingency basis."

Laurie and I had debated this, and we decided that we wanted Marcus to continue keeping an eye on the house, and Milo. I also like the idea of having Judge Catchings order the protection; it has the effect of making him at least slightly vested in the effort.

Catchings agrees to order the state police to provide the protection, if I consider it necessary. "But this is not a free ride," he says. "I don't want him taking in a Broadway show while he's in town. And if you can't determine in good faith that he has relevant and important testimony to provide for this trial, do not attempt to put this order into effect."

That is a reasonable condition to impose, and I agree to it.

"What is his name?" Catchings asks.

"Raymond Santiago."

Catchings picks up the phone and directs the clerk to reach Captain Robert Dessens of the New Jersey State Police. Once that is accomplished, he issues the protection order verbally, with the written order to follow.

The arrangement is made by which I will contact Dessens if protection is necessary, and tell him where they can pick up Santiago. The truth is that I have no idea if Santiago will willingly allow himself to be taken into custody. I may have to scare him into it.

Based on my performance in this case so far, the best way to scare Santiago would be to threaten to become his lawyer.

I head home after the meeting, fairly pleased with how it went. I believe that Judge Catchings will probably rule our evidence admissible, since it seems at least worthy of jury consideration. I also believe that in a first-

degree case like this, he would be loath to preclude what
is essentially the entire defense case. That would be the
kind of maneuver that appeals courts would take a very
careful look at.

I tell Laurie what transpired over an early dinner.
We're both anxious to talk to Santiago, a meeting that has
become even more important since I took what was a cal-
culated risk in the meeting with Catchings and Eli.

By dangling Santiago out there as I did, and by asking
for protection for him, I portrayed him as someone
important to our case. If he turns out to be a dud and provides nothing whatsoever that we can use, it will therefore make us look bad, and might make Catchings less
inclined to respect our position.

When we finish dinner, I take out the diagram from
the army report on the bombing. It places all of the victims in their positions when the blast went off, though the
way the bodies were scattered, I don't know how accurate it could be.

According to the diagram, the two closest victims to
the bomber were Iraqi bureaucrats. Next in order were a
French businesswoman, a German businessman, and then
Stanley Freeman and his protégé, Alex Bryant. Had the
bomber chosen to, she could have gotten considerably
closer to the oil minister, but she did not.

I'm far from ready to say that any of these people
were the targets, but it's something interesting for me to
follow up on.

Once I've finished with the file, I still have about half
an hour until Santiago's expected arrival with Marcus. I
use that time to do an abbreviated trust session with Milo.

It seems to go well; they always seem to go well. But

pretty soon I'm going to put it to the test, and then we'll know if I've been wasting my time.

"What's the story, Milo? You been playing me for a sucker?"

Milo just stares at me, stone-faced and noncommittal. He's playing it close to the vest, no doubt a tactic he learned at the police academy. I look over at Tara, who stares right back at me, defiant and still not about to give up her friend.

I'm locked with the two of them in a serious battle of the minds, and I'm coming in third.

•   •   •   •   •

MARCUS CALLS AND tells Laurie that he and Santiago are on the way. I was afraid the man would take one look at Marcus and decide he'd rather be back in the war zone, but that apparently is not the case. It's not a great early sign; if he's not afraid of Marcus, it's unlikely I'll scare him into submission.

Marcus pulls the car into my garage, and he and Santiago come inside. Santiago's a big guy, at least six two, 220 pounds, and he has an air of confidence about him that surprises me. It's hard to reconcile with Laurie's comment that he had sounded very frightened on the phone; he's obviously used the intervening time to compose himself.

Santiago and I go into the den, with Laurie and Marcus staying behind. Laurie and I have discussed this, and we think I'll have a better chance of getting something out of Santiago one-on-one.

Santiago wastes no time on chitchat. "Billy didn't do Erskine," he says. "No chance."

"Do you know who did?" I ask.

He nods. "I don't know who pulled the trigger, but I know who paid for the gun and the bullets."

"Who might that be?"

He answers a question with a question; never a good sign. "You find Jason?" he asks.

"Greer?" Jason Greer is one of the two soldiers we've learned nothing about in our investigation.

"Yeah. You find him?"

"Not yet," I say.

"Then I'm your only chance. Because they would have gone after him first."

"Why?"

"Because they think he's the only one who knows. But it ain't true. He told me."

"Told you what?"

"I want full immunity, and guaranteed entry into the witness protection program."

"I'm not a government official," I point out.

"So make it happen."

"You need to give me something; that's the only way I can help you. There are some things we know, but—"

He interrupts me midsentence, which is just as well, since I wasn't sure how to finish it. "You know nothing," he says. "And you have no interest in helping me. You want to get your client off the hook, and I can do that for you."

I decide to go at this from a different direction. "Who was the target that day?"

"In Baghdad?"

"Yes. Who was the target of the bomber?"

"I don't have the slightest idea, and I couldn't care less."

"So what was your job?"

"To make sure she got in. Once we made sure of that, whoever she went after was way, way above my pay grade."

I keep running into walls. "What do you want immunity for?"

"For the eighteen people who died that day. If I talk, the shit is going to hit the fan, and I want to be well out of the way."

"What about money? Nobody gets rich in witness protection." Since we know that the other two soldiers left large amounts of cash behind, I'm fishing to find out if Santiago has similarly enriched himself.

"Money's not a problem; don't worry about it."

I nod. "Okay, here are my terms. I'm going to get you protected by the state police; the judge has already ordered it. Once you're safe, I will try to get you immunity. It's not going to be easy, because generally a person in your position needs to reveal a part of his future testimony as a sign of good faith."

I expect him to rebel against the idea of state police protection, but he does not. Maybe he's not as confident and unafraid as he appears. He accepts my terms, which is not exactly a triumph for me, since those terms have been dramatically scaled back from my original goal. I've learned nothing, and according to Santiago I know nothing.

Business as usual.

I call Captain Dessens, who has disliked me for a

very long time. We've had run-ins on a few cases, and he makes no effort to conceal his disdain for me. Therefore it gives me some pleasure to be able to give him his marching orders in this case, and I tell him that Santiago is ready to be picked up.

It takes Dessens's officers about twenty minutes to get here, during which time Santiago and I sit in fairly uncomfortable silence. The frustrating part for me is that I believe him when he says he has the answers to my questions, and the logical extension of that is he probably can get Billy acquitted.

That is my primary goal, of course, but this situation has also become intellectually personal for me. If Billy were to get off tomorrow on a technicality, I would stay on this case, trying to find out the truth, for two reasons.

I don't want whoever killed eighteen people to get away with mass murder.

And I'm sick of being in the dark.

• • • • •

CAPTAIN ROBERT DESSENS was pissed
off. That would by no means qualify as breaking news;
after twenty-one years on the job "pissed off" had become his natural order of things. But the situation he was
now finding himself in kicked it up to a new level of annoyance.

First there was having to deal with Carpenter. As far
as Dessens was concerned, defense lawyers placed just
above pedophiles on the low-life scale, and Carpenter
was the worst of the bunch. Dessens fully understood that
defense lawyers had their job to do; he just would rather
they did it on a planet other than earth.

He was not opposed to all possible dealings with
Carpenter. For instance, he would take great pleasure
in arresting him. But having to wait for Carpenter's

phone call, and then having to take his instructions on when and where to pick up the witness, was asking too much.

Then there was the witness himself. Dessens didn't know Santiago, in fact knew almost nothing about him, which was precisely the point. The Erskine murder was a case that Dessens's state police were not involved in, not even peripherally. They had more than enough on their plate already; to have to use manpower to protect Santiago was a drain that contained no upside.

As if all of that were not enough to drive Dessens nuts, he was being forced to deal with the feds. Almost as soon as Judge Catchings issued the order, Dessens received word from the state chief of police that FBI and US Army investigators wanted to question Santiago the moment he was taken into protective custody.

If Dessens were more introspective, he might have seen the irony. It was commonplace for him to be resentful at what he saw as intrusion by the feds in his cases. In this situation, he was experiencing the same feeling even though it wasn't his case, and in fact he was resentful about being involved himself.

So Dessens found himself sitting in room 242 at the Marriott hotel, adjacent to the Paramus Park shopping center. With him were Special Agent Wilbur Briggs and US Army Captain Derek Meade. The room was what the hotel considered a junior suite, and sat at the far end of the hallway, flanked by two adjacent rooms that the state police had also taken over for their officers.

"You going to question him separately?" Dessens asked Briggs and Meade. Ordinarily he wouldn't care what they did, except for the fact that he was under instructions from his chief not to leave until they were finished with their interrogation.

"No," Briggs said. "And it won't take long, because he won't say a word without immunity."

Meade nodded his agreement. "It's jerk-off time."

Dessens checked his watch. Twenty minutes since his officers picked up Santiago from Carpenter's house. They should be showing up anytime. With any luck Dessens could be heading home in an hour, in time to watch the Yankees game from the West Coast.

While the men in the room did not expect Santiago to say anything when he arrived, the officers transporting him to the hotel couldn't get him to shut up. Maybe it was nervous energy, but Santiago was waxing semi-eloquent on baseball, politics, police procedure, and women, not necessarily in that order.

Occasionally the two officers would make eye contact with each other in the front seat, conveying their common feeling that they would be quite happy when they deposited Santiago and got the hell out of there.

They pulled up to the front of the hotel, where another two officers were waiting. The two in the front seat got out of the car, while the two waiting scanned the area for any sign of danger. Seeing none, they opened the door, and Santiago got out.

The moment Santiago's head rose above the car, it ceased to exist. A bullet crashed into it, entering through the right temple and exploding on impact.

The officers dove for cover. Neither was attempting to protect Santiago; they were not Secret Service, and he was sure as hell not the president. One look at him would have dissuaded them anyway; unless he had a spare head in the trunk, protecting him would be as futile an act as one could imagine.

M had used a silencer, and therefore the men in room 242 had no idea what happened outside. It was three minutes before the officers at the front of the hotel decided that the killer was no longer a present danger, and at that point they called Captain Dessens and told him what had happened.

Dessens immediately called homicide, which would come in with a full team. He, Briggs, and Meade rushed downstairs, but by that point there was nothing to be done.

Dessens knew that, just as certainly as he knew one other thing.

He was going to miss the Yankees game.

• • • • •

JUDGES DO NOT call me at home. Not ever. There is more of a chance that the president of the United States will call and invite me to a state dinner, or that Tom Coughlin will call and ask me to quarterback the Giants.

A judge would view such a call as somehow crossing a line that judges have no interest in crossing. If they have something to tell me, and I happen to be at home, they have the court clerk call and summon me to their office.

So when I hear Judge Catchings's voice on the other end of the phone, at ten PM, I immediately get a sick feeling in the pit of my stomach. I hate stomach-pit feelings, so I gird myself for the worst. I'm in bed with Laurie next to me, and I sit up leaning on one elbow, which is my preferred girding position.

When I say, "Hello, Your Honor," Laurie sits up,

knowing that this must be something important. Tara and Milo are at the end of the bed, but they seem considerably less concerned.

"Mr. Morrison is on the call with us," the judge says, referring to Eli. Eli stays quiet; he's here primarily to listen. "Raymond Santiago was shot and killed a little over an hour ago. His killer has not been apprehended, and at this point his identity and whereabouts are unknown."

My initial reaction to the news has nothing to do with the case. Instead I have what seems to be a surreal comprehension that the young man who was in this house a few hours ago, whom I was talking to and whose protection I arranged, is no longer alive.

Intellectually, I understand that these things happen, but when they do, they still don't seem quite real or possible.

"What happened to the protection?" I ask. It's a pretty ridiculous question, but the only one I can think of in the moment.

"He was in the process of being protected when he died," Judge Catchings says, drily.

Turning my attention to the trial, I would assess this news as an almost total disaster. I qualify it with "almost" because, while the loss of Santiago's information and testimony is devastating, his murder will surely compel the judge to let us put this line of defense in front of the jury.

"Your Honor, the jury needs to hear this."

"I agree. I'll be issuing a ruling to that effect in the morning."

"Your Honor," Eli finally says, "our objections to this have not changed."

"Noted."

"And we would like an opportunity to be heard once again."

"Denied. Anything else?"

"Yes," I say. "I would like to go down to the scene of the crime as soon as I get off this call. I'll need permission to be arranged for Laurie Collins and me to be allowed in."

"Mr. Morrison?" the judge asks, the implication obvious.

"I'll take care of it," Eli says.

"Good. See you tomorrow, gentlemen."

As soon as I hang up, I tell Laurie what has happened. We watch television as we dress. The news coverage has begun, and reporters are on the scene with camera crews. Santiago's name has not yet been released, and the reporters are obviously not aware of any connection between him and the Zimmerman case.

Laurie and I get in the car and head to the crime scene. The officers manning the periphery have been alerted, and we are let in, though cautioned not to interfere with the forensics people doing their work.

We look around, and not surprisingly Laurie sees the events from a cop's perspective, speculating on how the killer could have known where Santiago was going. "He had to have information," she says. "There's no way he could have followed him and pulled that off. He had to be in position, waiting for him to arrive."

"Where was he?" I ask.

She points. "I would say in either of those buildings. Probably in an upper-floor window. They'll be able to pinpoint it pretty easily. But the shooter didn't just show up; this was all set up in advance."

"Maybe Santiago told the wrong person," I say.

She shakes her head. "Not possible. Santiago didn't know where he was going; he didn't even know he was going into custody until you told him tonight."

I start to wonder out loud if I could have given it away to someone, but Laurie correctly points out that I didn't know where Santiago was to be held, either. "The leak had to be with the police," she says.

We walk toward the lobby of the hotel, which has been set up as a police command center. Captain Dessens and I see each other at the same time.

"Oh, shit," he says. I often bring out that reaction in people.

"Well, if it isn't the great protector," I say.

"What do you want, Carpenter?"

"I want to know who shot my witness."

"You'll be the first one I tell when we find out. So..."

"What are they doing here?" I ask, pointing to a uniformed army officer, talking to a man whom Central Casting would send in if I were looking for an FBI agent. I'm surprised they're here, and very surprised that the army could be here this soon.

"They were waiting to question your boy."

That really pisses me off, since Santiago was to be my witness. The fact that the feds were going to take first crack at him is both annoying and now moot. I try to talk to them about it, but they wave me off.

As we're leaving, I walk up to Dessens and say, "See you next week."

"Where?"

"You'll be on the witness stand, and I'll be walking around in front of you. Should be fun."

● ● ● ● ●

TODAY IS SCIENCE day, and Eli starts the morning court session by bringing in his forensics witnesses. The first is Police Sergeant Roger Halicki, a seasoned veteran who has no doubt spent more days in court than I have.

Halicki and Eli go through the rehearsed testimony without missing a beat, and the jury pays complete attention for the two hours it takes to go through it. Billy had gunpowder residue on his hand and blood on his shirt, both of which are thoroughly incriminating.

By the time I get up, I don't know whether to cross-examine him or change our plea to guilty.

"Sergeant Halicki, in the diagram you showed, am I wrong in thinking that the gunpowder residue was concentrated on the right side of the right hand of Mr. Zimmerman?"

"You're correct."

"Is that normal?" I ask.

"I'm not sure there is a normal. But it could be explained by various factors; for instance, the victim was shot at close range. He could have been grabbing for the gun as the trigger was being pulled."

"Did you find residue on the victim's hand?"

Halicki shakes his head. "No."

"But if he had such residue, that would have been a possible explanation for the pattern found on Mr. Zimmerman?"

"Yes."

"So if someone else was holding the gun along with Mr. Zimmerman, that would help explain it?"

"I'm not aware of anyone else who was holding the gun at the time."

I nod. "So therefore you didn't test anyone else."

"Correct."

I've gotten as much as I can out of this, which isn't much, so I change the subject. "You said there were two shots fired, one of which hit and killed Mr. Erskine. Where did the other shot go?"

I let him use the diagram of the scene that Eli employed, and Halicki shows that the other bullet was found down and across the street.

"So it was fired in a completely different direction from where the victim was standing?"

"Yes," he says.

"Any idea why?"

"Again, if the victim were wrestling for the gun..."

"Excuse me, Sergeant Halicki, but is this the same wrestling match we've already determined you have no evidence of ever happening?"

Eli objects that I'm being argumentative, and Catchings sustains.

"Can you tell if the gunpowder residue on Mr. Zimmerman's hand was from the first or second bullet?" I ask.

"No, we cannot determine that."

"Is it possible the second shot was aimed at the dog, Milo? Others have testified that he was running off with the envelope in that direction."

"I have no way of knowing that," Halicki says.

"Do you own a dog?" I ask, already knowing the answer.

"I do."

"As a dog owner, does it make sense to you that Mr. Zimmerman would arrange for his dog to take the envelope, and then try to shoot him once he had done so?"

"I couldn't say."

"But you would agree that the shot missed badly?" I ask.

"Yes."

"Sergeant, if Mr. Zimmerman were going to shoot Mr. Erskine, why bother to have the dog steal the envelope? Why not just take it from him after he was shot?"

Eli objects that Halicki cannot be expected to read Billy's mind, so I withdraw the question and move on.

"Now, where did you catch Mr. Zimmerman?"

"What do you mean?"

"I mean where was he, and how did you find him? Maybe an anonymous tip, or security trapped him at an airport trying to leave the country? That kind of thing."

"He was at the scene," he says.

I feign surprise; I am a terrific surprise feigner. "So there was a shoot-out?"

"No."

"Was he holding the gun when you arrived? Maybe threatening to shoot some hostages?"

"No."

"Where was the gun?"

"On the ground next to Mr. Erskine's body."

I'm wearing my most confused face. "About how long after the shooting did the police arrive?"

"Less than ten minutes."

"And he just hung out waiting for you?"

"He was on the scene," he repeats, making little effort to conceal his annoyance.

"So if I can sum up your testimony so far, your theory is that Mr. Zimmerman directed his dog to steal an envelope from the victim, which the dog did. Mr. Zimmerman then shot Mr. Erskine, after which he turned and tried to shoot his own dog, who had the envelope.

"Failing that, Mr. Zimmerman decided to hang out with the body until the police could get there to arrest him. Is that about it?"

Not surprisingly, Halicki argues with my version, and after a few minutes I move on.

"So let me try it another way. Here's a hypothetical, based on your testimony. If another person were there, wrestling with Mr. Zimmerman for the gun, could that explain the strange residue pattern, the fact that a shot was taken at Milo, and the fact that the shot missed badly?"

"I'm not aware of any other man being present," he says, which irritates me.

"Are you familiar with the concept of hypothetical questions?"

"Of course I am."

"Great, then please answer the one I asked. Hypothetically, could the presence of another man, the shooter, have caused all these factors to occur?"

He'd love to avoid answering the question, but can't figure out a way to do so. "It's hypothetically possible," he says.

"Glad to hear it."

As soon as court is over I call Colonel Mickelson, and I'm put right through to him. It could be due to his continuing desire to suck up to Kevin's brother-in-law, General Prentice, or it could be that he's very interested in any developments in this case. Or both.

"Too bad about Santiago," he says when I mention the murder.

I'm annoyed that an FBI agent and army investigator were at the scene to question Santiago, and I ask him if he had any part in it.

"Sure," he says. "Captain Meade was there on my orders. But I can't speak to the presence of the FBI agent."

"You were interfering with my witness."

"Back on the streets, I think the expression we would use as a response to that comment is 'tough shit.'"

I don't think I've fully intimidated him.

"You think our conversation was in confidence?" he asks. "What am I, your priest?"

"Santiago was—"

"Santiago was a soldier, and he was corrupt. And people died because of him, some of whom were in my command. Now, you may think I'm fine with that, and I'll just back off and let you go about your business. But that's not how the army operates; we take care of our own, and we deal with them when they need to be dealt with."

"So Santiago is dead," I say.

"That's not my fault."

"Somebody tipped the shooter off."

"And when we find out who that was, they will be dealt with. But if you're trying to find him in the army, you're wasting your time."

"Right, I forgot. Your men are pure as the driven snow. Erskine, and Chambers, and Lawson, and Iverson, and Greer, and Santiago, they were all choirboys."

"You left out Zimmerman," he says, a trace of amusement in his voice. My anger is having absolutely no impression on him.

"Billy Zimmerman is the only innocent one in the bunch."

"So go into court and prove it."

• • • • •

KATHY BRYANT HAD hoped never to see me
again. This doesn't exactly distinguish her from many
other women I've known in my life, but her reason is better than most. Talking to me rips the scab off the open
wound that is her husband's death.

This time she's allowed me into her Teaneck home,
probably having determined that even though I'm an ir-
ritant, I don't present a physical danger. She even offers
me coffee, a gracious gesture that I appreciate and accept.

"How is your trial going?" she asks. "I'm afraid I
don't follow the news much anymore."

"It's difficult," I understate. "But now we get to put
on our case."

"Good luck," she says. "If your client is innocent, that
is."

"Thank you."

"What is it you wanted to talk to me about?" she asks, with unconcealed wariness in her voice. If she weren't so polite, she would be cringing openly.

"Something you mentioned to me last time we talked," I say. "You said that Alex was stressed about work, especially in the last couple of months. You said he wasn't sleeping well, and that the quality of your lives depended on things like the price of oil and gold."

She nods, the memory all too fresh. "Yes."

"I know it can't be pleasant to think back on this, but I'd appreciate it if you'd try. Can you recall any specific things that upset him, or anything he mentioned to you about it?"

"No, it was always general; he didn't like to talk about work. He said he didn't want to bring it home with him, but of course it was with him all the time."

"Might there have been any conversations you over-heard? Anything that related to why he was stressed?"

"I need to ask you a question," she says.

"Of course."

"Why do you want to know all this? Alex was a bystander that day; he wasn't the target. How could it possibly benefit your case to know why he was stressed?"

Moment-of-truth time. I should gloss over this, not tell her what I'm getting at. It's a shot in the dark, and there's no reason she has to enter the tunnel with me.

On the other hand, if I were her I would want to know and judge it for myself. "He may not have been a by-stander," I say. "I'm not saying that for sure; I'm not even saying it's probable. But there's a chance."

She nods, but doesn't say anything for at least one full minute. Finally, "There is one thing that might help you."

"What is that?"

"We were watching the news one night; it must have been the ten o'clock news, because we were in bed. I think I was reading, so I wasn't paying much attention to the television."

"Okay…"

"Something Alex saw upset him; I could feel him tense up. He immediately grabbed the phone and made a call."

"Do you know who he called?"

She nods. "I heard him say Stanley, so it must have been Stanley Freeman. Alex walked out of the room as he was making the call, but I heard him say, 'Stanley, did you hear what happened?'"

"And you didn't hear any more of the conversation?"

"No. But he was on the phone for a long time…maybe fifteen minutes. For him to call Mr. Freeman at that hour, I knew it was something very important. But when Alex came back, he tried to shrug it off, as if it were nothing."

"Do you know what Alex saw on television that upset him?"

"No. But…"

She gets up and goes to the desk, opening the drawer and looking through some envelopes and papers. She seems to find what she's looking for, and takes a few moments to read it.

"I can tell you it was on Friday, March fourteenth."

"Are you sure about that?"

"Yes, because the next day was my niece's second birthday, and we were supposed to go to her party. But Alex told me in the morning that he couldn't go, that he had something he had to take care of at work. I knew it had to concern whatever he spoke to Mr. Freeman about, but I didn't ask him."

"Do you know what channel you were watching?" I ask.

"Definitely Channel Five. That's the only local news we watch."

I stand. "Thank you, this could turn out to be very helpful. If you think of anything else, please call me at any time."

"I will. And Mr. Carpenter, if you learn anything about Alex's...about Alex's death...that is different from what I've been told, I want to know about it immediately. Please."

"You have my word."

I call Hike on the way home, and relate my conversation with Kathy Bryant to him. I ask him to immediately get on to the task of getting a copy of that night's news broadcast. "If they give you any problem, ask the court to subpoena it. Judge Catchings will approve it in a second."

"I'm on it," he says. "And I'll get the other stations as well; if she was reading, she could be wrong about the station."

"Good idea. Thanks."

Hike just volunteered to do extra work. Can Edna be far behind?

"MILO, TODAY IS showtime." If Milo doesn't trust me enough to find the envelope by now, he's never going to. And since this is the Sunday before we present the defense case, there couldn't be a better time.

Laurie and Marcus are in charge of security, and Willie is along to provide extra backup. Hike has gone on ahead to prepare for his role, and I've allowed Laurie to hire two off-duty cops to help out as well. They are two guys Pete recommended, and whom Laurie already knew.

Billy had said that there was more chance that Milo would deliver if we did it late at night, so as to mimic the actual event. But that creates too many dangers, and I'm just not going to risk it.

It's a tricky operation to pull off. We are all cognizant of the danger to Milo; Santiago's death removed any doubt that our enemy is resourceful and ruthless. So maximum security is required, but we have to avoid freaking Milo out. We need him as relaxed as possible.

Laurie attaches the GPS device to Milo's collar, and we all examine a diagram of the neighborhood surrounding the bar. This is not the first time we've studied it; speaking for myself, by now I know it better than the Paterson streets where I live. We go over where each of us will be during the operation; no matter which direction Milo goes, some of us will be in position to follow him.

Of course, if he just sits there like he did last time, he'll be fairly easy to follow.

Marcus grunts a signal to Laurie that the coast is clear, and we're on our way in what amounts to a deceptive caravan, since we're pretty spread out to avoid attracting attention. Milo is in the backseat of my car with Willie, who has coaxed him into laying his head on his lap. Willie seems unconcerned that his own head remains in the line of fire.

When we arrive, we all go to our designated spots. Hike stands in the position where Erskine stood, in front of the bar. I stand where Billy stood, and Willie puts Milo in the place where he waited for the signal from Billy that night.

Today the signal will come from me, the guy Milo does or does not trust.

Everybody else fans out, in the general direction that Milo ran that night with the envelope. We all have GPS monitors and small walkie-talkies, so if he gets out of our sight, we'll be able to track him quickly. I'm very nervous about the whole thing, but Milo looks serenely confident. According to Billy, Milo is great under pressure. If I'm ever stuck in a war in a dog-hole, Milo is the guy I want next to me.

Of course, just as we're ready to begin the action, it starts to rain. Not a pleasant, drizzly summer rain, but a strong downpour, with the drops banging up off the pavement as they hit. As the commanding general of this operation, I have to make a decision: go or no go.

I opt for go; we've come too far to turn back now, and to do it again just increases the danger. Besides, Milo shows no sign of being affected by the rain. He's just sitting there patiently, waiting for his cue.

Hike looks somewhat less joyful than Milo; I'm assuming that standing out in the rain in front of a bar, and not being able to go in, dry off, and order a drink, is not his idea of a good time. It's becoming quite conceivable that Hike doesn't possess an idea of a good time. At least I haven't discovered it.

Laurie represents the command center; everybody is supposed to call in to her and report when they are set. Finally she gives me the signal...whenever I'm ready.

I motion to Hike, who nods and slowly starts to walk down to where Erskine stood when he was shot. Milo watches him and then turns to me, and I consider that a hopeful sign. He seems to be waiting for a signal.

Hike reaches the spot and stands there for a few moments. Milo seems to tense a little, maybe sensing that his moment is coming. As planned, Hike waits for about ninety seconds before taking an envelope out of his pocket. It's a letter-size manila envelope, which is what Billy believes Erskine was carrying. Inside the open envelope is a piece of Erskine's shirt; we are covering all the bases.

Once I see this, I make the hand motion to Milo that signifies he is supposed to make his move. He reacts immediately, jumping up and running toward Hike, who holds out the envelope while recoiling as if he is about to be run over by enemy tanks.

Milo launches in the air, truly an amazing sight each time I see it. He grabs the envelope out of Hike's hand, much as he did from Juliet the last time we tried this. Of course, last time he just sat afterward looking for a treat, so this is the moment of truth.

And he runs...full speed, the envelope in his mouth. He runs back past the bar, just as he is reported to have done that night.

"He's on the move!" I yell into the walkie-talkie, and I hear everybody's excited response on the other end. I start running after Milo, though I don't want to get too close, since I'm afraid he'll stop and come running back to me for a treat.

Within seconds it becomes obvious that my running is a waste of time and oxygen; Milo is out of my sight after a few strides. The last I see of him he is making a right turn at the corner and heading up a small hill.

I report this to the others, then run to my car. I start the car and drive in the direction I saw Milo run, checking my GPS periodically. GPS reading is not my strength; I certainly hope my fellow GPSers can do better.

They can. With Laurie directing the way, they keep close tabs on Milo, and I'm able to head in that general direction in my car.

"Roosevelt Park!" Laurie yells. "Near the tennis courts."

It's a park about six blocks from the bar, fairly small

and very quiet. At this time of day, there might be a few people playing tennis, and perhaps some mothers watching their children play on swing sets. Though I would imagine the rain would have scared them off already.

Except for Hike, I'm the last of our group to get there, so I just head for the collection of parked cars. I park as well, then jump out and run toward the tennis courts. I see Laurie, Marcus, Willie, and the two off-duty cops, but I don't see Milo. When I get closer, I realize that they are blocking the view, and he is just behind them.

Milo is digging furiously in some brush and dirt. The area has gotten muddy because of the rain, but he doesn't seem to mind. The envelope that he just took from Hike lies on the ground nearby.

Watching Milo dig is mesmerizing—his legs pump furiously, and the dirt and brush and mud go flying. He's like a canine shovel, and in seconds we see it, the envelope we've been searching for, lying there exposed.

Laurie reaches in, takes it out of the hole, and hands it to me. I wipe some of the dirt off and tear it open as neatly as I can. I can't imagine that the buried and now wet envelope could have fingerprints or other forensic material on it, but I'm careful anyway. Inside the envelope is a packet of papers, fastened together with a paper clip.

The cover sheet is blank. And so are the rest.

Except for the last one.

Which says, "Kiss My Ass."

• • • • •

"KISS MY ASS" is a phrase I am quite familiar with. Starting with teenage girls in high school, who certainly did not mean it literally, up through cops, prosecutors, and friends, it's a request I've become accustomed to hearing. So I wouldn't be particularly wounded if Erskine had meant it for me, though he certainly didn't.

Our caravan makes an uneventful return home, and Laurie, Hike, and I ponder what this latest discovery means. Clearly Erskine's killer did not arrange that clandestine meeting with him to get the contents of the envelope as we viewed them. He obviously thought there was something else, something valuable, inside. Erskine must have given him reason to think so.

But Erskine was reneging on that agreement. If it was blackmail, as we've suspected all along, then Erskine thought he could get away with not turning over the promised material in return for payment. If that is the case, it was a brazen and risky act, because surely Erskine must have known he was dealing with dangerous people.

Of course, the contents of the envelope did not figure in Erskine's death, since the shooter hadn't had a chance to open it before Milo intervened. The murder was committed as Milo entered the picture, which means that the shooter, or whoever sent him, still believed wrongly that Erskine would uphold his end of the bargain.

"Let's assume that they were killing Erskine for what he knew, and just getting the envelope wasn't good enough to make them feel secure," Laurie says. "They must have believed that the other soldiers knew the same thing, so they set about to eliminate them as well."

"Santiago asked me about Jason Greer," I say. "He claimed that he and Greer were the only ones who knew the truth, that Greer had confided in him."

Laurie nods. "But the killers didn't know that, or at least didn't want to chance it. If they eliminate everyone, then no one can hurt them."

"They think the envelope lost out there is just as dangerous, which is why they want Milo."

Milo looks up at the mention of his name. I think he's a little annoyed that no one is paying much attention to him or praising him for his performance. It's sort of like Eliza Doolittle's pique that she didn't get the credit from Professor Higgins for doing so well at the fancy party.

Milo, of course, has a point. It's not his fault the envelope contained basically nothing. He did his job, and this is the thanks he gets.

"What do we do with the envelope?" Hike asks.

It's a good question, and one I should have been thinking about. "What's your recommendation?" I ask.

"We sit on it. We have no obligation to turn it over to the court. It wasn't part of the prosecution's case, but even if it was, I think we're on solid grounds holding on to it."

I nod. "Agreed."

"The other positive in not revealing it is that the killers will be more likely to make a mistake and reveal themselves if they think the envelope is still out there and dangerous to them."

"Of course, their mistake could involve killing Milo and Billy's lead counsel, better known as me," I say.

Laurie turns to Hike. "I'd say that's a risk we have to take, wouldn't you?"

Hike shrugs. "No guts, no glory."

"How are you doing with the evening news show that his wife says upset Alex Bryant?"

"It was supposed to be delivered to my house this morning," he says. "I'm going to watch it now, unless you want to go over tomorrow's witnesses."

I shake my head. "I can do that myself. That tape is important; we're running out of things to count on." The envelope turning up dry was a big letdown for us. Had it contained incriminating facts about the bombing in Iraq, it could have gone a huge way toward making our case.

I was prepared for the envelope not to help us, because I thought it unlikely that we could get Milo to find it. The fact that he did, and we still received no help, is a major disappointment.

But I am feeling slightly more confident about the trial overall. We begin presenting our case tomorrow, and

I think there's a decent chance the jury will find Santiago's murder, as well as the disappearance of his fellow soldiers, to be relevant to the case before them. And if it's relevant, it certainly has the capacity to create reasonable doubt.

My problem is in connecting Erskine more closely to the other soldiers. They were found culpable and discharged from the army; he was not. They seem to have come into sudden wealth; we have found no evidence that the same is true for Erskine. And unfortunately, Erskine is the one Billy is accused of murdering.

I spend the evening reviewing my approach for our witnesses. I just try to go over the basic facts and make sure I can recall them completely and instantly. I never prepare actual questions to memorize or read during trial; it cuts down on the spontaneity. But even in direct testimony, surprises can take place, and I have to be prepared to deal with them instantly and effectively.

I close the file and go into the bedroom at eleven thirty. Laurie has waited up for me, which is a good sign. She is naked under the covers, which is an extraordinarily good sign.

"Everything okay?" she asks.

I nod. "Yup."

"Then take your clothes off and get into bed." This is a comment that would earn entry into the Good Sign Hall of Fame, if one existed.

Unfortunately, just as I'm ripping my clothes off, the phone rings. I am fully prepared to ignore it, but Laurie says I should answer it, pointing out that this late at night, it could be important.

I answer, and I hear Hike's voice, which is the audio

equivalent of a cold shower. "Sorry I called so late," he says. "I must have had a bad piece of fish; I've been puking my guts out."

"Hike…"

"This a good time?" he asks.

"Not anymore," I say. "What's up?"

"I went over the tape of the news show. There's not much there; mostly local shit. Murders, city council meetings, car accidents, weather forecasts…that kind of stuff."

"Nothing on a bigger scale?"

"A few things, but nothing obvious. I've made a list of everything, minute by minute. We can go over it tomorrow."

"Okay, thanks." What I don't tell him is that he's just given me an idea as to how we can narrow it down and figure out what Alex Bryant was reacting to that night. I don't tell him this, because it would prolong the conversation, and I would rather set my feet on fire.

I hang up and immediately call Sam Willis. He answers on the first ring, as he's done every time I've ever called him. "Willis."

"Sam, sorry to call so late, but I need you to access phone records." Sam has demonstrated the ability to do this in the past, and neither of us has let the illegalities of the process deter us.

"Sure, what's the number?"

"I don't remember," I say. "It's in my office. But the phone was registered to Alex and Kathy Bryant. They live in Teaneck, on Chapman Avenue."

"I'll get the number," he says. "Is it a landline?"

"I think so."

"What are you looking for?"

"Calls made from that number on March fourteenth between ten PM and midnight. I want to know who was called and the exact time the calls were made."

"No problem," he says. "When do you need it?"

"How fast can you get it?"

"Give me half an hour."

I look over at Laurie, who is still wide awake. "I'll give you until tomorrow," I say, and hang up.

"Anything you want to tell me?" Laurie asks.

"You look great," I say.

"I meant about the case."

"No," I say.

"Good."

• • • • •

OUR FIRST WITNESS is army captain Nathan Kershaw. He is from the inspector general's office, and will testify to the contents of the army's investigative report on the explosion in Iraq. Colonel Mickelson has arranged for this to happen, probably motivated by his desire to please General Prentice.

Captain Kershaw is at least six foot three, and looks like he weighs about 160 pounds. He's blond and talks in a slow, Southern drawl, peppering his answers with a bunch of 'sirs.'"

I take him through the events of that day in Iraq, which he is thoroughly familiar with, even though he wasn't there. In a sense he's an expert witness, with his expertise his knowledge of the report itself.

When I'm sure the jury has the proper context, I get to the meat of his testimony. "Captain, were any members of the army discharged as a result of this report and the events of that day?"

"Yes, sir. Five members of the military police."

"What are their names?" I ask.

"Sergeant First Class Jeremy Iverson, Sergeant First Class Jason Greer, Sergeant Raymond Santiago, Sergeant Donovan Chambers, and Corporal Tyler Lawson."

"Were they found responsible for the explosion?"

"Not exactly, sir. They were judged negligent for allowing the perpetrator inside the perimeter."

"So it was not determined that they acted intentionally?" I ask.

"No, sir."

"Was it determined that they did not act intentionally?"

He shakes his head. "No, sir. There just wasn't enough evidence either way. All the investigators could be sure of was the negligence."

"And they were dishonorably discharged for that negligence?"

"They received OTH discharges, which means 'other than honorable,' sir."

"I see. Does the army keep track of people with OTH discharges after they leave the service?"

He shakes his head. "We surely do not, sir."

"What did the report say about Major Erskine?"

"Very little; he was not considered culpable, though the overall command structure was held to be somewhat deficient."

"Did he resign?"

"Yes, sir. He did. Four months later."

I let Captain Kershaw off the stand, and Eli cross-examines. There's really nothing for him to gain, since Kershaw has simply and accurately reported on what was in the report. Yet Eli questions him for over an hour, probably because he likes being called "sir."

I've gone back and forth over who to call next. I could go with a witness to the Santiago killing. It just happened, and some jurors may even be familiar with it. It is likely to have the biggest impact, since it is the only certain evidence we have that one of the soldiers was killed. For that reason, I've decided to save it for last.

I call Lieutenant José Alvarez of the Albuquerque Police Department to testify regarding Tyler Lawson, who is still listed as a missing person. I would have been better off with an officer from Vegas, since that's where the disappearance took place. Unfortunately, but logically, it was a hell of a lot easier to lure someone to New Jersey from Albuquerque than Vegas.

Alvarez relates the basics: that Lawson had gone to Vegas for an apparent holiday, then went off with some guy and was never heard from again. The clincher, of course, is the safe loaded with cash that he left behind. The jury does not have to be filled with Rhodes Scholars to understand the significance of that fact.

Alvarez also reveals that a further search showed Lawson to possess assets of almost five hundred thousand dollars, sitting untouched in a money market account. The money had been wired in from a Swiss bank account that could not be traced back.

"So taking all of these factors into account, have you formed an impression as to where Mr. Lawson might be?"

"I believe that he is the victim of foul play, and is likely no longer alive."

Eli points out on cross that Alvarez has no real knowledge of Lawson's whereabouts, and that it is possible that he ran off with a woman, possibly to return any day. Alvarez admits that anything is possible, but his experience tells him that there is little chance that Lawson will ever return.

My last witness of the day makes me a little nervous, but I call Willie Miller anyway. He is there to testify about his trip to Nassau, and his conversation with Inspector Christian. I introduce the affidavit that Hike got the inspector to sign, and Willie's really up there as a witness seat filler, merely to recount and read from the affidavit.

I would have liked to introduce evidence that someone from Nassau, perhaps a rental car agent, had recognized and remembered M, but no such identification has been made.

I've gone over with Willie the importance of sticking to the facts and not going off on a tangent. He handles it pretty well, at least on the direct testimony. When I turn him over to Eli for cross-examination, my heart is in my throat. There is no telling what he can get Willie to say.

"I have no questions for this witness," says Eli.

Thank you, God.

Thank you, Eli.

Not necessarily in that order.

HIKE COMES OVER after court so that we can go over the tape. He brings with him his list of which stories could possibly have upset Alex Bryant and prompted his phone call to his boss. Sam is supposed to come over in a little while with the phone records; hopefully we can match them up.

It's almost six o'clock when Hike gets there, and Laurie asks him if he'd like to have dinner with us before we start on the tape. He eagerly accepts the invitation, a decision I think he regrets when he discovers that Marcus will be sitting across the table from him.

Laurie makes chicken parmigiana, one of her few hundred specialties. Hike spends the entire meal trying not to look at Marcus, who only says one word: "Yuh." But he says it three times, it serving as an affirmative response each time Laurie asks him if he wants more chicken.

Suffice it to say that this session will never be confused with the Algonquin Round Table.

I can see Milo and Tara lying on beds in the den and not looking too pleased. Milo's triumph in finding the envelope has resulted in the termination of the now unnecessary trust sessions. I don't think he or Tara would be too broken up about that, except for the fact that those sessions were treat and biscuit buffets.

This turn of events is really not fair to them, and I get up from the table and slip them each a couple of biscuits. I can do this secure in the knowledge that I won't be missing out on any conversational gems at the dinner table.

Once we're finished eating and Marcus has polished off three-quarters of an apple pie, he goes off to wherever it is Marcus goes off to. Hike, Laurie, and I settle down to watch the tape.

Local news is always boring, and local news that is months old is incredibly boring. It was raining heavily that day, and they kept cutting to field reporters standing in various parts of the metropolitan area, earnestly revealing that things were really wet.

National news barely made an appearance, mostly in snippets between rain reports. I agree with Hike on the four possibilities, though none seems particularly promising. There was a home invasion murder of a business executive and his wife, a rhodium mine explosion in South Africa that resulted in the deaths of two miners, a serious disease outbreak on a cruise ship off the coast of Mexico, and a congressional vote failing to renew a trade agreement with three Latin American governments as punishment for their alleged failure to rein in illegal drug production.

Sam comes over about ten minutes after we've finished with copies of Alex Bryant's phone records from that night. He called his boss, Stanley Freeman, at ten forty-seven, a call that lasted for twelve minutes.

The only two stories from the tape that were on our list and matched up with that time were the cruise ship, which ran at ten forty-one, and the rhodium mine explosion, which ran at ten forty-four.

"Can we get a list of the passengers on the ship?" I ask.

Hike frowns. "We could subpoena it, but we'd have to demonstrate relevance to our case. I'm not sure we can do that."

I turn to Sam, who is the person I was talking to in the first place. "Piece of cake," he says.

"Good. Now, what the hell is rhodium?"

"I think it's used in catalytic converters," Hike says.

"That doesn't quite clear it up for me," I say. "What are catalytic converters?"

"You know those harmful emissions that come out of your car? Catalytic converters make them less harmful."

"Doesn't sound like something people in high finance would be interested in," I say. "But you should check it out."

"I'll do that," Sam says.

"Still nothing on Jason Greer or Jeremy Iverson?" I ask. I'm especially interested in Greer, the soldier Santiago referred to as knowing the truth. In fact, he said that the killers would have gone after him first, and revealed that Greer told him the details.

Sam shakes his head. "No. They've both disappeared off the face of the earth."

I suspect that is literally true, that Greer and Iverson have been a few feet under the earth for quite a while now. I have no real hope of ever hearing from them, but evidence of their demise would be compelling to the jury.

Sam sniffs the air, as if first noticing something. "What's that smell? Veal parmigiana?"

"Chicken," I say.

"You got any left?"

"Marcus joined us for dinner."

"Oh. I'll stop for something on the way home."

"You've never seen anything like it," Hike says.

"Yes, I have," Sam says. "June twenty-eighth, 2003. I ate with Andy and Marcus at Charlie's; he ate everything on the menu and then started eating the menu. Cooks were collapsing in the kitchen. They have a plaque on the wall to commemorate the occasion."

"We've got some dog biscuits," I say.

"You want a tuna sandwich?" Laurie is asking the question from the doorway, having listened to some of the conversation. "I keep it hidden for emergencies like this. Marcus has no idea."

"No thanks," Sam says. "I'd be too nervous. What if he came back?"

Laurie tries to get Sam to have the sandwich, telling him that she replaces it every few days to keep it fresh, and this one is on its third day. But he begs off, choosing instead to go home to his computer. Hike leaves as well, and it will be up to Laurie and me to figure out what to do with the precious sandwich.

I stay up until almost eleven, going over the information for tomorrow's court day. Then I take Tara for a late-night walk. The grass is wet from dew, or from whatever makes grass wet, and Tara loves it. She rolls around on her back, feet up in the air, completely joyful.

For the five millionth time, I love and envy her.

Laurie is already asleep when I get to bed, so I pet Milo and Tara for a while and then go to sleep myself.

The phone wakes me at a little after twelve, and the voice is Sam's. He doesn't say hello, just starts with, "Guess what is a form of platinum but worth even more."

Even in my groggy state, I know the answer. "Rhodium."

"You got it. There's only twenty-five tons of it produced each year. The mine that was blown up was responsible for almost thirty percent of that."

"How much is it worth?" I ask, since I know Sam would have researched this fully before calling.

"The price generally fluctuates between one and four thousand dollars an ounce."

Now comes the key question: "What was it worth in the week after the explosion?"

"Over ten grand."

Kaboom.

• • • • •

"THE DEFENSE CALLS Captain Roger Dessens."

Dessens stands and heads for the witness stand, staring at me as he walks. He's expecting me to attack him and make him look incompetent, and the truth is it would give me great pleasure to do just that.

But I won't, damnit.

Frustrating as it is, Dessens is my witness, and he has things to say that will benefit my client. I don't want him reluctant to say them because he's pissed off at me. So I have to treat him with kid gloves, even though I've never really found a pair that fit.

I ask him to describe the circumstances by which he came to be responsible for the protection of Raymond Santiago the other night.

"Judge Catchings issued an order for the state police to take him into protective custody, at your request."

"Were you given background information on Sergeant Santiago?"

He nods. "We were." Dessens keeps using "we" rather than "I"; he doesn't want to take the fall for this on his own. He then goes on, at my prodding, to reveal that Santiago was one of the soldiers who was discharged from the army as a result of negligence that fateful day in Iraq.

After he describes getting the phone call from me and sending two officers to my house to pick up Santiago, I ask, "Were you waiting for him at the hotel?"

"Yes."

"With more of your officers?"

"Yes. We had six more officers assigned to the hotel detail."

"Was anyone else with you?"

He nods. "Yes. FBI Special Agent Wilbur Briggs and US Army Captain Derek Meade. They were planning to question Santiago when he arrived."

This is an important fact for the jury to hear. I want them to know that Santiago was not just some defense concoction; serious branches of the US government were anxious to hear what he had to say.

At the same time, the inconsistency of it puzzles me. First the feds were interested enough to have Milo guarded, then they backed off entirely, and then they were anxious to question Santiago. I'm not sure what Santiago could have told them that they'd be interested in, especially since they had obviously been content to conduct a whitewash investigation of the Iraq explosion.

"Had you notified them about Santiago being taken into custody?" I ask.

"No. I have no idea how they became aware of the situation."

I have no idea, either, and it's bugged me since that night. But I move on and get Dessens to explain that the shot came from a window in a building a good distance away. He describes the weapon as an advanced, high-powered rifle, and the shooter as an outstanding marksman.

"Is it your assessment that he was already in position when your men arrived with Santiago?"

"Definitely," he says.

"Do you have any idea how he knew where Santiago was being taken?"

"I do not," he says, firmly.

"Had you revealed the location to myself, any member of the defense team, or the court?"

"No."

"Thank you, Captain."

Dessens almost does a double take when I dismiss him; he still can't believe I didn't try to embarrass him. I'm having trouble believing it myself.

Eli starts his cross by asking if Dessens knew where Santiago lived.

"No."

"Do you know his occupation before he went in the army?"

Dessens shakes his head. "No."

"Was he married?"

"I don't know."

"So you know very little about him? Is that fair?" Eli asks.

"That is fair."

"Do you know if he had any enemies?"

"He had at least one." The gallery and some of the jury laugh at the answer, which is certainly not the reaction Eli wanted.

"But you have no personal knowledge of why that one enemy shot and killed him?"

"No."

"For all you know it could have nothing to do with the explosion in Iraq?"

"Correct."

"For all you know it could have nothing to do with this case?"

"Correct."

"Thank you. No further questions."

• • • • •

AS SOON AS court ends, I call Jonathan Chaplin. I
have to hold for almost five minutes, but he finally gets
on the line. I tell him I need to see him, and ask him if I
can come right over.

"What is this about?" he asks.

"Something has come up about the case I'm working
on, but I also need some investment advice, on an urgent
basis."

"Nephew Philip isn't providing satisfactory service?"
he asks.

"It's Edna's nephew Freddie. Let's just say he has his
limitations."

He tries to arrange a meeting for next week, but I
press him, telling him that the court schedule is such that
I really have no time. Finally, he agrees to see me at six

o'clock this evening, but warns that he will only have forty-five minutes before leaving for a dinner engagement.

"Perfect," I say.

Sam Willis is working on trying to find out if Chaplin's hedge fund, C&F Investments, was particularly active in the oil market at the time of the Iraq explosion, and the rhodium market when the mine blew up. I want to know if they made unusually large profits as a result of those events. But even Sam admits that it will be difficult. He must first penetrate the company's cyber security and then—if he's successful at that—read and understand the enormous number of transactions a company that size will conduct.

We could also try to subpoena the information, but we would need to offer the court proof that it is relevant to the case, and at this point we don't have enough to do that. Hunches are not usually a key component of offers of proof, and a wife's relating that she thinks her husband was upset by a news story won't carry much weight, either.

One of the problems is that C&F is a private company, and therefore has considerably fewer reporting requirements. The trades it makes on behalf of its clients are proprietary information, and correctly should not be allowed to be viewed by those that could be competitors.

One way or another we'll get the information, but if Sam can't do it, and the company contests it, we might not have it before Billy is up for parole. It's definitely a time to be aggressive.

Chaplin is actually wearing a tuxedo when I arrive, no doubt for the dinner engagement he spoke about. The only way I'd be wearing a tuxedo to dinner is if I were having it at Buckingham Palace, and I were going to be knighted as Sir Andy of Paterson.

"I feel underdressed," I say.

He smiles. "I envy you. These charity dinners...sometimes I wish I could just stay home and write a check. So what can I do for you?"

"Well, if you don't mind, can I just borrow your phone for a minute? I left my cell in the car, and I just have to tell my co-counsel something."

He nods and points to the phone on his desk. "Use my private line."

"Thanks." I pick up the phone and dial Sam Willis's number, and he of course answers on the first ring. "Got the number," he says.

"Hike, it's Andy. I need the forensics documents for tonight, but I left them in the office. Can you get me copies?"

Sam laughs. "Sure. No problem."

I hang up and turn to Chaplin. "Thanks. So I have money to invest, and I'm thinking of putting it into rhodium."

He actually flinches at the word, though he regains his composure quickly. "Rhodium," he repeats.

"Rhodium," I say, probably breaking the record for the most times "rhodium" has been said consecutively.

"I don't really know much about it," he says.

"Really? My information is that your company was heavily invested in it when that mine blew up in South Africa. Congratulations on that, by the way. I hear you cleared up. That's exactly the kind of thing Freddie misses out on."

"Can't help you," Chaplin says. "So if you'll excuse me…"

"Between that and the money you made on oil when your partner and Alex Bryant got killed, you've had quite a year."

"What are you trying to say, Carpenter?" His voice is cold, and his whole attitude has convinced me that I am right in my suspicions. There's plenty I don't know yet, but what I believe is that this guy is dirty. And that he was involved in the deaths of a lot of people, including his partner and Alex Bryant. He's a piece of garbage, dressed in a tuxedo.

"I'm trying to say that pretty soon you won't have to go to any more charity dinners looking like an asshole."

As exit lines go, I've had worse, and I turn and walk out the door.

I get in my car and drive around the block. I park in a spot from which I can see the parking lot of Chaplin's building. I don't know what kind of car he drives, and over the next twenty minutes three cars exit the lot. It's too dark to see if he's driving, but I don't follow them because they're relatively inexpensive, domestic cars.

Not Chaplin's type.

Finally a Jaguar comes out of the lot, and I follow it at a distance. This is not my strong point, and a couple of times I almost lose him. But I manage to stay with him, and he leads me to the Woodcliff Hilton Hotel.

I follow him into the parking lot, and watch as he leaves the car with the valet. The valet is busy, and almost all his other customers are dressed in formal attire as well, so my assumption is that Chaplin was not so distressed by my visit that it caused him to miss the charity dinner.

I head home, calling Sam on the way. "He didn't make a call," Sam says. "At least not from that phone."

My hope had been that Chaplin would have called a co-conspirator from the phone I had used, which Sam could then have traced. That has worked for us before, but Chaplin was either too smart or too lucky.

"Okay...it was worth a try."

"I tried to get his cell phone number," he says. "But there's none in his name; they're all registered to the company. More than eighty of them."

My next call is to Willie. "You ready to play private eye?"

"You'd better believe it," he says. "What have you got?"

I ask him if he can come right over, and he's eager to do so. Rather than talk to him on the phone, I'd like Laurie to be around, so I can update her on my meeting with Chaplin and in the process get her input.

Willie is at the house before I am; he and Laurie are in the kitchen with the dogs, and he is eating what I am sure was meant to be my dinner. Between him and Marcus, if this case doesn't end soon, I'm going to starve to death.

I bring them up to date on everything that has transpired, right through Sam's lack of success in getting Chaplin's cell phone number. When I'm finished, Laurie asks, "Who were you hoping he would call?"

"Somebody else involved in the operation. A co-conspirator."

"Maybe he doesn't have one; maybe Erskine was the only guy. With M doing the dirty work."

I shake my head. "I don't think so. This feels bigger than that. If I had to guess, I think Chaplin's company was used as the conduit for investments in oil and rhodium. Maybe Freeman and Bryant were complicit in it, but I don't think so."

"Why?"

"Because Kathy Bryant said that Alex was upset when he saw the report about the rhodium blast."

"So maybe he and Freeman were considered a risk to blow the whistle, and that's why they were killed in the explosion."

I nod. "Which would have made it three for the price of one. The blast sent the price of oil way up, and killed the two guys who were a danger to the scheme."

Willie has been sitting patiently through this, and when there is a lull he asks, "So what do you want me to do?"

"Follow Chaplin wherever he goes. Take pictures of anybody you see him meeting with. But don't let him see you."

Willie nods. "Cool."

Laurie seems a little worried about this, as I knew she would be. "You comfortable with this, Willie?"

"Sure. No sweat."

I give him the address of Chaplin's home and office, which Sam had gotten for me. We go online and find a bunch of pictures of Chaplin, so Willie will recognize him. Finally, I give him my digital camera; it's not CIA-issue, but it should work. He promises to get started first thing in the morning, and then leaves.

"This may not be the best use of Willie's talents," Laurie says, probably understating how she really feels.

"I know," I say, "but I think he can handle it. And there's not much downside if he can't."

"How is that?"

"Well, I don't see Chaplin as savvy in these matters, so he probably isn't good at spotting a tail. But if he does, then he'll feel pressured and worried, and that's a good thing. Maybe it will force him into a mistake."

She seems unconvinced. "You may be right, but I'm worried about Willie."

"He can handle himself even better than I can," I say.

"Is that supposed to make me feel better?"

I guess not.

• • • • •

ALAN LANDON COULD have reacted to the call from Chaplin with anger, but that wasn't his style. He certainly would have been justified in being furious. He had covered every base, thought of almost every eventuality, but was in this difficult position because of the incompetence of others.

Landon knew Carpenter was a danger from day one. He was smart, and he had resources, and once he took on a client he did whatever was necessary to defend him. That was why Landon had ordered Zimmerman murdered in the prison; if Carpenter's client had been killed, he would have had no reason to keep going. But that attack had failed, and this was the result.

Landon knew this was coming eventually; there was too much money at stake, too many people involved, too many moving parts, for it to have remained under the radar forever. He had planned for this moment, and he would be fine. He just wished it had waited another seventy-two hours to happen.

"Carpenter knows about the rhodium," Chaplin had said, a trace of panic in his voice. "He's putting the whole thing together with Iraq."

"Does he know the details?"

"No," Chaplin said. "I don't think so. If he did, he wouldn't have been trying to pressure me. He'd be talking to the feds instead."

"Good," said Landon. He agreed with Chaplin's assessment. "Then it's important you not give in to that pressure. This will all be over very soon."

"For you, maybe. But I've got to go on with my life. I can't disappear."

"You won't have to," Landon said, even though his plan all along was for Chaplin to involuntarily disappear when the time came. "Everything is under control."

"That's not how it looks from here."

"You need to continue to trust me. By next week, this will be behind you."

"Right. Okay," Chaplin said, not very convincingly.

"You have done nothing wrong. You made investments on behalf of your clients, investments you were directed to make."

"People died," Chaplin said. "Stanley died, for Christ's sake."

"That was an unfortunate accident—"

Chaplin interrupted. "Was it?"

"—that you had nothing whatsoever to do with."

"I don't want to go to jail, Alan."

"That won't happen." What Landon didn't add was the rest of his thought. *Because you will be dead.*

Once they were off the phone, Landon called M. "Carpenter is making Chaplin nervous."

The news came as no surprise to M. "I told you Chaplin couldn't be counted on."

"He'll make it for the next week," Landon said. "And then it won't matter."

"I hope you're right," M said. He was noticing less confidence in Landon's voice, a sure sign that he was more worried about Chaplin than he was letting on.

"Are things under control on your end?"

"Totally. We're just waiting until the target is in place."

"Good. When you're finished, we start cleaning up. Chaplin, Carpenter...everyone."

M couldn't help but smile. Landon had no doubt that he was in charge, that M would do whatever he asked.

Wrong on both counts.

• • • • •

WILLIE MILLER WAS surprised at how easy
it was to follow somebody; he just wished it wasn't so
boring. He was down the street from Chaplin's Short
Hills house when he left in the morning, and followed
him all the way to his office.

He waited outside the entire day, but Chaplin never
left, not even for lunch. Willie figured they must have
one of those executive chefs he'd read about; maybe he
should hire one of them for the Tara Foundation. That
person could cook for him and Sondra, and maybe make
homemade dog biscuits the rest of the day.

At least it was something to think about during the
endless hours he spent waiting for Chaplin to leave. Finally at six thirty his car pulled out, and Willie followed
him. He went straight home, and when the lights went off
on the house's lower level at ten fifteen, Willie left.

Willie was not particularly introspective, but he knew enough about himself to realize that more days like this would drive him crazy.

If tomorrow repeated this pattern, Willie would just have to make something happen.

• • • • •

W<small>E</small> A<small>RE</small> I<small>N</small> deep trouble. I probably shouldn't say "we," since it is my client, Billy Zimmerman, who is really the one in trouble. If we lose this case, and that's the direction we're heading, he is the one who will have to spend the rest of his life in prison. I will still get to go home, and sleep with Laurie, and play with Tara, and watch Giants games in the fall.

I will be upset, and I'll feel guilty, but my life will go on. Billy's, for all intents and purposes, will not.

I have a few minutes' time for conversation with Billy before the start of court, and he broaches the subject straight-out. "How do you think we're doing?" he asks.

"At this point, we're behind."

He seems surprised. "Really? I think you're getting your points across."

"I probably am, but they're the wrong points. I'm

talking about conspiracy theories and people missing and murders happening halfway around the world. Eli's talking about a guy on an Edgewater street with a gun and a dead body."

"So we're going to lose?"

"At this point it's more likely than not. But we're making good progress in our investigation outside of court, and that gives us a fighting chance."

I start to detail what we've learned, but I don't get to finish because Judge Catchings enters the courtroom. Today is going to be a short day, because the judge has some personal business to attend to this afternoon. I'd be fine if he had a month's worth of personal business.

My first witness is Nina Rodriguez, a patron at the bar that night who is one of the few people who saw the events remotely close to the way I want them to be seen.

She testifies that she was walking out of the bar and across the street when she happened to look over and see Erskine talking with a man. Less than thirty seconds later, gunshots were fired and chaos erupted.

"Was the victim talking to the defendant?" I ask.

She shakes her head. "No. This man was taller; I mean, he could have been a basketball player. The other man, the man who died, looked up at him when he talked."

"You could see that from where you were?"

"Yes."

"What happened after you heard the shots?"

"Well, I thought it was firecrackers, but my boyfriend, he knew what it was. So he pulled me behind a car, and we waited a couple of minutes. Some men ran by us at first, toward the shooting, but we waited. When we finally looked up, there were people everywhere, and Mr. Zimmerman was standing next to the body."

I turn her over to Eli, who has little difficulty in diluting the effect of her testimony. He demonstrates how difficult it is to tell height from that distance, in that light. Besides, as he points out, Billy is six foot two, and Erskine was five ten. Erskine would have been looking up at Billy as well.

Next I call Pete Stanton, whom I will use as a character witness for Billy. They came up in the force together, and Pete was anxious to do it. I haven't gotten a chance to do a final prep session with Pete this morning; he arrived as court was beginning. But I have no doubt that he'll handle things fine. He's an experienced witness.

As he walks toward the stand, he passes me and whispers under his breath, "We need to talk."

I don't know what to make of that; I'm certain he doesn't mean the talk we're about to have in front of the jury. I'm worried that he somehow has ominous news, but I'll have to wait until court is over to hear it.

Pete handles himself very well, powerfully defending Billy's character, courage, and honesty, and Eli's cross-examination is quick. He points out that Pete and Billy had spent very little time together since Billy got back from Iraq, the implication being that Billy's injury and desire for revenge turned him into a different person.

But basically Eli has little desire to tangle with Pete on the stand, and he knows that the testimony is just not that damaging. Fortunately for me, he's taken enough time that Pete is the last witness of the day, and Catchings adjourns the session.

I walk over to Pete, but before I can say anything, he says, "Let's grab a sandwich."

We go over to the diner near the courthouse. If Pete is taking me to such an inexpensive place to eat, it means the goal is not to drain me of my money. It's to tell me something important.

Even before we order, he gets right down to it. "If anybody finds out where you got this, I will chop up your body and feed it piece by piece to sharks."

"I don't think I'll order the fish."

"I mean it. They won't be able to identify you with dental records."

"Pete, you have my word. Now, will you land the plane already?"

That's good enough for him, so he continues. "A good friend of mine on the force, who shall remain nameless, told me something today. A body was fished out of the Passaic River, and he took the call."

I have no idea where this is going, but I don't want to interrupt and ask questions. It will only delay hearing the rest.

"The body had ID on it. A guy by the name of Jerry Harris. He's a hired gun out of Philadelphia; doesn't come cheap. I checked it out, Jerry Harris was six foot six."

This completely gets my attention, but Pete isn't finished.

"My friend is upset, because since he found the body he hasn't heard a thing. Nobody's been assigned to it, and as far as we know, a case file hasn't been opened."

"When was the body found?" I ask.

"Three days after Erskine was killed. So my friend

asked the captain why he hasn't heard anything, and the captain said he couldn't talk about it. That the feds put a lid on it."

I let this sink in for a few moments. It can have monumental implications for my case, though at this moment I don't know what they are, or how I can manipulate them.

"You know I have to use this," I say.

He nods. "Yeah, I know."

I thank Pete and leave, after doing two things that he insists on. One is to promise once again that I will not mention his name in this, and the other is to pay the check. They seem of equal importance to him.

When I get home, I tell Laurie what I've learned. "The FBI has been all over this from day one," she says.

I nod. "It's time to find out why."

I call Cindy Spodek, who can tell from the fact that I don't engage in preliminary banter that this is serious. "Cindy, I need to meet with the agent at the FBI who is in charge of the Erskine case."

Cindy certainly has not been involved in it, so she's not sure what to make of the request. "How do you know there is such a person? Just because you have an Erskine case doesn't mean the bureau does."

"Take my word for it. Please ask your boss to get the word to the agent in charge that we need to meet."

"Why would that person agree to it?"

"Just say I want to talk about three things. Oil, Jerry Harris, and rhodium."

● ● ● ● ●

THIS WAS NOTHING like the detective shows
on TV. Willie knew that was true, even though he didn't
watch anything on TV except sports. Because if detective
shows were this boring, nobody would watch them, and
they would be taken off the air.

Willie had been outside Chaplin's home when he left
in the morning, and had once again followed him to his
office. As he had the day before, Chaplin spent the entire
day there, not leaving until it was time to go home.

It was while following him home that Willie had an
idea. He figured Andy would be pissed off, but that was
something he was willing to risk. It's not that he wasn't
okay with following Chaplin for weeks; it was a job and
Willie was willing to do it. It's just that it didn't seem like
it would accomplish anything.

Willie followed until he was comfortable that Chaplin

was heading home, and then he pulled ahead of him. It was easy, because Chaplin was a slow and careful driver, something Willie would never be accused of.

He got to Chaplin's house a full ten minutes ahead of him, and parked down the street. He ran on foot to the house, positioning himself at the end of the winding driveway. He made the assumption that Chaplin would park in the same place as he had the night before; if he didn't, Willie would just abort the plan.

Willie waited for Chaplin to arrive. He wasn't nervous; in fact, he couldn't remember the last time he was nervous. Certainly it was before he went to prison. That experience had changed him in quite a few ways.

Chaplin pulled in and parked in the exact same place as the night before. When he got out of his car, Willie hit him in the temple with his right hand. He came from the side, which he wished he didn't have to do, since he had never sucker-punched anyone like that in his life. But he couldn't afford to be seen.

Chaplin literally did not know what hit him, and he was out cold before he reached the ground. Willie caught him before he landed, preventing his head from hitting the concrete.

Willie quickly looked through his pockets until he found his cell phone. He was going to leave it at that, but then made the decision to take his wallet as well. This way it would be possible that Chaplin might think this was a real robbery, and that getting the cell phone was not the goal.

Within two minutes, Willie was in his car and on the way to Andy's. Knocking out Chaplin and getting his phone was the easy part; now he had to deal with Andy.

M HAD NO idea what was going on with Chaplin or Willie, and really wouldn't have been terribly interested anyway. He was holed up in a hotel room in Everett, Massachusetts, with nothing to do other than watch television.

M had a simple job before him, and once it was done none of the other bullshit would matter. There would still be some cleaning up to do, some people to kill, much money to collect. He would then leave the country, possibly never to come back, but he was fine with that either way.

As M stared out the window toward the harbor, he smiled to himself at the exquisite irony of it. He was waiting for his ship to come in, both literally and figuratively.

When it did, all hell would break loose.

Which most definitely was not his problem.

●　●　●　●　●

"You what?"

It's nine o'clock, and I've had a long day, but it sounded to me like Willie just said, "This is Chaplin's cell phone. I took it from him." So I've asked him again to be sure.

"This is Chaplin's cell phone. I took it from him." I hear this coming out of Willie's mouth again, which significantly increases the chance that I heard it correctly the first time.

I look over at Laurie, who seems amazed to have heard it as well. Tara and Milo obviously expected something like this from Willie, because they appear only mildly amused.

There is a seemingly endless list of questions for me to ask, so I might as well start with the one-word ones. They're quicker.

"How?"

"I waited for him in his driveway, and when he got out of the car I knocked him out and took it from him. I got his wallet also, to make it look like a robbery."

"It was a robbery," Laurie points out.

"Did he see you before you knocked him out?" I ask.

"Nope. No chance. And he was still in dreamland when I left."

"Are you sure you didn't kill him?" The image of Childress's crushed skull behind the Tara Foundation flashes through my mind.

"No way; worst case I busted his jaw. You didn't want me to kill him, right?"

"Right," I say. "Killing as a general rule is a problem."

"Knocking out and stealing also are somewhat problematic. As is jaw busting," Laurie says, the ex-cop in her coming out.

"So I shouldn't have done it?" Willie asks. "I figured you guys might be pissed."

"Why did you do it?" I ask.

"Well, I was going nuts, you know? I'd follow him to the office, sit there all day, and follow him home. This happened every day."

"Today was the second day."

Willie nods vigorously, as if I'm proving his point. "Right. Anyway, I wasn't finding out anything. I didn't know what he was doing, or who he was doing it with. And you wanted Sam to find out who he's been calling, so I figured a good way to do that would be to get his phone."

"But you committed a crime."

He shrugs. "Last time I didn't do nothing and I got seven years in jail. They owe me a few."

"Did anyone at all see you?" I ask.

"Nah. I don't think so. The only one there was Chaplin. And it was dark."

"Willie, this was a mistake."

"Now you tell me."

"Come on, Willie. You know damn well you shouldn't do this kind of thing."

"Andy, these guys are doing bad shit, right? They almost killed Sondra. So we should play by the rules when they don't?"

I'm not going to get anywhere by continuing to reprimand him, and I need to start thinking about where to go from here. "Okay, if you hear from the police on this, you don't speak to them. You got that? Just call me, and I'll do the talking."

He nods. "I know the drill. But don't worry, they can't follow this back to me."

"I hope not... let's talk some more tomorrow."

"You want me to keep following this guy?" he asks, apparently seriously.

"No thanks."

Once Willie leaves, Laurie says, "I don't suppose you're going to report the commission of a crime, Mr. Officer of the Court?"

She knows full well I'm not; she's just having a little fun at my expense. "I don't suppose I am. I just hope nobody saw Willie or his car."

"Willie's DNA is on file because he was in prison," she says. The implication is that if he left any DNA on the scene, or on Chaplin's face, the trail could lead to him fairly quickly. Either way, there's nothing we can do about it short of turning Willie in and plea-bargaining on his behalf.

"Let's think only sunny thoughts, okay?"

Laurie points to Chaplin's cell phone on the table. "The question is what to do with the stolen merchandise."

"We could throw it out, or we could look at it and possibly get valuable information. Not exactly a tough call."

"You won't be able to use anything you find in court," she points out.

"Such is life."

Laurie and I between us have the technological knowledge and skills of a slow-developing four-year-old, so I call Sam Willis and ask him to come over. He seems eager to do so; maybe he thinks we're going to go out and shoot some people. Sam lives on Morlot Avenue in Fair Lawn, about ten minutes away if he drives quickly. He makes it in eight.

Once he arrives, I show him the cell phone and say, "Is there any way to find out what calls have been made from that phone in the last four days?"

"Is that a joke?" he asks.

"No. Why?"

He just shakes his head, picks up the phone, and presses a few buttons. In less than twenty seconds he hands it to me. "There's a list of the numbers he called, and when he called them."

I turn to Laurie. "See? I told you Sam and I could do it."

"Is this Chaplin's phone?" Sam asks.

"Sam, that phone was obtained illegally. People could go to jail."

He laughs, apparently not intimidated by my statement. "That Willie is a piece of work. You want me to trace down these numbers?"

I nod. "Yes, but can you write them down? I want to keep the phone here."

"Sure," he says, and starts to do so. "You want an update on Chaplin's company now, or do you want to wait until tomorrow?"

"You've got it already?"

"Yeah, although the news isn't great. There's no doubt that the company profited heavily from both the oil and rhodium events. They made trades that slowly built up their stake in each over about six months, and then sold everything off within a month after the stock shot up."

"How much did they make?"

"Hard to say exactly, but probably eight hundred million on the oil, and two billion more on the rhodium. Turned the company around; a couple of years ago they almost went under."

"You're sure of all this?"

He nods. "Yeah."

"How come you said the news isn't great?" Laurie asks, beating me to the punch.

"Because I don't know who made the money. The investments were made on behalf of clients, most of which were foreign companies. There's no way to crack that and find out who's behind them; they're probably dummy companies."

"Sam, you did outstanding work on this," Laurie says.

Sam gives his best aw-shucks look and waves her off. "Come on, it's not like I shot anybody."

"Keep at it, Sam," I say. "If you work hard enough, someday you'll leave somebody bloody in the street. That will be a proud day for all of us."

• • • • •

My PLAN IS to spend the weekend making the key decision of the trial. It's actually the key decision of every trial, though technically it is not mine to make. I am going to have to either call Billy Zimmerman to the witness stand, or rest our case. The question to be answered is which option is worse; both are very bad.

The decision is Billy's to make, and we've had a few conversations about it. He wants to testify, but once again his experience as a cop works in our favor. He's been around enough trials to know that the defendant rarely takes the stand, and when he does the defense is likely desperate. More significantly, the testimony usually hurts rather than helps.

In Billy's case there is even more downside than usual. I have already conveyed to the jury our claim that there was another man present, and that Billy wrestled with him. So Billy's saying it, while having the advantage of being straight from the horse's mouth, wouldn't add very much to the record.

Then he would have to suffer through a cross-examination by Eli that would not be pretty. Billy is an admitted thief; in fact, that's why he was there that night. Eli would harp on this until Billy looked like Jesse James. Then he would turn to the grudge Billy had against Erskine, which others have already testified to.

There is no question in my mind that the downside is greater than the upside. Laurie agrees with my assessment, and I call Hike to get his view. I have to take it with a grain of salt, since Hike is "Mr. Downside," but he agrees as well.

I'm about to leave for the prison to have a final discussion about it with Billy when Cindy Spodek calls. "You've got your meeting," she says. "Special Agent Dan Benson is waiting for your call."

I'm not surprised. "The rhodium did the trick, huh?"

"It was like telling Superman that you knew where a kryptonite mine was."

"You want me to bring you up to date about what's going on?" I ask.

"Not particularly, unless you need help. This seems like a need-to-know situation. Benson was already pumping me for information that I was glad I didn't have."

"So he's anxious?" I ask.

"Let's put it this way. It's Saturday, and he told me to give you his cell phone number. An FBI agent giving a defense attorney his cell phone number...does that strike you as anxious?"

I hang up and head down to the prison to talk to Billy.

I call Benson on the way, and we set a meeting for early afternoon at his office in Newark.

I lay things out for Billy. I tell him our situation is grim, for reasons we have gone over repeatedly. I go on to say that I think his testimony would make things worse, but that it's his call, and I'll support him either way.

"But you're against?" he asks.

"I am."

"Then we don't do it." Billy is pretty much the ideal client, logical, unemotional, and realistic. I wish I could be doing better for him.

I tell him the latest developments in our investigation, which cheers him up, since it's obvious we're making more progress outside the courtroom than in. "The FBI agent is meeting with you on a Saturday?"

I nod. "As soon as I leave here."

"He needs something."

"So do we."

As I'm about to leave, he asks, "How's Milo?"

"Doing fine."

"It just hit me that I'll probably never see him again."

"I'm nowhere near prepared to say that," I say. "But either way he'll be well taken care of, safe, and loved."

"Thanks. I appreciate that."

FBI Special Agent Dan Benson is a tall, dignified-looking man, probably in his midforties, with a touch of gray starting at the temples, preparing to advance. He has the demeanor of a man who has seen everything there is to see, at least twice, which makes his anxiousness to see me all the more surprising.

I thought I'd have to force my way into a meeting, and here they are laying out the red carpet. I think they would have sent a limo to my house.

Once I'm settled in, Benson gets right to it. "You wanted this meeting."

I nod. "I did."

"Why is that?"

"I want to see my client acquitted, and I think you know he didn't murder Erskine."

"How would I know that?" he asks.

"Seconds after the fatal shot was fired, three men were on the scene. One checked on Erskine, and the others ran after the shooter, a guy by the name of Jerry Harris. Based on the way they were dressed, they were either FBI agents or on their way home from a hardware convention."

I wait for him to respond, but he stays silent, so I push on. "Right after the murder, you were so interested in Milo that you intervened to have an armed guard stationed in front of his cage twenty-four hours a day. A few days later, I went to court to get him released, and you did absolutely nothing to stop me."

"And you read that how?"

"Between those two events, Harris's body was discovered. You had been tracking him; my guess is you wanted him to lead you to his bosses. But you lost him in the chaos after the murder, and when he was found dead, you covered it up. By then you needed something else to draw those bosses out. You were hoping Milo could do that, but he couldn't do it in a guarded cage."

"It's Saturday, and it's been a long week," he says. "Can you move this along?"

"Sure. Your men know my client is innocent, yet you've let him sit in jail and face this trial. Using a technical legal term, that was a shitty thing to do. So you need to step forward and fix that."

I'm far from sure that I'm right in all the things I'm saying, but I learned a long time ago that in these situations it's best to sound confident. That confidence is increasing because of the fact that he hasn't thrown me out or laughed at me yet.

Instead he changes the subject, though the two subjects are going to be related in any negotiation we might have. "You mentioned rhodium."

"I did."

"What about it?"

"The mine explosion in South Africa and the explosion in Iraq were caused by the same people for the same reason," I say. "To move the market and make money."

"Do you know who those people are?"

I shake my head. "Not yet; not all of them. But I will."

"If you share with us what you know, and if it's accurate, then we can use our resources to find out the rest."

"Did you forget the part where I said my goal is to get my client acquitted?"

"This is the United States of America," he says. "We can't intervene in a criminal trial."

"First of all, that's bullshit; you can get the charges dropped if you want to. Second of all, that's bullshit; your men were on the scene; they were eyewitnesses and can clear Billy with their testimony. Third of all, that's bullshit; you know damn well that Jerry Harris killed Erskine. And fourth of all, that's bullshit."

"Carpenter..."

"Why do you care so much, anyway? You and the army whitewashed the Iraq report. I can't imagine the South Africa explosion is a national security issue, and..."

Just then it hits me why he's so interested, and I can't believe I didn't realize it earlier. "...you care about what's going to happen next. You think there's a third shoe to drop."

"You don't want this kind of blood on your hands," he says, an almost direct admission that I'm right.

"Here's what I've got on my hands," I say. "I've got a client who is depending on me. I am legally bound to represent him to the best of my ability, and right now that requires me to tell you to kiss my ass."

I turn and leave the office and go to my car. It takes me a few seconds to get the key in the ignition, because my hands are shaking so bad.

• • • • •

"I HAVE NO idea what to do." I make this admission to Laurie and Hike, gathered at the house for a Sunday-morning strategy session. "Usually I know what the right thing to do legally and morally is, and then it's up to me whether to do it or not. But this time I don't even know that."

"So he implied that there was going to be another incident, and that you could help prevent it?" Hike asks.

"He did more than imply it; he beat me over the head with it. He said I don't want to have this kind of blood on my hands."

"Let's take it legally first," Laurie says. "Am I right that your first obligation is to your client?"

"In part; I have to defend him as best I can. I could be disbarred if I didn't. But as a citizen, I also have the obligation to do my best to prevent a future crime from happening."

"You have no information about such a crime," she says.

"Benson thinks I do."

Laurie nods. "And two years from now you don't want him saying it to some congressional committee, with the next day's headline, 'Carpenter Could Have Stopped Massacre.'"

I'm floundering here. "So I need to cave and tell him whatever I know?"

"I don't think so," Hike says. "He has the power to find out what you know by intervening in the trial. If he doesn't, the blood is on his hands, not yours."

"Looking at it morally, it would be nice if we could stop blood from being on anyone's hands," Laurie says. "Including Billy's."

We decide to hold off on making a decision for now, mainly because we can't come up with a satisfactory one. I don't think I've ever been in a situation like this before, and it's scaring the hell out of me.

I don't want to turn on the television and see breaking news about some catastrophe that's killed a bunch of people, with an imaginary graphic across the bottom saying "Andy Carpenter's Fault." But I also don't want to wake up every morning for the rest of my life knowing Billy's waking up in a seven-by-ten cell.

For now, the only action I can take is to focus on figuring out what the hell is going on. To that end I call Sam, who says he is working on the phone numbers, and should have the people that Chaplin called on the cell phone in a few hours.

"Good," I say. "Then I've got another job for you."

"What's that?"

"You know how you told me C and F positioned itself to profit from the oil and rhodium events? How they formed positions in it over some months?"

"What about it?" he asks.

"I want to know if it's happening again; if they've put themselves in a similar position. And if they have, I want to know what commodity they're looking to profit from."

"That's not going to be easy, Andy. It's a huge company operating in all different markets. And if I don't know what I'm looking for..."

"For now, limit it to the companies that bought the oil and rhodium. Only look at their trades. Does that make it easier?"

"Much," he says, relief in his voice.

"Great. Call me when you have anything."

When I get off the phone with Sam, I go into the office, where Laurie is sitting at the computer terminal. She's also on the phone, or at least she has it to her ear, though she's not saying anything.

Finally she says, "Thanks, Rob," and hangs up. She turns to me. "Chaplin didn't file a robbery report. The guy is definitely dirty."

"Or maybe he's still lying in the driveway."

"If he's not, he's dirty. A guy gets mugged and robbed in the driveway of his house, in that neighborhood, and he doesn't even report it? That's a guy who doesn't want the police anywhere near him."

When I get off the phone, I don't do what I should do, which is prepare for my closing statement to the jury. Instead I obsess over the meeting with Benson, and the predicament it's left me in.

Benson is playing a game of chicken with me, and I

feel like I'm losing. At some point I'm going to cave; my fear of being even indirectly responsible for mass deaths is too great. I'm not ready to do it yet, which I realize on some level is silly. The next disaster could come at any moment, and any delay could make me too late.

Intellectually, I know that Benson is under at least as much pressure as I am. He has the power to find out what I know, which he believes could help avert a tragedy. Yet he is resisting doing so, just as I am resisting on my end.

I hope he's as scared as me.

I finally get started on the preparation for my statement at nine o'clock, and Sam calls five minutes later. "I got something good," he says, which is one of my favorite ways for a conversation to start.

"I'm ready."

"This guy uses his cell phone a lot. He made two hundred and fifty-eight calls in the last six days. A lot of the calls were to the same number, so he called a hundred and sixty-one numbers."

"You've got a printed list?" I ask.

"Sure. More than half of the numbers he called were companies, and they went through the company switchboards, so I can't know who he talked to. And of course, there's no way for me to know exactly who he spoke to when he called personal phones; more than one person could answer, you know?"

The Declaration of Independence has a longer preamble than this. "What happened to the I've-got-something-good part?"

"I'm getting there. There are three phone calls to a phone registered to Alan Landon."

Alan Landon is a very prominent investor-financier, and

evidence of that prominence is the fact that I've heard of him. That is not a world that I understand or have much familiarity with. Even with Freddie's help, I haven't become wealthy by investing. I've done it the old-fashioned way: I rolled up my sleeves and inherited it.

"You're sure it's *the* Alan Landon?" I ask, though it makes sense. Chaplin is a major player in that world; Landon is someone he could be expected to talk with at least occasionally. For all I know, Landon could be a client.

"Positive. And *the* Alan Landon is the person that Chaplin called four minutes after you left his office. They talked for fourteen minutes, and then again the next morning for seven."

"Sam, you're a genius."

"You're just figuring that out?"

Sam gets off the phone to get back to work on studying C&F's recent trades, and I relate the information he gave me to Laurie. She is even more excited by it than I am, which is really saying something.

"So you meet with him, he's on the way to a black-tie dinner, and you scare the hell out of him. Then you leave, and he immediately makes a fourteen-minute phone call."

"It could have been a call he was making for business," I say. "It might have had nothing to do with me."

"That's true," she says. "That's what he might have done if he was innocent. If he's guilty, he'd be doing something to protect himself in those moments. Even if it meant just sitting and thinking of a way out of the problem you created for him. Or if it meant calling someone he thought could help him."

"If Chaplin were innocent, he would have reported the mugging," I say. "We know too much about him at this point to believe he's innocent."

"Yes, we do."

"And under the you-have-to-have-money-to-make-money principle, Landon fits perfectly. He's a guy with the resources to make those kinds of investments in oil and rhodium."

"We're getting somewhere with this, Andy."

"We'd better hurry up. The world could blow up any minute."

• • • • •

"THERE ARE MANY, many victims in this case" is how I start my closing statement. "There have been at least twenty-one deaths of people drawn together by fate or bad luck. Probably more. Most of the victims were innocent. Some were not.

"Mr. Morrison has told you that you should be focusing on only one of those deaths, that of Mr. Erskine, and he is partly right. That is the crime you are here to rule on, to decide beyond a reasonable doubt whether Mr. Zimmerman is guilty.

"But common sense requires you to look further. Because eighteen people died in the explosion that cost Billy Zimmerman his leg. And at least three people were murdered after Mr. Erskine, while Billy was sitting in a jail cell. If you know that others killed twenty of those people, how can you believe beyond a reasonable doubt that Billy Zimmerman killed the twenty-first?

"I said it in my opening statement, and I'll say it again. Billy is not perfect; he committed three thefts. But balance that against all the good he has done, as a decorated police officer and a combat veteran. And while you're doing the balancing, throw in the shameful way that we as a society treated him after he protected us for so long. After he lost his leg in the horror that was Iraq.

"We may never know who pulled the trigger in front of the bar that night. We may never know the identities of the men who appeared mysteriously after the shot was fired, only to run off and never be seen again. The police decided they had the killer and looked no further. They may have been well intentioned, but they were hasty, and they were wrong. It is a wrong that you have the power to right.

"In the interests of justice, please right that wrong."

I sit down at the defense table, and Billy leans over and says, "Outstanding." Hike hands me a note that says, "You're as good as Kevin said you were."

But I'm not paying attention to what they are saying, nor am I doing what I usually do after my closing statement. I ordinarily obsess that I haven't done enough and panic at the fact that there's nothing left for me to do. There is nothing I hate more than when a case goes to the jury's hands, and that's what is happening now.

This time, however, I'm thinking of something different, something I realized when I was talking about the men running onto the scene of Erskine's murder that night.

I had been assuming that the men were FBI agents, following Harris but losing him in the chaos after the murder. The way Billy described the scene, though, three men came out of nowhere, as if they had been lying in wait.

I can't imagine the bureau would have the inclination or manpower to have three people following a guy like Harris, nor do I know how they would have known to follow him in the first place. Pete described him as a hired gun out of Philadelphia; M likely employed him on a freelance basis.

To use that much manpower, and to have them in place as they did, must mean that they were watching Erskine. And there is a damn good likelihood that Erskine knew they were there. That he even planned for them to be there.

Erskine was smart; he was not the kind of guy to walk around with a truckload of FBI guys following him, watching him commit illegal acts. He would have been much more careful, if he had any reason to be.

If I'm right, Erskine was working with the FBI. Maybe he was getting immunity in return for turning in his bosses, and the apparent blackmail was part of a sting operation. I'm far from sure about why they were working together, but I still feel like I've figured out another piece of the puzzle.

Our game of chicken has a long way to go.

Judge Catchings gives a standard charge to the jury, and since it is almost four o'clock when he finishes, he sends them home. Neither Eli nor I had made a request to have them sequestered, not that I think the judge would have agreed anyway. Sequestering is pretty rare these days, and in the absence of special circumstances, judges usually don't force it on juries.

He does, however, give them a strong dose of the

same admonition he's been giving throughout the trial: that they are to scrupulously avoid all media coverage of the case. I've never believed that jurors completely do that; I know I wouldn't. I'd hide in the basement and watch everything.

The jurors all nod as he says this. My guess is they'd nod an agreement to stick toothpicks in their eyes if that's what it would take not to get stuck in a local hotel. Then off they go, to reconvene tomorrow morning and start deciding whether Billy Zimmerman is going to live the rest of his life in a cage.

"You did a hell of a job," Billy says as we shake hands.

"That remains to be seen," I say.

He shook his head. "I've seen it already. No matter what the jury says."

It's a generous thing for him to say, especially with the stress he must be under, but it's consistent with his attitude throughout the trial. He's done nothing to make me sorry I took the case, even though he hasn't paid me a dime.

I go home and Laurie greets me with a kiss and a glass of wine. "It's been a long time since I've been around while you're waiting for a verdict," she says. "Are you still as nuts as ever?"

I nod. "Some things never change." I become a complete basket case while waiting for a verdict. I adhere to ridiculous superstitions and am generally impossible to be around.

"You want me to move into a hotel?" she asks. It's a serious question; she doesn't want to intrude on my space or make things more difficult for me by my feeling I have to be civil.

"That nuts I'm not," I say. "Besides, we still have a lot of work to do."

We are going to continue our investigation, even more energetically now that I'm not tied down to being in court every day. If Billy is convicted, then I will use the results of that investigation for an appeal. If he's acquitted, I'll turn over everything we know to Benson and be done with it. Then he can have the responsibility for preventing whatever is going to happen for himself.

Usually I dread hearing that the jury has reached a verdict, but this time I'm semi-eager for it. The sooner I can tell Benson what I know, without damaging Billy's interests, the better.

• • • • •

CHAPLIN NEVER REPORTED the mugging to law enforcement. He immediately decided not to contact the police, and never regretted that decision.

But he did tell Landon about it, and that was a move he did regret.

Landon did not believe in coincidences, and even if he did, this one would have been so over-the-top as to defy credibility. For Chaplin to have been mugged, and for the muggers to take his cell phone, simply had to relate to what was going on. And it had to do with Carpenter.

Landon's number was on that cell phone, of that he was certain. It had to be there at least three or four times. Which meant that Carpenter would come after him. And when he did, it would be through Chaplin.

Chaplin was scared; Landon could tell that from the first sentence of their conversation. This had hit home, more powerfully than even the death of his two colleagues. Someone had invaded his property, had hit him in the head and knocked him out, and that scared the hell out of him.

It was no longer just numbers moving through computers and bank accounts, and it had become personally dangerous. And Chaplin was not the type to handle that kind of danger.

"We need to meet," Landon had said.

"Why?"

"To plan our strategy. We have to keep the upper hand in this."

Chaplin couldn't believe that Landon felt they still had the upper hand, and he certainly didn't want to meet with Landon.

But he wasn't capable of refusing, so he tried another approach. "I don't think we should be seen together right now," he said.

"I agree," Landon said, giving Chaplin momentary hope before dashing it. "So it needs to be someplace out of the way."

Landon suggested they meet the next night at a place just outside Stamford, Connecticut. It was an empty building, originally a medical center, but it had been foreclosed on when the economy went bad. Landon owned the building and could get a key.

Best of all, there was a long, narrow road for almost half a mile leading to the building. If either of them was for any reason being followed, he would be able to detect it and could abort the meeting. "But we won't be followed," Landon said, departing from his norm and saying what he really believed.

Landon's next phone call was to M, to explain what was going on and what he needed him to do. He detailed it clearly and concisely, and it took him almost three minutes to do so.

M's response was a little shorter. "Got it," he said.

"No problem?" Landon asked.

"I don't believe in problems."

They got off the phone, and M got ready to go. He was actually looking forward to it; sitting around and doing nothing was starting to drive him crazy.

"You okay here without me?" M asked, although he already knew the answer.

"Of course," Jason Greer answered. "It will be good to get rid of you."

M smiled, partially because he knew Greer was telling the truth. M was not an easy guy to hang around with; he made people uncomfortable. Always had, always would. "If for any reason I'm not back in time, you can handle things?"

"I can handle things," Greer said, and M also knew that was true. For this specific job, it was M who was unnecessary. Greer was well trained and more than tough enough to do the job.

M got ready to leave, fully prepared himself to handle what had to be done. But first he made a phone call to find out exactly what that consisted of.

The answer made him very happy.

What would not have made him happy, had he realized it, was that as he was leaving the hotel, he was seen by one Jesse Barrett. Barrett and M had briefly worked together on a job in Chicago, a job that resulted in the untimely death of two people.

M didn't notice Barrett, and Barrett was not about to call out to him. In the moment, Barrett considered M a source of potential profit, mainly because the word was out that Joseph Russo was looking for him.

• • • • •

TODAY SHOWS EVERY sign of being worse than yesterday, and that is really saying something. All I did yesterday was hang out in the house, grumbling occasionally and waiting for the phone to ring.

Laurie kept away from me, and Milo and Tara made the intelligent decision to stay with her. We've sent Marcus away as well; with the trial over, our being at home all the time, and the envelope found, his protective services no longer seem necessary.

After coming over for a while to talk about the case, even Hike said I was too downbeat to spend time with. Hike!

Each hour feels like a week, and what I plan to do is break up each day by going to the prison to talk to Billy. He has to be a bigger basket case than I am, since it's his freedom on the line. But I also have the added pressure of worrying about Benson's ominous prediction of "blood" being shed, while Billy is appropriately only worried about Billy.

Just as I'm about to leave I get a call from Benson. "We need to talk," he says.

"We already talked." Since he called me, rather than the reverse, I may have the upper hand, so I don't want to blow it by seeming too anxious.

"Now we really need to talk. How fast can you be here?"

"It'll take a while," I say.

"Come on, all you're doing is sitting with your thumb up your ass waiting for a verdict. Get down here."

I agree to do so, and forty-five minutes later I'm in his office. He doesn't waste any time. "We have reason to believe that there will soon be a strategic attack on a key element of the infrastructure of the United States. We don't know what the target will be, when the attack will take place, or who is behind it."

"You have my attention."

"Good. If you have information that can prevent this event, you need to tell it to me now."

"We've already had this conversation. My client is facing life in prison for a crime that you know he didn't commit. You need to fix that first."

"That's going to be taken care of," he says.

"What the hell does that mean?"

"I can't say. Just trust me; it's being taken care of."

"When?"

"Today."

"When it happens, I'll tell you what I know."

"Carpenter, people are going to die. Is that what you want? Your client will not be convicted; I give you my word."

I have no idea where this is coming from, and I'm torn as to what to do. I believe that Benson is telling me the truth as he sees it, but that does not mean it will turn out as he says. Too many things can go wrong; he's got too many bosses that can potentially intervene.

I make a decision that I'll give him part of what he is looking for, and hold back the rest for now. "I don't know that much," I say. "But the guy you should be looking for is Alan Landon."

"Alan Landon." He doesn't say it as a question; it's more like he's letting it roll around in his mind, thinking about it.

"My belief is that he has been investing heavily in commodities like oil and rhodium, and then taking advantage of incidents that have sent the prices way up. There may be other examples, but I'm only aware of those two."

He nods. "Okay. What else?"

I reach into the briefcase I brought and take out the envelope that Milo dug up, and that Erskine gave to his killer that night. It's in a clear, plastic cover, to preserve any trace evidence that might still be on it.

"This is what Erskine was carrying that night, although you may have seen it already."

He looks at me as if he's about to say something, but then stays silent and opens the envelope. He looks at the empty pages, and then the "Kiss My Ass" type on the last page. He then makes a facial expression, somewhere between a frown and a grin, and puts it back in the envelope.

If I had to guess, I'd say he was surprised by what he just saw, and I'm surprised that he's surprised.

"You got the dog to find it?"

I nod. "Milo." For some reason, it irritates me when people refer to him as "the dog." I am aware that the irritation is not a sign of mental health on my part. "I got him to trust me."

"What else do you know?"

"I have suspicions that I'm working on. When I confirm them, we can talk again." I'm not being straight with him. For instance, I'm more sure that Chaplin is dirty than I am Landon. But I think Landon is more dangerous, so that's why I gave him to Benson. When Billy is out of jail, I will be more forthcoming.

"Maybe you'll confirm them when the trial is over," he says, understanding the situation.

"We can hope," I say.

On the way back, I call Hike and relate my conversation, and tell him that something is about to happen.

"How the hell can they stop a trial?" he asks. "After all this time they're going to say, *Damn, we had agents who saw the whole thing, but we forgot to mention it?*"

"It'll be interesting to see," I say, and I head home. I'm not going to go to the prison, because Billy will ask me a million questions that I won't be able to answer. We're going to find out soon enough.

"Soon enough" is at two o'clock in the afternoon, when Rita Gordon calls from the courthouse. "The judge wants you here in forty-five minutes," she says.

"A verdict?" I ask, though I doubt that's what it could be.

"No."

"Then what?"

"Andy, just get down here, okay? It's important."

• • • • •

HIKE AND I get to the courtroom with five minutes to spare.

Eli shows up looking confused, and he shrugs at me as if he has no idea what's going on. I return the shrug, but I'm sure I'm more informed than he is. While I don't know exactly what's going to happen, I know it's going to mean the end of the trial.

Billy is brought in, looking nervous and concerned. He's afraid that a verdict is reached; I think he's been hoping for a hung jury. "What's going on?" he asks.

"I don't know, but it's not a verdict."

"Does the jury have a question?"

"If they do, I haven't heard it."

The bailiff comes over and informs first me, and then Eli, that Judge Catchings wants to see us in his chambers. He doesn't say lead counsel only, so I bring Hike with me, and Eli brings his second counsel as well.

I always hate going to a judge's chambers. It feels like I'm being dragged to the principal's office, mostly because I'm usually being called there because the judge is pissed off at me. That's not the case this time.

Judge Catchings sits behind his desk, not wearing his robe and looking weary. "I've been informed of very serious juror misconduct, and I've confirmed it to be true."

"What kind of misconduct?" Eli asks.

"One of the jurors visited the murder scene on his own, though I had prohibited it repeatedly. The same juror watched media coverage of the trial."

Eli is not completely getting it; or maybe he just doesn't want to. A mistrial is a nightmare for the prosecution, in some ways worse than an acquittal. "You can bring in one of the alternates, Your Honor. It's only been a day and a half; you can instruct them to commence their deliberations from the beginning."

Catchings shakes his head. "The juror has conveyed to the other jurors his feelings based on his visit to the scene, and the coverage he watched on television. The entire panel is contaminated."

We throw out some more questions, until all the details come out. In addition to going to the scene one night last week, the juror had watched the CNN coverage, in particular an appearance by Douglas Burns, a defense attorney often called upon as an expert commentator by various networks. I've seen him many times; he's got an outstanding legal mind, honed by his earlier days as a prosecutor.

His point of view on this case was basically that Billy should be acquitted, and I assume he gave cogent arguments that I would have agreed with. More importantly, the juror seemed to agree with them, and came in and tried to convince his colleagues on the panel.

Somebody had conveyed this information anonymously to the court, and Catchings confirmed all of it. "I have no choice but to declare a mistrial," he says.

"Which juror was it?" I ask.

"Number nine," he says, confirming my hunch. He was the juror who seemed far too anxious to be on the panel.

"Had the jury taken any votes?" Eli asks. "Did you happen to find that out?"

Catchings nods. "Ten to two for conviction."

It's all Eli can do to stifle a moan, and we head back to the courtroom for Catchings to announce it officially. As soon as I see Billy, I tell him the news.

His relief is obvious. "I'll take the mistrial; I thought we were going to lose."

"We were," I say. "The jury was ten–two against."

Billy's no dummy; he knows how this works. "With those kind of numbers they'll retry the case."

"Billy, I'm going to tell you something, but at this point I can't answer the questions you'll have about what I'm going to say. Okay?"

"Okay."

"I strongly believe you will never be convicted of this crime. You will not even be retried for this crime. You're going to stay in jail for a while, but it will be a short time."

He grins. "I can think of a few questions to ask, but for now I'll just sit with this awhile."

"Thank you."

Billy is taken away. I'm happy he's going to get off,

but I'm feeling very uneasy about the turn that things have taken. For all my cynicism, I believe in the criminal justice system, and I take my role as an officer of the court seriously.

This has been an abuse of the system. Juror number nine was planted there by the FBI, to be used as they saw fit. There might have been others as well, since it was possible that number nine might not have made the panel in the first place.

This worked out in my favor, and in Billy's.

But it stinks.

• • • • •

ALAN LANDON WAS already waiting in the
deserted building when Chaplin arrived. Chaplin was surprised when he saw him, because Landon's car was not
there. Perhaps a limo dropped him off and would come
back for him; nothing that people with this kind of money
did surprised Chaplin.

"Sorry if I'm late," Chaplin said, though he knew that
he wasn't.

Landon looked at his watch. "You're not late. Thanks
for coming. Sorry I can't offer you anything to drink."

"No problem."

"This situation has the potential to become a bit of a
mess," Landon said.

"There's no way Carpenter can prove anything. These
are foreign companies, fully insulated. No one can tie
you to them, and all I'm doing is executing trades for a

client." Chaplin believed what he was saying; he'd had time to think it through, and his confidence increased in the process.

"I'm not sure I agree," Landon said.

"Why not?"

"Because there are people who know the truth, and people have a tendency to talk."

"Who are you talking about?" Chaplin asks.

"Well, for instance, you."

A quick flash of panic hit Chaplin, but he recovered quickly. "I'm certainly not going to say anything; I'd wind up going to jail."

"Unless you got immunity in return for turning me in."

"Come on, Alan. I would never do that."

"Do you believe him?" Landon asked.

Chaplin was confused. "Do I believe who?"

"Not for me to say." The voice was coming from behind Chaplin, and he whirled to see who it was. It was M, and though Chaplin had never met him, he was scared to death. The gun in M's hand told him all he needed to know.

Chaplin turned back to Landon. "Alan, please..."

"I'm sorry, Jonathan. When it comes to money, I'm a risk taker. But in things like this, I don't take chances."

"But I swear I won't say anything. Please, Alan, I'm begging you."

"Don't, Jonathan, it's unseemly. M..."

M didn't hesitate; he fired three shots. All three hit Alan Landon directly in the chest, a grouping separated by no more than a few centimeters. Landon was blown back against the wall, dead long before he hit the ground.

And long before he had time to realize what had happened.

It took Chaplin a moment to process what he had just witnessed, to try and understand why Landon was dead and he was still alive. It did not give him a feeling of safety; his instinct was that M was there to kill both of them.

He started to move toward the door, which was twenty feet away, way too far to get to in time.

"Hold it!" yelled M, and Chaplin froze. "Turn around," said M, and Chaplin did just that.

To his surprise, M did not have the gun raised. "You've got nothing to worry about," M said. "As long as you keep your mouth shut and do what you're told."

"I will. I swear."

"So go home, and make sure the trades are executed as planned. Then you're finished with this."

"So I can leave now?"

"As soon as you help me clean this up."

Which is what Chaplin did. And after they had wrapped Landon's body in plastic, they carried the body together and placed it in M's trunk.

"You can go now," said M.

Chaplin drove off, and did not look back.

• • • • •

"ANDY, I KNOW where M is. Or at least where he was a couple of days ago."

Willie Miller has called to tell me what he obviously considers important news. I know he thinks it's important, because he's waking me at six fifteen in the morning. I look over and see Laurie awake and pedaling furiously on the exercise bike. It's as if the world and I are in different time zones.

"Where?"

"Just outside Boston, a place called Everett."

"Why did you say 'was'? You don't think he's there anymore?"

"My source saw him leaving a hotel," Willie says. "He doesn't know if he'll be back."

"Who's your source? Russo?"

"Yeah. He put out the word, and some guy called in

and said he saw M. Russo said the guy is pretty reliable."

I hear noise in the background, as if someone is talking on a loudspeaker. "Where are you?" I ask.

"LaGuardia. My flight is in forty-five minutes."

I'm torn as to what to do here. If M is really there, it would be extraordinarily dangerous for Willie to go chasing him. Everyone familiar with him tells me he's an ice-cold killer, the kind of guy it would require an army or Marcus to take down.

On the other hand, there seems to be a very good chance that the informant was wrong, since I know of no reason for M to have gone off to a small Massachusetts town. Also, the guy reported that M may well have left, thereby covering himself nicely if he was wrong. The report could have been just to get on Russo's good side.

Making my decision considerably less important is the fact that Willie wouldn't listen to me anyway. He's going to Everett, with my blessing or not.

"Willie, be careful. This is not a guy to fool around with."

"I hear you," he says.

"If you find him, you call me, and I'll get the FBI to move in. Cindy Spodek works out of the Boston office."

"I hear you."

"But my recommendation is that you not go at all."

"Can't hear you," he says, and hangs up. I'm beginning to think that I am not Andy, the Supreme Leader.

I no sooner get off the phone than Sam calls. I'm going to have to sit my crack staff down and explain to them that we are a nine-to-five operation.

"I think I've got it, Andy. It's gas."

"Sorry to hear that, Sam. Why don't you take a Pepto-Bismol and call me later?"

"Come on, Andy. You know what I mean. Chaplin's company has been taking positions in natural gas. It's mostly on behalf of the same companies that made the killings on oil and rhodium."

"You're sure about this?"

"Well, I'm sure that they have big positions in natural gas. The problem is that they are a large company, so they have a lot of investments. So there could be something else I'm missing that's even bigger; it will take me a while to make sure."

"How much do they stand to make on the gas?" I ask, knowing that he can't really answer the question, since it would depend on how much the price of natural gas were to go up.

"A lot" is his answer. "They've got bigger positions than the other two times combined. If it goes down the same way, they're going to make a killing."

His choice of words is uncomfortable for me. I still have a dilemma; a mistrial is not an acquittal, so Billy is far from off the hook. But telling Benson Landon's name may not be enough to prevent whatever is going to happen, and I am tempted to tell him what Sam has learned about the natural gas investments.

I decide to wait the rest of the day to see what the fallout is from yesterday's mistrial. The media has latched on to the news that the last vote the jury took was heavily in favor of conviction, and their unconfirmed general belief is that juror number nine was one of the two dissenters.

I have an early-afternoon appointment at the prison to

see Billy, who is craving information about his situation. I tell him I'm in negotiations with the FBI, trying to get them to reveal information that can exonerate him.

"Information they've had all along?"

I nod. "Yes, I believe so."

"Bastards. They just let me sit here?"

"I'm working on changing that, but it's a little tricky."

"Work hard, okay? I'm getting a little sick of this place. And I'm looking forward to seeing my man Milo."

I nod. "Okay."

"It's time you started earning the money I'm not pay-ing you," he says.

I've come to like Billy a lot, but I'm looking forward to the day that he's no longer a client. For both our sakes.

I leave the prison and get a phone call from Eli's as-sistant, asking if I can come to his office right away. He's in a meeting, but he'll be back in twenty minutes, just about the time I would get there. The message is that it's very important.

I'm there in fifteen minutes, and Eli is waiting for me. If he's happy to see me, he's hiding it well. He looks like Hike on a particularly bad day.

"You okay, Eli?"

"Yeah, I'm giddy with happiness. Thanks for coming, Andy. I wanted to tell you something before you heard it in the media." He looks at his watch. "Which will be any minute."

"What's going on?"

"We're officially dropping the charges against Zim-merman. There won't be a retrial."

I'm shocked, not at the decision, but at the timing. To drop charges hours after word is released that the jury was ten–two in favor of conviction is to invite public anger. "Why?"

"Between us?"

"Of course."

"I have no idea. The word came down from up high that it was going to end this way."

"How high?"

"The attorney general of the State of New Jersey. I believe that he was in very intense discussions with agents of the federal government."

"I'm obviously pleased about this, Eli. But you know it's going to look bad."

He nods. "Tell me about it. They're going to say that some new information has surfaced, and then hope it all blows over. But anyone with a brain will know there's something wrong."

I stop at the prison to tell Billy the great news, and he hugs me in relief upon hearing it. Man-hugs are among my least favorite things, and prison man-hugs with large men are the absolute worst. Since the prison officials haven't received notification yet, I tell Billy that it probably won't be until morning that he is officially released.

"Me and Milo," he says. "You saved us both."

His saying that makes me realize that Milo and I are soon going to be parting company. I'm going to miss him; he's a lot of fun, and he's one of the few living creatures who trusts me completely. I'm sure Tara is going to miss him even more.

I'm almost home when I hear on the radio that the government has decided to drop the charges against Billy. As Eli said, they are claiming additional information has come up that would make a conviction im-

possible, but they cannot reveal what it is, for fear of
jeopardizing a "continuing investigation." God forbid.

I call Benson's office and am told that he is "out in
the field" and is not expected back until the morning. I
don't have his cell phone number with me, but I'm not
sure I'd call him anyway. Agents may not like to be bothered when they're in the field. Instead I leave a message
for him to call me, that I have information for him that
could be significant.

I'm having a weird post-trial reaction. Usually I am
either euphoric by a victory or devastated by a defeat,
but this is somewhere in the middle. I'm happy that Billy
is free and that justice was served, but I'm very disappointed and uneasy with the way it was served.

It is ominous to me that members of the FBI can
manipulate the justice system the way they did, with apparent ease. I can't imagine that they broke new ground
here; they must have done it before. And if they can do it
in favor of the defendant, why not the prosecution? The
implications are chilling.

The only even slightly mitigating factor is that they
knew Billy was innocent, and their actions served to
eliminate the possibility of a wrongful conviction. I don't
know if that was their motivation; I can only hope it was.
But I still don't like it.

After every victorious trial we have a tradition of having a party at Charlie's to celebrate. I'm not inclined to
do so this time, even though whenever a client goes free
I consider it a victory. Not only am I not in a partying
mood, but Charlie's has not yet reopened.

Also, a couple of Laurie's Findlay friends are vaca-
tioning in New York, and Laurie is having dinner with

them tonight. A party without her is definitely starting at a disadvantage in my mind. Besides, with Marcus off the case, I don't want to leave Milo and Tara alone. I have no reason to think Milo is still in danger, but you never know.

All in all, it's not party time.

• • • • •

I MAKE MYSELF a frozen pizza, then throw tennis balls to Milo and Tara. It's not exactly mentally taxing, which is fine with me at the moment. It feels good, though it would feel better if Laurie were here.

Laurie's told me not to expect her until ten o'clock, since their dinner reservation was at six thirty. I hope she likes her friends, because if I had to have a three-and-a-half-hour dinner with Vince and Pete at a restaurant without televisions, I would go into the kitchen and stick my head in the oven.

Actually, I should have asked her if her friends were female. For all I know, she could be with some old boyfriend. She's off wining and dining some guy, and I'm sitting here with a frozen pizza.

I go upstairs, lie on the bed, and turn on the Mets game. It's in the fifth inning when Hike calls. "Turn on the television," he says.

"I'm watching television."

"Turn on CNN."

I do so and immediately see his point. The graphic across the bottom of the screen says, "Financier's Body Found." Then, "Alan Landon Is Murder Victim."

Within five minutes I've gotten as much of the story as the media has. Landon was found by a jogger in a Connecticut park with three bullets in his chest. He's believed to have been dead for approximately twenty-four hours, though it is thought that the body was killed elsewhere and then dumped.

It's amazing how many bodies seem to be found by joggers. If I were a detective looking for a missing person, I would recruit marathon runners and deputize them.

According to reports, the jogger called in local police, who then brought in federal authorities.

Now I know what Benson is doing "in the field."

It's about nine thirty when I think I hear Laurie downstairs, but then I realize it's only the television, which I left on when I was in the kitchen. I go down to turn it off, mainly because it will give me an excuse to be near the refrigerator again. I'm a growing boy; one frozen pizza apparently doesn't do it for me.

I fill a dish with chocolate ice cream. It's nonfat and sugar-free, so the dish that I have probably is no more than two thousand calories. I head back out of the kitchen through the den, on the way to the stairs.

I hear a noise off to my left, and suddenly the front door comes crashing open. Bursting in behind it is a large man with a gun. He falls to the floor from the impact, and I drop the ice cream and run back toward the kitchen.

It was the only place I could go, but it does little to improve my thin chance of survival. I hide behind the stone island in the middle of the kitchen, but there is no escape from there. The man with the gun, whom I think is M, merely has to follow me in, walk around the island, and shoot me.

I'm also not near a phone, and to get to one would expose myself to the intruder. That would not be an answer anyway; unless the emergency officers are hiding in my living room and waiting for my call, they couldn't get here in time to save me.

"Nowhere to run, Carpenter. Nowhere to hide." Then, "This I'm going to enjoy."

I can hear him enter the kitchen, and I expect that he will walk around the island. I try to sense which side he'll come from, so that I can move the other way and make a break for it out of the room. But he must be walking quietly, because I can barely hear him, and there's as much chance that I'll guess right as wrong.

If I guess wrong, I'll walk right into him. Guess right, and he'll shoot me in the back.

I'm so busy guessing that I don't realize he's already found me. When I look up, he's standing there, pointing the gun at me and smiling. It is M, and he is the person that is going to kill me. The feeling of panic is overwhelming.

"I should have done this a long time ago," he says, and he raises his gun. I brace myself for the impact, though I know that bullet bracing is not a terribly effective defense.

But there is no bullet. Instead something flies across the room and knocks the gun out of M's hand, shoving M down in the process. It is the amazing Milo, doing what Milo does.

Except this time Milo takes it a step further. He jumps

on M and starts to bite at him around the face, and M is screaming in pain. I've been frozen watching this, but I finally force myself to move, and I pick up the gun, which is lying only a few feet away from me.

Once I have it in my shaking hand, I yell, "That's enough Milo! Milo! That's enough!"

Milo actually listens and moves away, and I can see that M is bleeding from his scalp, forehead, and cheek. I point the gun at M and scream, "Get up! Get up!" though I'm not sure why. I was probably better off with him lying on his back.

He slowly gets to his feet, dripping blood. I notice Tara has ambled into the room, probably assuming that with all the commotion, there are treats to be had. I briefly fear that she'll walk near M and he'll grab her, but she seems content to watch from afar.

"Don't move," I say to M. "Stand there." All the while I'm pointing the gun, and my arm is getting a little tired. I reach over with my left hand, pick up the cordless phone, and dial 911. When they answer, I quickly tell them my name and address, as well as the situation. "Please hurry" is how I end the call.

M hasn't made a move, but I'm worried that he could have another gun, maybe strapped to something like an ankle or his back, like Bruce Willis in *Die Hard*. I don't say anything else; I just keep pointing the gun and praying that the cops will hurry the hell up.

"Give me the fucking gun," he says.

"Shut up" is my witty response.

"You don't have the guts to shoot me," he says, and he takes a step toward me.

"You're about to find out," I say.

M laughs, and takes another step forward, as if taunting me. He thinks I'm scared, which makes him 100 percent correct.

"One more step and you are a dead man," I say, without having any confidence whatsoever that I could actually shoot him.

He seems to quickly look behind me, and then does more than take a step; he rushes me, taking me by surprise. The bullet hits him square in the forehead and for one sickening instant reminds me of the scene in *The Godfather* where Michael shoots Sollozzo and the police captain in the restaurant.

I must have acted on instinct, evidence of a reflexive, almost primitive defense mechanism that I didn't know I had, because I don't remember deciding to shoot, or even shooting.

That's because I didn't.

Laurie is standing in the doorway, dropping her gun to her side. I hadn't even seen her come in, but perhaps M had, and made his move because of it.

"How was your evening?" I say.

"Are you okay, Andy?"

I try and come up with a witty response, but I'm out of them. The impact of what just happened is hitting me, and it's all I can do to keep myself together. I walk over and hug Laurie, and then Tara, and then Milo. I hug Milo twice.

By the time I'm finished hugging, the police are arriving.

• • • • •

WILLIE WAS SITTING in the hotel lobby bar, drinking beer and watching television. He'd been there most of the night, trying to limit the number of beers he had, since he wanted to stay alert. He hadn't seen M all day, and was beginning to think that he was no longer there. Russo's guy had said he might have left, and it appeared to Willie that he must have.

All of a sudden staying alert became easy when a breaking news story came on the screen reporting that M had been killed in the process of breaking into Andy Carpenter's house.

Willie watched for five minutes, but they didn't mention whether anyone other than M was hurt. He then went out to the lobby, where he could hear better, and called Andy on his cell phone.

His relief when Andy answered was palpable. "Andy, you okay?"

"Yeah, I'm fine," Andy said. "Where are you?" In the excitement he had momentarily forgotten that Willie had gone off in search of M.

"Everett. Up in Massachusetts."

"Right. I think it's safe to come back now."

They talked for a brief time, since Andy had to get off to answer more police questions. Willie promised to get a flight back the next morning.

But there was plenty of time until morning, so Willie went back to the bar to have a few more beers and watch the TV coverage. He wasn't going to be chasing M that night, or ever, so he could drink without worrying about staying alert.

Jason Greer came into the hotel a few minutes later. He had been repeatedly admonished by M to stay out of public view as much as possible, since his picture had been one of those that Carpenter had shown on Larry King.

But M hadn't called in the two days since he left, and Greer had been going nuts in the room. So he went out to a fast-food restaurant, using the drive-thru so that customers wouldn't see him.

Then, when he returned to the hotel, he did what he had been doing all along, which was self-park the van rather than use the valet. This was far less to avoid being recognized than to prevent anyone from seeing what was in the locked rear section of the van.

Greer walked down the lobby toward the elevators, casually looking into the bar and the televisions that were on in there. He stopped in his tracks when the first thing he saw was the picture of M, and a graphic saying that he had been killed.

Trying to control his rising feeling of panic, Greer went into the bar to watch the television and find out whatever he could. He didn't notice Willie Miller drinking a beer at the end of the bar, nor would it have meant anything if he had. He didn't know who Willie was, or what he looked like.

But Willie noticed him.

He couldn't be sure, but he had a good eye for faces, and he thought he recognized Greer from the picture Andy had shown on television. And the way Greer was staring at the screen, trying unsuccessfully to hide the look of confusion and fear on his face, made it far more likely that he was right.

Willie went out and called Andy again, doing so from a vantage point where he could see the bar. No one answered, so Willie left a message in which he said that he thought he was looking at Greer, but he wasn't sure.

As he was getting off the phone, Greer was leaving the bar. Willie followed him and got on the same elevator. Greer pressed 9, and Willie briefly debated whether he should press a different floor so as not to look suspicious. He decided to go to 9 as well, since Greer would have no reason to think that Willie was tailing him. If a potential tail, probably a cop, knew Greer's whereabouts well enough to be in the hotel, there would be little reason to follow him to his room. They would have other ways of learning the room number, if they didn't know it already.

Willie caught a break when Greer got off the elevator and went to room 942, which was almost directly across from the elevator. Willie was thus able to walk past him as if heading for a different room.

Willie then went to his own room, which was on the third floor, to watch more of the coverage and figure out his next move. He couldn't be sure it was Greer; his mind and memory could have been playing tricks on him and causing him to be overly suspicious.

But it would be worth a day or two to find out, even though the idea of more time alone in Everett was not all that appealing. Regardless, he would stay and keep an eye on Greer.

The question he needed to answer was how.

• • • • •

Aʟᴍᴏsᴛ ɢᴇᴛᴛɪɴɢ ᴋɪʟʟᴇᴅ can be exhausting, and I would love to get some sleep. Unfortunately, detectives usually have a lot of questions to ask when they find someone with their head blown open on a kitchen floor. The media have set up camp on the street outside, but they're easier to avoid.

Even though Pete Stanton is in charge, and therefore we are obviously not under suspicion, the process is very time consuming. This is especially true since two people, Laurie and me, are very much involved. Milo, arguably the key player in the entire incident, escapes unscathed, and he and Tara are in the corner, sleeping together.

When we've finally answered everything there is to be answered, and when forensics and the coroner have concluded their respective business, my need for sleep is put on another hold. That's because Benson and two

other FBI agents show up at around two AM to make a
long night much longer.

Benson talks to Pete for a while, probably getting an
update, and when they're finished Pete comes over and
asks me if I want him to hang around as a buffer. I thank
him but say it's not necessary; I've had plenty of experience going one-on-one with Benson.

"You've been a busy boy," Benson says when he
comes over to me.

"As have you. Any chance that with Landon and M
out of the way, we're out of bad guys?"

"We're never out of bad guys," he says. "You called
my office before."

I nod. "Speaking of bad guys...Jonathan Chaplin is
somebody for you to check out. He runs a hedge fund
called C and F Investments. Landon was making the
investments through that fund, and they were doing it
through a bunch of different brokerage houses."

"Chaplin know what was going on?" he asks.

I nod. "Definitely. But I've got something else for you
that's more important."

"What is it?"

"First we need to make a deal," I say.

"What a surprise" is his dry response, which I ignore.

"I want your word that an announcement will be made
tomorrow stating in no uncertain terms that Billy Zimmerman is innocent. I don't want people thinking he's a
murderer who was released on a technicality. The truth
is he's been a goddamn hero all his life, and when Erskine got shot he ran at the killer and disarmed him, even
though he couldn't stand Erskine."

Benson nods. "Fair enough. Done."

"And I want him taken care of financially."

"Kiss my ass, Carpenter."

"That's what Erskine's note said...did you write it for him?"

He ignores the question. "You want me to give Zimmerman my pension?"

"I don't care how it happens. Zimmerman has been sitting in jail for a crime you knew he didn't commit. Beyond that, the FBI committed jury tampering. I don't think that was your call; I'll bet it goes high up to people who will be seriously pissed and embarrassed to have it made public. Well, I'll go on *60 Minutes* to get the story out, if I have to, and you'll have every reporter in America digging for more."

"I'll do what I can," he says.

"You'll do better than that." I'm trying to extract a promise from Benson, though he wouldn't be above breaking it if it suited him. My threat to go public is my insurance.

"Okay," he says. "Are you finished now? Or do you want my firstborn?"

"I'm finished."

"Okay, now here are my terms," he says. "As long as I deliver on my end, you tell no one about FBI involvement in this case. And you tell me everything you know, right now."

"Deal. I have reason to believe that the next commodity that Landon was hoping to profit from is natural gas."

"Why do you say that?" he asks.

"The same companies that profited from the oil and rhodium through C and F are poised to make an even bigger profit on gas."

"Do you know what they're planning?"

I shake my head. "No. But with Landon and M gone, I would hope there's no one else to plan anything."

"You keep hoping," Benson says, the implication being that he plans on doing a lot more than that.

Once Benson leaves, Laurie and I get into bed. The implications of what happened here hit me full-bore, and being able to hold her is a substantial comfort. Of course, momentous events are not a requirement for me to enjoy holding Laurie, but tonight it seems even more necessary.

It's not until the morning that I think to check my phone messages, and I have one from Willie, telling me that he thinks he has seen Jason Greer. My very strong hunch is that he's imagining things, especially since it now seems very unlikely that the M sighting in Everett was real.

I call Willie back, but his cell phone doesn't answer. I leave a message expressing my doubts, in gentle terms, and tell him to call me.

Now it's time to experience the absolute best part of my job. I head down to the prison to get Billy, who is being processed out. I have to wait less than twenty minutes, a blip in prison time, and there he is.

We do a real firm handshake, and he grabs my left arm with his left hand, but we avoid the full-on man-hug. Then we head outside to my car, with him stopping briefly to look up at the sky and take a deep breath. I can't imagine what it's like to be cooped up in a cell, so I have no insight as to how it feels to be finally let out of that cell.

But if Billy's expression is any indication, it must feel great.

BILLY DOESN'T WANT to go out for a big breakfast. He also doesn't want to have a beer, or go to a park, or see any friends. He wants to go directly to my house, because that's where Milo is.

On the way he asks me to tell him what has gone on, and I tell him I will when we get home. For the time being I describe how Milo saved my life last night.

He smiles and says, "I know what that feels like. He saved mine when I got back from Iraq."

We pull up in front of the house, and I tell Billy to hurry up and get inside. I say this because Milo is at the window, clawing at it and going nuts at the sight of Billy, and I'm afraid he's going to come crashing through.

I open the door and let Billy in first, and Milo re-creates the flying-dog trick he did on M. Except this time he's not after anything in Billy's hand; he's after Billy. They roll around on the floor for a while, with Billy laughing the whole time. Tara looks at me as if wondering who these two lunatics are on the floor.

Laurie hears the chaos and comes downstairs, laughing when she sees Billy and Milo. I wait until they've calmed down before introducing her, since she and Billy have never met.

Laurie makes pancakes, her specialty, and Billy inhales them in Marcus-like fashion. "I never thought I was going to have food this good again," he says.

Billy pauses chewing long enough to again ask me to fill him in on everything he's missed relating to his case. I do that in some detail, only leaving out the parts about the FBI's being on the murder scene that night, and the jury tampering. I promised Benson I would keep that to myself, and I don't want to jeopardize the financial payoff I've arranged for Billy.

"So it's over?" Billy asks.

"Yes. You'll be fully exonerated today."

He shakes his head. "I don't mean my case. I mean the operation they were running."

"I think so, but I certainly can't be sure. And I don't think Benson agrees, though he's not in a position to just assume the best."

"I agree with Benson," he says.

Laurie nods. "So do I."

"Why?"

"Two reasons," Billy says. "One, there's a lot of money that's been made, and a lot more to come. If Landon and M were alone at the top of this, then that money has no one to collect it, and no one to spend it. In my experience money is always surrounded by people."

"And the second reason?" I say, though I am formulating my own.

Laurie provides it for him. "Erskine. He doesn't figure. If he was bad and in on it, then he would have no reason to blackmail them; they were his money source and there was plenty to go around. If he wasn't bad, then who recruited the other soldiers?"

Billy nods. "Right," he says, though I already knew that. "There's got to be someone else, someone who could get to Erskine's people, who also has the smarts to handle the financial end of this."

It hits me like a ton of bricks. I know exactly who that someone is. My mind is racing such that I can barely hear Billy continue.

"You know who worries me right now?" he says, but doesn't wait for an answer. "Greer."

I grab the phone, in the moment deciding which of two crucial phone calls I should make first. I call Willie, but again his phone goes to voice mail. I leave another message, this time far more urgent.

As I'm dialing the second call, I say, "Laurie, please Google 'Everett, Massachusetts' right away. I want to know what industry they have there."

"What am I looking for?" she asks.

"You'll know when you find it," I say, as she rushes over to the computer.

I call Benson, but he's not in his office and not answering his cell phone. I leave a message that it's absolutely urgent that he call me.

When I get off the phone, Laurie is getting up from

the computer. The look on her face says it all. "Everett has one of only five liquefied natural gas terminals in the United States. It's where the tankers dock."

That is exactly what I was afraid of. "Shit," I say, substantially understating the case.

"The terminals are considered prime targets for a terrorist attack."

"Shit."

"It's only four and a half miles from Boston."

This time I don't say *shit*.

I say, "Willie."

• • • • •

WILLIE SET A wake-up call for six o'clock in the morning. He figured that would be early enough to keep track of Greer, unless Greer was in Everett to do dairy farming. Not being used to tailing people, he was faced with a dilemma. If he waited inside the hotel to see him, then he might not be able to get to his car in time to follow Greer wherever he might go. If he waited outside, then he was worried that he'd have no idea at all where Greer was.

Willie solved the problem by giving the valet fifty bucks to let him park his car on the hotel driveway, where he could get to it quickly. He then waited in the lobby near the only elevator bank that stopped at the ninth floor. If Greer came down, Willie would see him and be able to get to his car in time.

At around eight o'clock Willie realized that he had

left his cell phone in the room. He debated whether or not
to go get it, and came down on the negative. If he did, he
could miss Greer, and then wind up spending the rest of
the day waiting for someone who was already gone.

By noon Willie was bored and starving, not necessarily in that order. He saw a room-service waiter pushing
a cart, and asked if he would consider bringing him food
there. The waiter seemed generally okay with it, and his
enthusiasm increased when Willie gave him another fifty
dollars as an incentive.

Willie ordered just about everything he could think of,
and ate quickly, since he knew that sitting in the lobby
with all those trays looked weird. He finished and called
for the trays to be picked up, and that was accomplished
by one o'clock.

One hour later, Geer came off the elevator and went
outside. Willie followed him and watched him walk to
the self-service parking lot. Willie then went to his own
car, and when Greer came out driving a van, Willie followed after him at a decent distance. Fortunately for
Willie, the van was large and therefore distinctive and
easy to pick out in the traffic.

Greer drove north for about a mile and a half, and then
east toward the water. He drove slowly and carefully, so
Willie had no trouble following him.

But losing him wasn't what Willie was worried about;
he was trying to figure out where Greer was going and
why he was going there. And in the back of his mind was
the very real possibility that it wasn't Greer at all; that
he'd been mistaken all along.

But every instinct Willie had told him he was right.

Greer reached an area above the water, and then

turned onto a winding road that led downward, past a sign that said NO THROUGH STREET. Willie decided not to follow him; since it was a dead end he would be easily noticed at best, and a sitting duck at worst.

Instead he parked along the road at a spot from which he could see the rest of the road below. He watched as Greer parked his van almost directly below Willie. Both of them overlooked the pier and had a view of the water, though Willie's was from a higher elevation. Off to the left was a huge industrial plant with enormous tanks, though Willie did not know exactly what its purpose was.

This seemed to Willie to be suspicious behavior, and reaffirmed his feeling that it was, in fact, Greer. But it didn't tell him what to do, and worst of all, he had no way to call anyone for advice or backup.

So he waited, by himself, without even a room-service guy to provide sustenance.

• • • • •

I TELL CINDY Spodek's assistant to interrupt her meeting, that it's urgent I speak with her. Apparently it isn't FBI protocol to interrupt important meetings when defense lawyers call, and he resists doing so. So I up it a notch and describe it as a matter of life or death, and he relents.

Fifteen seconds later Cindy is on the phone. "Life or death?" she asks. She doesn't sound that worried, since she knows I'll say anything to get what I want.

"Many lives and many deaths," I say, and relate the situation as quickly as I can, without leaving out anything important.

"Have you spoken to Benson?" she asks.

"I can't reach him."

"So what do you want me to do?"

"Make sure that nothing is happening at that terminal, and maybe find Willie in the process."

"Andy, I can't order an FBI terrorist operation on your hunch. That's not how we operate."

"Cindy, this is real; I can feel it. If you don't stop it, we could be looking at a catastrophe. If I'm wrong, we'll be embarrassed. I'll take whatever heat I can take. But I know if I spoke to Benson, he'd move on it."

"Hold on," she says, and I wait for about three and a half endless minutes before she gets back on the phone. When she does, the stress in her voice is unmistakable. "Andy, I'm on it; I have to go."

"What's going on?"

"There's a tanker due in port in twenty minutes."

I hang up the phone, then I stare at it and mentally beg for it to ring. Billy and Laurie do the same; we are silent, knowing that there is nothing more we can do, other than wait.

It is five minutes later that Benson calls, and I quickly tell him what has happened, and that I have already spoken to Cindy, who said she was on the move. If he's annoyed by my intervention in bureau affairs, he certainly doesn't sound it.

What he sounds is worried.

As he's about to get off, I say, "I believe the guy behind all this is Colonel William Mickelson; he's based at the Pentagon."

"How sure are you?" he asks.

"Eighty percent. But if I'm right, he's about ready to leave the country."

Click.

Benson has hung up on me. I hope and believe he

did so because he was in a desperate hurry to act on my words. The other possibility is that he hung up for the same reason that people have been hanging up on me my whole life, that they find me an insufferably annoying pain in the ass.

So we wait again.

THE SHIP HEADING in was the largest Willie had ever seen. It seemed to be a tanker of sorts, and Willie guessed that whatever it was carrying would be transferred to the tanks looming over the industrial plant. He thought it might be something like oil, and if so it would make an inviting target.

There was still no movement from the van. Willie was sure that Greer was still in there, but he couldn't see him in the driver's seat.

Small tugboats went out to the tanker to bring it in. At least they looked small next to the tanker; Willie figured the *Titanic* would have been dwarfed by it as well.

The tanker was about a quarter mile from the pier when Willie saw the back of the van open. Greer climbed out the back, pulling something behind him. It was covered in canvas, and Greer dragged it out on to the road, carefully placing it down.

Willie's mind was racing, not sure when to act, and more importantly not sure how to act when the time seemed right. For the moment he watched, transfixed, as Greer looked around warily and saw no one. He did not think to look up at the road in the distance where Willie stood, but would not likely have perceived him as a threat anyway. Finally, secure that he was alone, he took the cover off.

It was a missile.

There was no doubt in Willie's mind; he had seen enough war movies to know for sure. It was the type that you put on your shoulder and fire, the type that can bring planes down. And if there was something combustible in those tanks, the kind that could do unbelievable damage.

There wasn't going to be any way for Willie to approach Greer unseen; there was only one way in, and his presence would be obvious. He also felt that there was no time to move in on foot; if Greer was taking the missile out now, with the ship so close, he was about to use it.

Willie jumped in his car and pulled away, the tires screeching from the sudden burst of speed. Willie feared that Greer would have heard it and prepared himself for Willie's arrival, but there was nothing he could do about it.

Willie came flying around the curve, leading down to where Greer was standing. He was going so fast that he almost lost control of the car, but he managed to straighten it out.

Up ahead, Greer was paying no attention to him. He had hoisted the missile launcher to his shoulder; it seemed larger than he was. He was standing just behind the van, turned toward the pier, facing the tanker and apparently ready to fire at any moment.

Willie made the instant assessment that he had no time to stop the car, jump out, and prevent Greer from firing the missile. And he had no time to worry about whether the missile would explode as a result of the impact it was about to have.

Greer was intent on his mission, and if he knew that Willie was bearing down on him, he didn't show it. When Willie was just a hundred yards away, traveling at more than sixty miles an hour, he finally sensed it and turned to look.

That turn caused him to take the impact head-on. Willie crashed into Greer and the missile, crushing them into the van, and totaling both the van and Willie's car in the process. Greer was killed instantly, but the missile did not explode; it just fell harmlessly to the ground.

Willie was slammed into the front of his car, breaking four ribs and a kneecap, and smashing his head into the window. Just before he lapsed into unconsciousness, he had one thought.

That better have been Greer, and that better have been a real missile.

● ● ● ● ●

IT'S AN HOUR and forty-five minutes before we get the phone call. They are the longest hour and forty-five minutes I've ever spent; the same time on a treadmill would fly by in comparison.

The call is from Cindy. "It's over, Andy. Willie stopped it, and Greer is dead."

The feeling of relief I have is overwhelming, and I repeat Cindy's words for Laurie and Billy. Then, "How is Willie?"

"He's hurt pretty badly; he smashed up his car. The medics say he'll be okay, but he's going to be recuperating for a while. He just regained consciousness."

I put her on the speakerphone, and the three of us ask Cindy at least fifty questions, all of which she painfully answers. She ends it with, "Andy, I'm sorry I doubted you. Thousands of people could have died today."

"All to make somebody rich."

Laurie, Billy, and I watch CNN until three o'clock in the morning, and their coverage of the incident is constant. It takes a few hours for them to get confirmation of Willie's identity, and a while longer for them to connect him to me and the Zimmerman case.

Benson calls at about two o'clock, to thank me and tell me that Colonel William Mickelson was arrested at Dulles Airport, just before he could board a flight to the Cayman Islands. Chaplin was taken into custody two hours before that.

"How did you know it was Mickelson?" he asks.

"I didn't know for sure, but it made sense. He had access to the conspirators in Iraq, and he was smart and sophisticated enough to deal with Landon as an equal."

"That's it?"

"No. When I talked to Santiago, I asked him who the target was that day in Iraq. He said that he didn't know, that it was a decision way, way above his pay grade. Santiago was a direct report to Erskine, so he wouldn't describe him that way. Mickelson was the next one up the ladder, and he was in Iraq that day."

"Not bad" is Benson's grudging admission.

"Also, when I had talked to Mickelson, I told him that one of the soldiers was coming in to talk. He assumed it was Santiago, even though Greer and Iverson were also missing. It's something I remembered today; I should have done so earlier. And Mickelson knew from me that the state police were going to be protecting Santiago."

Benson promises to call in the morning to resolve the other aspects of our deal, and we get off the phone. Laurie has overheard the conversation, and asks, "Are there any spoken words that you don't remember?" She asks it with a smile on her face, which is good.

Billy realizes that he doesn't have a place to stay, since his rented apartment has long since been re-rented to someone else. I offer him an upstairs bedroom, and he gratefully accepts. He and Milo go trudging upstairs, and Laurie, Tara, and I head to our own bedroom.

Before we go to sleep, I call Cindy back to find out what hospital Willie has been taken to. Then I call and wake his wife, Sondra, to tell her what happened. She's understandably very upset, and since one of my strengths is not talking to upset women, I put Laurie on the phone.

It's four o'clock when we finally get to bed, and thirty seconds later I'm asleep.

Without setting an alarm, we're all up by seven thirty in the morning. I call the hospital and am pleasantly surprised to actually get Willie on the phone. "You're a goddamn national hero," I say.

"Bigger than that guy who landed the plane in the Hudson?"

"Much bigger. You talk to Sondra?"

"Yeah. Man, how do you talk to women when they're crying? I can never figure that out."

"It can't be done," I say. "I've tried a bunch of different approaches, but it simply cannot be done."

"They want me to go on the *Today* show. From right here in the hospital."

"Are you going to do it?"

He laughs. "What do you think?"

My guess is that Willie is about to break the all-time

record for television appearances. I tell him that Laurie and I are going to fly up later today to see him, and we'll bring Sondra with us.

"Cool," he says. "Thanks."

"No, Willie. Thank you."

Benson holds a televised news conference during which he reveals very few of the details, citing an ongoing investigation. He does credit Willie's heroism, reveals Mickelson's arrest for murder and about a hundred other counts, and unequivocally states that Billy is innocent.

Benson calls soon after and tells me that the second part of our deal is arranged. I am going to threaten to file suit against the Department of Homeland Security for false arrest, even though they're not the people that arrested Billy. They are then going to avoid the suit by settling for two and a half million dollars.

Because it's under the banner of Homeland Security, everything is going to be classified and under seal, so no one will have to answer any questions about it. As Billy's lawyer, I'm thrilled with it; as a citizen, less so.

"Plus ten percent for my fee," I say.

"You're a pain in the ass," he points out, but promises to get it done.

"I'm a pain in the ass with questions," I say.

"Answering questions was not part of our deal."

"I'm going to ask them anyway. Was Erskine in on the explosion in Iraq?"

He hesitates, as if deciding what he can tell me and what he can't. Finally, "No; he must have found out about it from one of his men, probably Chambers. But he was trying to profit from it."

"Blackmail," I say, more a statement than a question.

Benson tells me that Erskine was trying to play it both ways. The FBI was threatening to charge him with the Iraq bombing, but he was holding them off, first by giving them M's identity, and then by promising to name the top guys, though he only knew about Mickelson, not Landon.

"But first he wanted his money, and he had documents showing that Mickelson had arranged to get his hands on the missile that was to be used in Everett. He hadn't shared them with us, or told us about Mickelson. I don't even know if he had documents at all."

"But that's what was supposed to be in the envelope?" I ask.

"Yes. But of course they didn't trust Erskine, with or without the envelope, so they killed him."

"And you didn't trust him, so you had him followed that night," I say.

"Not our finest hour. Are we done here?"

"Almost," I say. "Who was the bomb in Iraq meant for? The oil minister, or Freeman and Bryant?"

"All of the above. The minister was the key, because that would move the price of oil. Freeman and Bryant were an extra bonus, because they had figured out what Chaplin was doing, and were likely to expose it."

"Last one," I promise. "Why did you plant the juror?"

"It was a mistake," he admits. "And it was my mistake. I just couldn't take a chance that Zimmerman could be convicted. I wouldn't have been able to live with myself."

Billy comes back from a walk with Milo, so I let Benson off the phone. Billy wants to talk about my fee, and the fact that he can't pay it. He also is unsure how he is going to make money to live, though he has ruled out a return to canine thievery.

"What would you do if you had a lot of money?" I ask.

He thinks about it for a few moments. "Probably become a private investigator." Then he smiles. "And take on Willie as a partner."

"I don't think you can count on Willie for that," I say, "but you can get your own shingle ready."

He asks what I mean, so I tell him. Suffice it to say, he's pleased. "Man, am I glad Pete is your friend."

"Do me a favor?" I ask.

"Anything."

"Even after you're a millionaire, make him buy the beer."

• • • • •

KATHY BRYANT IS going to be richer than Billy Zimmerman. I instruct her to tell her civil attorney to be very aggressive with their lawsuit, that I know for a fact the government will never allow it to go to trial, and will settle for major dollars.

So she'll be rich, but it will be a long time before she'll be anything close to happy.

At the very least, though, she'll be happier than Jonathan Chaplin. He's confessed, and is fully cooperating with the Justice Department, helping them to understand the financial intricacies behind the scheme.

Most of it has been made public, and there is a general clamoring in Congress for regulations to provide more financial transparency so that something like this will never be attempted again.

Yeah, right.

Mickelson's fate is being handled within the military system of justice, but it's safe to say that he will never be heard from again. A real shame is the bad light this is putting the army in. It sounds like a cliché, but the many thousands of brave soldiers who have gone halfway around the world to fight, and die, and lose a limb like Billy, don't get nearly the attention they deserve.

It's the few bad ones that the media focus on, and everything else gets drowned out. I went on Larry King last night to make that point, but I don't really think anyone heard it.

Laurie and I miss having Milo around, and Tara misses him even more.

I'm not sure I've ever met a more charming thief.

About the Author

DAVID ROSENFELT was the marketing president for Tri-Star Pictures before becoming a writer of novels and screenplays. His debut novel, *Open and Shut*, won Edgar® and Shamus award nominations. *First Degree*, his second novel, was a *Publishers Weekly* selection for one of the top mysteries of the year, and *Bury the Lead* was chosen as a *Today Show* Book Club pick. He and his wife established the Tara Foundation, which has rescued over four thousand dogs, mostly golden retrievers. For more information about the author, you can visit his website at www.davidrosenfelt.com.

VISIT US ONLINE AT

WWW.HACHETTEBOOKGROUP.COM

FEATURES:

**OPENBOOK BROWSE AND
SEARCH EXCERPTS**
•
AUDIOBOOK EXCERPTS AND PODCASTS
•
AUTHOR ARTICLES AND INTERVIEWS
•
**BESTSELLER AND PUBLISHING
GROUP NEWS**
•
SIGN UP FOR E-NEWSLETTERS
•
**AUTHOR APPEARANCES AND TOUR
INFORMATION**
•
SOCIAL MEDIA FEEDS AND WIDGETS
•
DOWNLOAD FREE APPS

BOOKMARK HACHETTE BOOK GROUP
@ WWW.HACHETTEBOOKGROUP.COM